Echoes from Shady Mountain

The wolf spirit roams Shady Mountain and calls out to Echo Valley below. Those who listen will learn.

Copyright

Echo from Shady Mountain by Clarice Cook was written from notes and character creation beginning in the 1990's. The collection formed into chapters on a word processor, transferred to a manuscript on the website WEbook.net and slowly evolved into the finished novel on files.

©CCCWriter Clarice Cook 2013 First Edition on Amazon ebook. March 2014 Re-edit for ebook and paperback edition. Re-edit and

Note that all content and images are the sole property of the author and infringement of the copyright is in violation of copyright law.

This rendition is the only true version of this book. Any other works that may have been hacked into and trashed are not the works of the author, Clarice Cook and would be considered as identity theft if the name Clarice Cook or CCCWriter is used on such works.

Second Edition: Published by Morrowpond Publishing 12/31/2015.

Echo from Shady Mountain
Dedication

Thank you to all the great WeBook.com feedback members who took time to encourage, critique and nudge me on in writing Echo from Shady Mountain. In the beginning first draft that I wrote in the 1990's, I asked We Book members to give honest feedback. As a result, this is the first of a two part series. Justice for Echo Valley was published January 2015.

My friends at Webook, wherever and whoever you are, thank you. SEdenttus, Eddie Tol, Travis, Salukis32, MLegrande, Evelyn Keaton, Totally Batty, Sixteen Pages, Jane Austen, Kayzzaman, Angel24, Elixir, Stokes, the dainmaster, RobHanson, stef_nalton, Andy_07bug, amandab, Sushuti, wayahowl, mayfield, Wally_Smith, Satyr, patimari

I also appreciate those in my life, who have been there for me, who have been patient while I have grown, have forgiven me when I was wrong and loved me through it all. I love you, Seymour, my children and my friends. Chrissy K. McVay, as an excellent author, you continue to shine a light for me.

Echo from Shady Mountain

Description

Echo from Shady Mountain is totally fictional, including the main setting. Echo Valley, Shady Mountain, Echo Valley College, and Clarksville, Pennsylvania are all a figment of my imagination. If a resident of the lower Alleghany Mountains were to be asked about wolves, they would deny their existence in the mountains. This fact adds to the mystery of this story.

This novel has been fabricated purely on the 'what if's' in life in the lower Alleghany, Mountains. What if a college had been available in the mountain community? 'What if' there had been wolves there? Are the wolves really just spirits and part of the folk lore? Would life be pristine and pure?

It is the beginning of November 2000, and the college is gearing down for the semester and gearing up for mid-term exams and holidays. Young people, both local and from other areas are in the midst of learning about life. Some are in college to better their education, but many have nothing better to do and some gain attention and bring many problems with them.

These chapters are a beginning to the sequel to Justice in Echo Valley, another novel that will grow out of this work.

MAIN SPEAKING CHARACTERS

Eliza Hardigan: Aunt and guardian of Angela Pike
Angela Pike: College student and niece of Eliza Hardigan
Joseph (Joe) Hardigan: Eliza Hardigan's father and Angela Pike's grandfather
Rachel Brooks: College student and daughter of Dorothy and David Brooks
Detective Lieutenant Greg Yoder: Investigating police chief of Echo Valley
Dorothy and David Brooks: Missionaries and parents of Rachel Brooks
Brent Morse: Antagonist college student at Shady Mountain College
Julie Thompson: Friend of Rachel Brooks and college student
Stephan Brooks: Brother of Rachel Brooks
Dianna Brooks: Sister of Rachel Brooks
Jerrod Showalter: Rachel Brooks' friend

Other Speaking Supporting Characters::
Zeb Greenway, Joe's friend;
Dean Johnson, Dean of Student Services;
Edna Gray, Nurse Practitioner;
Joanna Scholtz, School Counselor;
Dave Taylor, campus security officer;
Eugenia Frye and her daughter, Delilah Wray;
Samuel "Ray" Taylor;
Justus, Policeman;
Prosecuting Attorney, April Donovan;
Herbert Snow, local lawyer;
Sadie O'Reilly, dormitory counselor,
Sheldon Grimes, mortician;

Dan Bolger, Detective,
Sam Gibson, driver,

Mentions: Dog; Joe's devoted canine;
Carrie Hardigan, sister of Eliza and mother of Angela Pike;
Ila Bence, college English teacher;
Cedric Pike, Angela's father;
Chad Ellerton, Eliza's superior in Chicago;
Benjamin Snow, Herbert Snow's brother;
Other Snow family members, and others.

The above characters may or may not appear in the sequel, Justice for Echo Valley, which is due out in 2015. Certain characters from another novel, Legacy from the Wake Journals will appear in Justice for Echo Valley.

FOREWORD
In Chicago

"Eliza, dear friend, why haven't you ever married?" The young lawyer sitting across the desk leaned forward as she scanned the document in front of her.

"Because, dear friend, I never met anyone who would want to take the responsibility of raising a child and put up with the hours I have to put in to support the two of us." Eliza paused to motion her finger at the papers. "But what has that got to do with you taking over my case loads until I get back from Pennsylvania?"

"Just curious. I'm happy for the work, actually. But don't be surprised if I move in and take your future promotion away from you."

"Linda, go for it. I'm too stressed over a family matter right now to worry about what happens when I get back. I just need to be in Pennsylvania as soon as possible."

"You're from that area, right?"

"Yep. I came here with my sister about eighteen years ago. I thought that it would be the best here, away from the superstitions and laid back slow pace of the mountains. However, I thought that sending my niece to my old alma mater, Shady Mountain college would give her time to study and focus on learning. I'm not so sure she's learned anything.'

"So is this about Angela? What has that hot little red head done to get you all upset?"

"I don't know that she's done anything. There was a message on my answering machine stating that they needed me to come right away. When I tried to call back, I had to leave a message. I'm just a little concerned because of the way Angela acted this summer. Angela didn't want to leave Chicago, but when she came home for summer break she was totally silent and moody, and then giddy all the way back to Pennsylvania and her dorm. She was acting a lot like her mom did when I brought Carrie to the big city, but in reverse."

Linda looked up sharply from the paper with a startled look. "Oh my. Well, get out of here, woman. I've been briefed and I'll handle all this." Eliza grabbed her briefcase and stood up.
"Thanks, Linda."
As Eliza headed for the door, Linda hugged her. "Do you need someone to drive you to the airport?"
"Oh no, I'm driving."
"Be careful out there alone."
As she turned onto the freeway toward the east, Eliza felt a few tears escape. Her sister's daughter had become a handful when she became a teen. She hoped that she had made the right decision in sending her little hot head to her old college to get her away from the criminals that she helped prosecute every day. The teenager had kept her busy trying to steer her away from drugs, alcohol, and the wrong elements that come with the big city.
Angela had one year at the college. When she came home to spend the summer with her at the lake house, Eliza noticed a real change in Angela. Angela didn't want to come home and she stayed to herself in her room or lying on the beach. After only two weeks after Eliza dropped her back at the college dorm, the school calls her to come for some kind of emergency.
Eliza sighed and leaned back in her seat. Perhaps the dean didn't want to give her too much to worry her on the road, but the not knowing was distracting to say the least. She hoped he'd call her on her car phone number that she left on the voice mail.
After driving a few more miles, the phone rang. "This is Eliza." An unfamiliar voice on the other end says, "Hello, this is Lieutenant Yoder of Echo Valley, Pennsylvania. Are you Rachel Brooks mother?"
"No, I'm not. I'm the guardian for my niece, Angela Pike."
"Oh, I'm sorry. I was given the wrong name for this number. Nevertheless, please, you were the next call I was

going to make. We need to talk to your niece and we haven't been able to locate her. Do you have any other number to reach her or any idea where she might be?
"Do you mean that the college has lost her?
What's going on?"
"We just need to question her, Ms. Hardigan, on a matter concerning another student."
"I'm on the highway from Chicago. I'll be there by tonight." Eliza put the phone down. Perhaps she would find the whole thing solved when she got there, but Eliza didn't want to take the chance since the dean had asked her to come. Where was Angela that they couldn't find her? Yes, it was good that she was going back. "Drugs or alcohol?" She muttered.
Angela's reports were average. She was running a 2.0, which was a better GPA than she was getting in her private high school in Chicago, but Eliza knew that she was capable of more. The psychologist that Eliza had hired and all the childhood testing over the years proved that Angela was capable of 4.0. "Perhaps it is time to move back to the mountains, at least to the valley." She said aloud. She leaned over and dialed on the radio. Time to listen to her favorite reaffirming radio program and settle in for the long ride.

Chapter One

The warm autumn, mountain air whirled across the picnic for two. Dry leaves blew all around and swirled up over the boulders and down toward the valley below. Rachel Brooks felt invigorated by the magnificent view overlooking the valley. She turned and looked out to the east across the craggy rock ledge toward the eternal blue mist that engulfed the valley. She shivered at the thought of stories she'd heard about the wolf spirits that howled from the mountains, perhaps from the rocks just steps from where she now sat on a blanket.
Her mood changed to mellow as she looked toward over the entire boundaries of a distant lake and the morning sun peeking through the mist just above the mountain tops far beyond the shorelines. The beauty of the taller mountain range against the clear blue sky was breathtaking.
"Is that the college campus?" She asked her companion as she pointed to the buildings far off into the distance.
"Uh, huh," answered the smile with perfect teeth.
She turned her attention toward the mountain peaks covered with the gold, and reds of the maple and oak trees intermingled with the evergreens. White steam puffs came up through the tops of trees in the distance, reminding Rachel of campfire smoke. A subliminal feeling came over her. The mystic feeling that greeted her on the first day she entered the valley through the blue haze overcame her.
"How indescribably gorgeous the mountains are today. I didn't think to bring my camera."
"Yes, beautiful, just like you." Her companion said. His voice was husky with just a slight southern accent. She realized that Brent had been staring at her. She turned and smiled sweetly across the picnic blanket at the incredibly sexy, dark haired, college senior finishing his wine in sips. He smiled seductively back at her.
He looked harmless enough now. Rachel looked into the deep, dark pools of his eyes. Her body took on a new

tenseness. She raised her hand and pressed her fingers into the throbbing beat in her neck.

Rachel looked away as she remembered what the self-defense instructor had taught her. Never make eye contact with the assailant. Keep your head up, look at the top of the head, and look for any signs of aggression in the face, watch the body movement, but don't look directly into their eyes.

"You didn't drink the wine I poured for you." He picked up the plastic glass and handed it to her. She took a tiny sip and held the glass away from her.

"You don't realize how gorgeous you are, do you?" His voice was still deep, but smoother.

She flipped her blonde bangs back from her short forehead and started to pack the picnic basket with urgency.

Something stirred deep inside Rachel and she smiled back nervously. "Thank you."

"Drink the rest of the wine, so that we can get on to better things."

Rachel looked at the wine glass. She mentally scolded herself. 'I meet a guy in the library, have coffee with him in the student lounge, and end up in a secluded mountain park area. What was I thinking?'

The wine in the glass enticed her. She had never tasted anything quite like it.

"Come on, Rachel. Drink your wine."

She looked up into his big brown eyes. 'Yeah, there's chemistry.'

She searched her mind for a distraction, something that covered the flushed feeling in her face.

"It was a great hike up here. Did you say that this is Starlight Plateau? I heard that the wolves howl from the ledges up here."

"Yep, and you'd better stick close to me. It's where all students come to howl and make out during the day, and if the chicks don't make out, the guys turn into wolves."

Rachel chuckled nervously. "Oh? What do they make out?"

Brent snickered. "Hey, you're naïve, but not stupid.

"No, I'm not naïve; I was just pulling your leg."
"I've got something you can pull."
Rachel's mouth dropped open and she stared at Brent. 'Red flags. Stay in control. Mother and
Father... a perfect opportunity to witness Christianity, but…no, that's pious. Stephan warned me.'
Rachel swallowed hard. "Brent, we came up here to help each other with the history mid semester essays."
"You can't possibly be that lame?" He rolled over onto his back and stared up at her. "You're one mixed up chick, you know that?"
Rachel struggled to control her nerves and her thoughts. 'He's right. I am mixed up. But I've still got to stay in charge of my actions.'
"It's just that I'm flattered by your compliments, but I'm just as God made me. No more, no less."
"As God made you? Well, he didn't miss a beat. Beautiful art is what you are."
Rachel felt her face flush. "It's not God's will that such things should be said to a woman without benefit of marriage. Again, I thought we came up here to study."
Brent started laughing uncontrollably and with mockery. "You're kidding, aren't you? Why would I, a senior, want to come up here to this romantic setting with a pretty, freshman to study? Isn't it a sin for a woman to lead a man on? Drink the wine."
Rachel looked back at the glass. "I don't drink alcohol."
"Why not? Didn't Jesus make water into wine?"
Red flags. Sister Dianne's lectures on chauvinistic pigs. Dumb, I'm stupid. O.K. it's time. She tried to hand the wine glass back to Brent.
"Look. This is how it's going to be. I was raised in a strict Christian home. This conversation is making me uncomfortable."
Brent put his hand up toward the glass.
"Well, your smile and that light in your eyes tell me something different."

Rachel put the wine glass on top of the picnic basket. She shifted uncomfortably on the blanket.

'What is this primal feeling I'm having? Jezebel. Control yourself.'

"Yes, well, Brent. I'm sorry that you got the wrong idea. I'm just trying to be friends. Obviously, my expectations are different from yours. I do need to study. We'd better get into our test study papers before it gets too windy up here."

" We'll have plenty of time. Here I'll help you," Brent's voice continued to be deep and smooth as he moved closer to her.

He picked up the wine glass and brought it up to her lips. "The wine can help you relax and open up your brain. Come on."

Rachel backed away and moved up on her knees. "No, Brent. I don't need the wine. Besides, I had a sip. I don't like it." Brent stood up over Rachel. She looked up at him. She put her hand on her book bag. "I'm going to study."

"Rachel, this is a make-over class for me. I've had plenty of time to catch up. I don't need to study and I didn't bring you here to this beautiful setting on this great Saturday morning to keep my head in a book."

Rachel got up on her feet and put the repacked picnic basket down on a corner of the blanket. When she felt Brent's arm around her, she pulled away turning to face him defiantly. "Come on Brent. Chill out. I'm sorry if you had other ideas, and I didn't mean to lead you on, but...come on, let's get to work or let's just pack up and go back to the library."

He shrugged his shoulders. "I thought you might need some help."

"Yeah, well, let's get busy." Rachel pulled out her notebook and library books from her satchel and sat back down by the picnic basket, motioning Brent to the other side.

"So what's it like to be a do gooder's child? Your parents must make pretty good money to be able to afford to send you to this college."

Rachel thought, none of your business, but if it gets you on a different subject.

She said aloud, "No, they don't have a lot of money. My parents are just quiet missionaries."

"Didn't your mother teach you about the facts of life?"

Rachel shook her head. "No, but I learned all I need to know from the media, from friends, from books, and from my older brother and sister."

"And what did they teach you?"

"Well, my older brother defends women's rights, and my sister has always lectured me about the dangers of dating."

Brent chuckled. "Dangers of dating?"

Ignoring the question, Rachel used the flat top of the picnic basket for a desk. She started to write in the notebook.

"I wish that I'd brought my laptop. It would have been so much easier. But I doubt that the reception is very good up here."

"I think the reception is super." Brent grabbed her long, slender hand and put the wine glass in her hand. Startled, she pulled back, knocking the glass to the blanket. She gasped and looked at the red stain seeping into the fleece fabric.

Brent put his hand on her chin and moved her head to look into her face. Frightened by the glazed look in Brent's eyes, Rachel scrambled to get up onto her feet.

He grabbed at her legs. "You're just one of those little teases, aren't you?"

Rachel's voice was shaky. "Brent...no...really. I'm flattered and I think you are a great catch, but I really did think that we came here to study. We're just friends. I was raised to be friends first, and then if there is chemistry...a calling from God..."

Brent leaned back his head and laughed hardily.

Then he calmed.

"Ah, but I know what all the teasing is about. When girls are raised so strict, they become wild. I plan on finding the wild part of you."

In one explosion, Rachel was hurled backward. The taste, the smell...the smell of leather and wine. The heavy, metal zipper pull scraping against my face, oh, what a putrid odor smothering me. Rachel felt nauseated.

"Awwgh," Rachel screamed falling heavy onto the ground, Brent's six-foot frame on top of her five foot five slender figure.

"We both know that you didn't come up here with me to research mid-term papers. I've better research in mind and so do you. Right? Little Miss Innocence?" His voice was low and his breathing heavy.

Rachel pulled back the pencil that was in her hand. As the adrenalin rushed to her head, she lunged the point into his groin area with as much strength as she could muster, hoping that it met close enough to the mark. Brent yelled and rolled away.

Oh, God. Short of breath, she jumped up immediately and started running down the trail. Her fleeting thoughts came fast and furious. 'Thank God for women's defense classes Dianna made me take... these jeans... A Quaker dress...ah-h, impossible thought.'

She dodged trees and brush, stumbling on the gulley-washed earth and screaming to the top of her lungs.

'Oh, forget screaming,' she told herself. 'No hikers on this trail.'

As she ran, her every step sounded like thunder in the quiet forest. The swishing of the brush as she pushed through the woods and the snapping of the branches cut out any evidence that she was being followed.

'My God. Is that him, I feel?' She prayed.

'Please help me.'

Reaching Brent's old, red van she jerked the door open, jumped inside, and locked the door. Her body throbbed from fear and exhaustion.

"Oh, no," She gasped out. Brent had the keys.

She was no safer in the van than in the woods.

"How could I have been so dumb?"

Rachel's thoughts came fast and furious. She pondered what her parents would say. Will they believe their one hope, an obedient servant of God, their late in life child, would be so stupid to go to a mountaintop alone with a boy? I want to please them, but how can I connect with them in all things.'
Still breathless from the run, she started to pray. 'Dear God, I know that this is the only time I pray, but I'm in trouble here. I feel like a hypocrite, but please help me anyway.'
Just as Rachel started to open the door, Brent exited from the woods and was outside the door before she had a chance to unlock it.
She stiffened her body. 'Control this shaking.
He can't know. I'm scared.'
Dianna's voice emerged in her thoughts. 'Never show fear to a mad dog. He's a mad dog...a raging wolf.'
He stood on the outside of the van grinning at her with arrogance. Her body was so rigid her bones ached.
"I'm sorry," he yelled. He wasn't opening the door.
He held up his empty hands. "I lost my keys. If we're going to get back to the dorm, you'll have to open the door so that you can help me find the keys."
He looked harmless. Is this all my fault? She thought. Did I lead him on? Rachel looked into the deep, dark pools of his eyes. Her body took on a new tenseness. She raised her hand and pressed her fingers into the throbbing beat in her neck.
She looked away as she remembered what the self-defense instructor had said, 'Never make eye contact with the assailant. Keep your head up, look at the top of the head, and look for any signs of aggression in the face, watch the body movement, but don't look directly into their eyes.'
"Go back and look for them, yourself." She yelled back, her voice shaking with terror and contempt. Her fear was betraying her.
Brent rolled his eyes at her, turned, and waved his arm in disgust, disappearing back into the brush.

Rachel lay back on the seat and breathed heavily. 'Think fast.'
She looked in the rear view mirror back down the trail. 'If I run... No... the bushes, he could be...
Looking ahead at the opening through the woods, she searched for the color of his bright green and brown school jacket. Open the door slowly...see if the brush moves...No, too risky. Maybe he's truly sorry. Maybe he is going to be decent now. Her mind continued to reason. She pressed her hands to the heavy feeling in her chest.
The memory of Brent's eyes haunted her. She spoke out loud. "No, Brent Morse is not to be trusted. He's like a Pied Piper, an opportunist. Maybe even a rapist."
Think fast. She put her hands to the pressure in her head. "How could I have been so dumb? What is wrong with me? I am so naive. Oh, God, I'm talking to myself."
She put her hand on the door handle. 'Got to stop shaking and be confident.'
'O. K. I'm going to get out now. I've got to make some distance between me and that jerk before he gets back with the keys. God forgive me, but he's a jerk.'
Slowly, she unlocked and cracked the door open.
Seeing no movement in the brush, she swung it wider. Simultaneously, the crashing of the trees stirred her reflexes. Brent's hand came through the opening. She brought the heavy metal door crashing back on his hand.
The curdling scream from the male predator echoed across the valley and vibrated down Rachel's back. Holding onto his wrist, he fell to the ground. Rachel slammed the door shut again and locked it.
His face pinched in pain, Brent rose up again yelling obscenities toward the window at her. He disappeared back into the woods.
Rachel leaned against the seat again and closed her eyes. 'What was that...that thing Stephan did?'

A picture came to her mind of her brother with his hands under the dash of an old car. He couldn't find the keys...Oh, yeah... hotwiring.

She looked down at the floorboard at her purse that she had left lying there before that fateful hike up the mountain trail. Tools, I need tools. 'Ah, the manicure set that Dianna gave me for Christmas.'

Nervously, she dumped out the contents on the adjoining seat and found the little brown pouch. Unsnapping the closure and getting down on the floorboard, she reclined on her back and grabbed the wires to the starter.

'O.K. Don't electrocute yourself,' she warned herself.

The stripping completed, she touched the two wires together, and sparks flew.

'Thanks Sis for the gift, and thanks Bro, for teaching me this trick. The two of you may have saved my life.' Her hands shaking, she broke the wires away and tried again. Then it happened. The starter hummed and she leaned an elbow against the gas pedal. The engine roared.

Climbing back up behind the wheel, she shifted the van into reverse just as Brent came running out of the woods, waving the keys in his hand. With a sense of urgency, she shifted into drive and turned back onto the highway in the direction of town without looking back.

Chapter Two

The road into town seemed to be miles away. She pressed her shaking foot harder on the pedal, slowing for curves. One hand released from the wheel at intervals to wipe away tears and rub her aching head. She kept watch of the rear view mirror as she drove.
"So cold, but yet so hot. Maybe Brent was right. Maybe I am a mixed up chick. One thing I'm sure of, I am more frightened than I've ever been in my life." She said aloud. She grabbed her phone from her purse and punched her mother's speed dial number. As Rachel listened to the rings, she thought, 'What am I doing? Even if I can get a signal out of these mountains, Mother will just start crying and go into a panic. She's so far away.'
Realizing the futility of it all, she pushed the off button and turned to put the phone down. The howling from the mountain indicated more than one animal. As she rounded a curve, a white animal peered out from the Rhododendron. Distracted for a moment, she looked up to hear the blare of a horn blowing and to find that she was over the line. She swerved to avoid the near miss of a large white truck. She pulled sharply to the right and felt a jolt.
Rachel felt a sharp, but throbbing pain as her head hit the side windowpane. Shaking, she pulled the van over to the side and sat sobbing. Everything was blurry. The mountains normally held a lot of fog in the morning. However, this was different. She looked up at the strange eerie blue mist that surrounded her.
A knock on her window on the passenger's side made Rachel jump. She had not noticed before, but there seemed to be a house on a hill. A woman stood looking in at her. The woman's face seemed to be transparent.
"Are you alright?"
Rachel wiped her wet face on her coat. She found the button to roll down the window on the passenger side. "I'm ok. I'm

so sorry to have blocked your drive." She rubbed the side of her head.

The woman shook her head. "No, it's alright. Can I get you to come up to the house and get some tea? You shouldn't be driving like this. You look like you could use a friend right now."

"No, I'm fine. Thank you anyway." She lied. She glanced in the rear view mirror at herself. She was holding her hand to her head, her eyebrows were furrowed, and her face dirty. She thought, 'Yeah, sure I'm fine'.

The woman's face in the van window looked vaguely familiar, but Rachel could not place her. Something told her not to explain much to her. Her instinct told her to take flight. Go! She politely said, "I need to get back into town. Thanks again."

Then she rolled up the window. 'Oh God, I need to keep my cool. I could have killed someone.' She looked back at the woman's wrinkled brow, into her blue eyes and lips turned down into a deep frown. Rachel thought the woman looked worried.

Rachel turned to look forward, buckled her seat belt, and put the van in drive. She turned to look at where the woman had been standing. She was gone.

Rachel calmed herself and took her foot off the brake. She drove slowly and on course for the rest of the trip.

She put her right hand on her leg. She spoke loudly to herself. "I've got to stop my legs from shaking." She shivered. Cold, dear god, I'm so cold and clammy. The woman's face kept creeping back into her thoughts. 'Why can't I remember where I've seen her?'

Her mind searched for a name for the face. I might as well forget trying to remember...employees, vendors, non-traditional students...professors...so many on campus...professors. Now professor does seem familiar. A sharp pain stabbed her head.

Her thoughts turned to her parents. 'What are they going to say?' She sighed and continued her thoughts.

I know what they're going to say. They're going to ask me how I could've made such a mistake in going up on that mountain with a strange young man that I'd only just met. That most definitely is what they are going to ask.
Rachel drove past an old barn that had caved in.
I don't remember seeing that or anything else that I've seen for miles...where am I? Is there a fog, or...
She pulled over into a roadside park and sat there with the motor running. Looking around, she thought, I have never felt so lost. Somewhere in her mind, she could hear the echo of a canine howl.
She gasp as a large animal came bounding out of the woods. 'Is that a wolf?' Then she could see a man...or was that a man...a large gray furry face came closer. 'Was it a wolf man standing up with a staff to walk?' The creature was forming what might be words with the bearded covered lips and motioning with large paws... like hands. The smaller animal turned and headed back to the man wolf. Fear mounted and she drew back away from the door.
The man wolf walked up to the van window. The lips formed words. Now he became more like a man, as Rachel understood the sounds he was making. "Hello" and something else she couldn't make out. Rachel relaxed and moved back to the door as she stared at the white beard. All she could think about was Santa Claus. Maybe he had toys in his backpack. Her parents never made a big deal out of Santa. Maybe he was real after all. Crazy thoughts kept shooting through her brain.
The man moved his lips forming words she couldn't hear, and motioned, rolling with his hands, pointing at the closed window. She found the left window down button after fumbling for a while, and the glass gave way to the open air.
"Hello, are you waiting for someone?" Rachel thought his words sounded like he was in a tunnel.
She nodded no.
"What's your name?" The man asked as he looked inside toward the back seat of the van.

"I'm..." She had to give him an answer.
She struggled. Then it came. "Rachel, I'm Rachel."
"Are you alone, Rachel?" He asked, looking straight into her eyes.
Her thoughts were jumbled. "I don't...no... I need to go. I guess I need to get back to my room at the dorm."
She wondered, am I talking? I can't hear my voice.
The man rubbed his beard. "Oh, so you're lost. If you had kept going down this road, you would have come to the freeway. You don't want to get on that highway. You'd be driving a long way out of your way. You need to go back up here to the fork." The man pointed in the direction that Rachel had just come.
"A lot of people miss that and take the wrong curve as they're coming down the mountain. You should've stayed to the right, but you followed the road to the left. Let Dog and me get into your van, and I'll guide you back up to the fork. You can let me out there and I'll get you started down the mountain again."
"Who are you?"
"I'm Joe. Many people call me the old wolf man, some just call me a hermit. I live a little ways up here on Shady Mountain. Dog here and I walk the trails every day."
Rachel hesitated for a moment. She thought, 'What is it that I've been told about picking up people on the road...he's a strange man. I don't know...I'm so confused...so lost. He seems so gentle...honest.'
She finally spoke. "O.K. Joe. Hop in." She thought, feeling a sense of gratitude and fear of risk at the same time.
As Rachel drove the van around the curves back to the fork, Dog stuck his head through from the back seat and Joe rubbed his head.
"We're almost there. See where the road joins up here... yeah...just pull over here...Good." Rachel pulled over on the side. "Now you see where that point there curves to the left? Yeah? Just go left there and it takes you right down past the college entrance. You can't miss it."

The van door squeaked as the man called Joe got out and opened the side door for Dog. She glanced back through the rear view mirror to see the man and dog, as they seemed to evaporate in the blue mist. She stopped at the fork and turned left down the main road. The cool air brushed her face and she shivered as an eerie howl echoed across the valley.

Chapter Three

The landscape of the sprawling college campus was never so welcome. Set on the edge of town, the dormitories were located in the center of the campus on a hill surrounded by the teaching, chapel, and administration buildings. Soon she would be in her room. Then she could take some aspirin and lay down to get rid of this increasing headache.

Rachel passed the main administration building and drove up the winding hill. She almost missed the entrance. For some reason, the fog had not lifted. She pulled the old van into her dormitory parking lot. She found an empty parking space in front of the large, glass dorm door. Pulling the gearshift into neutral, she sat trying to sort her thoughts out.

She sat staring out the window and she couldn't remember how she got back to the college entrance. Now the tears came and she didn't know what to do next.

Rachel wondered. 'Why can't I remember? Rachel started sobbing again, I was attacked. I remember...' She paused again.

Shaking, she finally stepped out, leaving the motor running. Her roommate, Julie, was suddenly there beside her. She bounced around, her curly black hair bouncing with her.

"Hi, Rachel. What are you doing driving this van?"

Julie stopped when she saw Rachel's wet, scratched face and her long, tangled, blonde hair.

"What's wrong?"

"Julie. It is you, Julie." She sobbed.

"What happened to you? Isn't this Brent Morse's van?"

Rachel stopped sobbing and rubbed her forehead. "I remember..." Rachel stopped and stood. Her forehead furrowed as she stared at the front of the van.

"Go on, Rachel. Where's Brent?" Julie stepped around to the driver side door that was still open.

She looked in and backed out with Rachel's purse. Her manicure items were scattered everywhere.

Julie chucked in a dry humor sort of way. "I was going to shut it off and found no keys. Looks like someone hooked the starter wires together.
Was that you Rachel?" Rachel took the purse. She looked inside.
"Brent was chasing me."
Julie continued opening doors and peering inside the van. Making the full circle around the vehicle, Julie stepped back to where Rachel stood.
"Where's Brent?" Julie asked her again.
"Why is there so much fog?'
"There's no fog this morning, Rachel. What's happened to you?"
"The guy...Brent, Julie, he was so forceful. I didn't know what else to do, but get back down the mountain."
Rachel started to panic. "What if he's so mad that he's going to come after me, Julie?"
Julie took charge. "Come on. We are going to the security office. You have got to report this. You can tell Dave the whole story. Maybe it'll all come back to you when you feel safe."
Rachel stood stiffly, not moving.
"Well, come on. We need to go now." Julie put her arm in Rachel's.
"Oh, please, Julie. I just wanna go take a shower and lay down. My head's pounding. I feel like it's in a vise, and I need a couple of aspirin."
"No, you don't have a choice. You're going with me."
"Oh, God, Julie. Everyone's staring at me. I look awful."
"And if you walk into the security office all clean and rested, who's going to believe your story?"
Rachel felt too weak to argue further so she followed her. Halfway down the hill from the dormitories, her phone rang.
"Rachel, did you try to call me?"
"Hello Mother. Yeah, I pushed your speed dial by mistake. I'm sorry." Rachel voice shook as she lied. She started

wheezing. She grabbed her chest and started to cough. The jolts from the coughs caused more pain in her head.

Julie stopped beside her and took the phone while Rachel caught her breath. "Do you want me to talk to your mom?" She asked her.

Rachel shook her head 'no' and took the phone back. She took a deep breath and said, "I'm fine,
Mother."

"Well, you don't sound too good. Are you sure that you're ok? "

"What? I think we're losing signal. I'm ok, Mother. I'm just hurrying across the campus and I swallowed too much air. I'll call you back later when we can have a better signal. I promise."

After she pushed her off button, Julie scolded. "I don't think you sound fine. What was all that coughing about? You need to come clean with your mom."

"It must just be tension. I've done that since I was a kid. You know...hyperventilate when things got a bit frantic, especially when I'm trying to smooth things over with Mother."

"What's there to smooth over? Rachel, you're not making sense. I suggest that you call her back as soon as we talk with Dave."

The two girls started walking again. Rachel was moving slower than before and Julie was walking a little ahead of her. "You know, Mother will probably forget all about my phone call in a few hours. It won't matter if I call back or not. She's got so many church projects; she won't have time to give anything else much thought. Mother and Father have that trip within the month. They've just got too many things on their plate right now. It's just not necessary that I talk to her."

"You most certainly are going to call her back.
And you're going to tell her the truth, Rachel."

Rachel made a what-ever gesture. "Sure."

"I'm serious, Rachel. Your mom could be a big help to you, like mine was."
Rachel grabbed Julie's arm and turned her toward her. "What're you saying?"
"I'm saying that I have a similar story. When I was a junior in high school, I was the victim of an attempted date rape. I tried to be cool and handle it on my own. I only made matters worse. Believe me you're not going to be able to work this out without your mom's help."
"Listen, Julie. You don't understand my Mother. First, she'd have a nervous breakdown. Then she and Father would be dropping everything to come up here, or they'd be ripping me out of school. I just can't tell her this just yet."
"Suit yourself, Rachel. Nevertheless, your parents are going to be blazing mad when this comes out. I know that from experience." Julie said as they entered the building lobby.
Rachel's brows furrowed. "It'd be a disaster, Julie. My parents should never find out. They're semi-retired missionaries, and their reputations are at stake. I don't want to be the third child in a row who disappointed them."
Julie stopped and turned to her in the lobby. "How've they been disappointed? Are your brother and sister that bad?"
"No. They've never been in trouble. They just didn't have the same moral or life values as our parents. That's reason enough for me to try to protect the family ties."
"Well, let's discuss this later. Your eyes are blood shot and your skin is as gray as a ghost." Julie stepped toward the security office door and turned back as she heard Rachel groan.

Chapter Four

Rachel sat down on a bench and held her head. "I don't feel so great, Julie. Can't I just go back to the dorm and go to bed?"

Julie sat down beside her and put an arm around her. "Do you want me to get someone to send for a nurse?"

"No, I'm fine. I just need to rest."

"As long as we're here, we might as well go inside when you feel like walking again."

Rachel took a deep breath and slowly let it out. She stood up. "O.K., I can see you're not going to leave me be until I talk to the security officer. So let's go get this over with."

The security front lobby was quiet. A work-study sat at the desk, chewing gum with her head in a book. She turned her big dark eyes up, almost without lifting her head.

"What can I do for you?"

"We need to talk with an officer about an incident."

The girl at the desk leaned over and pushed a button. "Dave. There are two students here to talk with you."

Rachel was thankful that the receptionist didn't get a good look at her face and hair. However, she was caring less by the minute. With every footstep, she was getting sick to her stomach and her headache just would not go away.

Julie and Rachel sat down on a long row of chairs along the wall and almost immediately stood back up as the tall man with a buzz cut walked in and motioned them back to his office. He politely introduced himself as he directed them to the two chairs sitting in front of his large desk. Julie and Rachel introduced themselves. Julie interrupted the awkward silence that followed by prompting Rachel to speak, "Rachel, tell him what happened."

Dave put up his hand. "Wait just one moment Rachel. Do you mind if I record this. I'm not very good at taking notes."

"Sure. Go ahead." Rachel's toes were pressed hard on the floor and her knees were bouncing up and down. She rubbed the side of her head with one hand and bent forward holding her other hand on her churning stomach.

Dave clicked on his machine. "What's the story, Rachel? How'd you get all those scratches?" He pushed a box of tissues toward her.

"Thank you." Rachel brushed some tissues over swollen eyes and blew her nose. "I was running from Brent Morse up on Shady Mountain." She took a sip of water from a cup that Julie sat down in front of her.

"O.K. Why don't you start from the very beginning, Rachel? Just start from what happened to cause you to run from Brent Morse."

Dave stopped her ever so often to clarify facts. Then she found herself letting it roll. As she spoke, she moved to place her feet flat on the floor. Her body stopped shaking. She brought her hands to her lap. Her fists balled tightly together.

Her speech became louder, more pronounced and forceful. "He...He jumped on me. That dirty rotten scum jumped on top of me and pinned my arms down." Rachel could feel the tension in her neck and jaw as she tried to contain her anger. Suddenly she had thought of her Mother and Father and what they would say if they knew how furious she was. The lifelong lessons loomed over her, turn the other cheek; anger is not of God; speak ill of no one. She stopped. She started to cry violently again. Then she took a deep, quivering breath.

"God forgive me, I brought a pencil up, and I jabbed it into him." She sobbed. "That act is against the Quaker teaching. I was so angry. I had to stop him."

Dave was leaning forward with his elbows on the desk. "I'm sorry that you're going through the retelling of this, Rachel. However, we need to know the rest. Tell me how you got down the mountain."

"When Brent rolled off, I got up and ran as hard as I could run. I broke through away from the trail in places and ran as straight as I could toward where I knew the van was parked. That's how I got the scratches."

Dave wanted to sympathize with the girl, but he reminded himself that he had to keep an unbiased attitude and just get the statement. His heart went out to her as she told about how she sat in the van, locked in and scared to death. A strange thing happened as she told how she got the van started. Hotwiring a vehicle did not fit in the profile of this young woman. The security officer watched as the face of the girl started to glow. He noticed that her pupils were dilated. Was she on drugs, or maybe she had a good deal of that alcohol. Her annunciation and slightly slurred words indicated something more than anxiety. The more excited she became, the less he could understand. Then, young people talked too fast and ran words together a lot these days.

She sat up straight and held her shoulders back. Her hands were on the arms of her chair.

"I don't know what happened inside me. I guess people must get a shot of adrenalin to the brain when there is trouble. But it worked and that's why I'm here now." At that point, Rachel realized that the telling of the act of hotwiring the van gave her a sense of pride in herself.

Then her tears came back and she held her head. A prideful soul is a sinful soul, Mother's voice echoed in her mind.

"I left Brent there, but he had his cell phone. I knew he'd get back somehow."

Dave prompted her. "Did you send anyone back for him? Sometimes the cell signals don't work here in the mountains."

"No, I guess I should have, but after what he did..." Rachel started rubbing her head again. "Look. Part of me is telling me to be a good Christian and let this go. On the other hand, it scares me to death to think of what could happen if I do not do something. What if he comes back here and tries to get revenge on me?"

Dave leaned back in his large office chair. "Sounds like you've got a huge argument between right and wrong going on in your head. I will check into what happened to Brent. Don't worry about that now."

Dave leaned forward. "I need to know one more thing. You said you were studying on the mountain. Give me a little background on how it came about that you were with Brent. For instance, how long have you known him? Have you dated him before? What made you decide to go up there with him in the first place?"

Rachel wiped her eyes and cleared her throat. "I met him for the first time in the library this morning, and then we walked over to the Student Union Hall. It was noisy there and he led me to believe that we could study better up on the point. He said that we would be able to think more clearly up on the mountain where the air is fresh. But all he was after..." Her voice started to shake. "Well, I made it clear to him that I only wanted to study." Julie stood and went to put her arms around Rachel. "You did the right thing, Rachel."

Dave leaned back toward his desk. "How old are you, Rachel?"

"I'll be eighteen next month. But I don't understand why that matters." She put her face in her hands and rubbed her forehead.

"What's your home state?"

She looked up at him. "We just moved to Ohio from northern Pennsylvania last November. And why does that matter?" her voice was strained.

"The age of consent laws for college students are different state by state. Legally, we're bound by the laws of Pennsylvania. However, I'm not a lawyer. As for school policy, we're obligated to let your parents know what's going on if you're still living at home and they're paying your tuition, regardless of your age."

"No. No. No. They don't need to know." Her voice became elevated. "I have scholarships and money from a trust fund left by my grandparents."

"Your parents, what're their names?"
"David and Dorothy Brooks."
"Are they still considered your legal guardians in the trust?"
"Yes, they guide me in the trust until I'm 21. However, they do not have to know what I do while I am here. The only thing they have to know is that I'm using the money for college."
Dave bit his lower lip. "Do you want to press charges, Ms. Brooks?"
"Of course she wants to press charges." Julie interrupted.
Rachel voice started to shake. She almost shouted. "Wait. Will this be in the news if I press charges? Do you absolutely have to report this to my parents?"
Julie rolled her eyes to the ceiling. "Rachel...."
Dave interrupted while looking directly at Rachel. "Your name can be withheld from the press. No information will leak out of this office. However, I'd advise you to talk with your parents about this, with or without legal action. I am not sure that I can keep this from them, whether you file papers or not. However, I'll look into it to see what I can do. I'm sorry, but I'm obligated to report the incident to the Dean of Student Services."
Julie exploded. "How many other women on this campus are going to have to deal with this jerk if something isn't done? What if he succeeds next time? The evidence is all there. Why does she need?
To go through all that paper work. She's the victim here."
Rachel began to cry again. "Just look at me. My…my clothes are torn. I'm all scratched up." Dave's face was showing signs of aggravation. "Calm down. We have to be legal here. A court order is necessary to give to the city police. Besides, it happened off campus. That makes it harder for me to deal with it...but I will deal with this. Rest assured, I'm taking this seriously, Ms. Brooks."
Rachel's hope was leaving her and she felt a sudden let down. She threw up her hands, her long fingers extended in a defeated gesture. "This is a waste of time, and I'm not

even sure it's the right thing to do." She turned to her companion seated in the chair next to her. "Come on Julie. I need a nice hot bath." She started to get up.

Dave continued as he leaned forward. "With your consent, I'll call the college nurse practitioner. We'll need her evaluation. My advice to you is not to be taking any baths or showers yet. Just go back to the dorm and wait for her to call you. We'll need that paperwork from the nurse to continue with this report. Don't worry about it. If you decide to press charges, this report will be on file with our unit, the unit downtown, and the unit around Shady Mountain. Regardless, I'll talk with Brent, and we'll get back to you."

The tone of his voice showed fatherly concern. "This is all up to you. I'll get papers for you to fill out, Rachel. If you decide to press charges, just complete them as fully as possible, and with as much detail as you can remember, and get them back to this office as soon as you can."

Rachel started to cry again. "Please, isn't there any way that you can keep this from my parents?" "Believe me, Rachel. I'll talk to the Dean of Student Services when he comes back on Monday. I'll be as discreet as possible. But we do have to stay within the law, for your sake as well as for the school."

"I'm worried that it could happen again. What if Brent succeeds next time? What if he murders some innocent child, perhaps your niece or your daughter?" Rachel was starting to take Julie's attitude.

"Will you trust me, Ms. Brooks?" Dave talked with a subdued tone. "But I can't help you if you don't file the proper papers.

Julie leaned forward. "Do you realize how long that process would take? By the time the papers get to the court, we'll be out of here and at home. In the meantime, that jerk will be on the loose to assault other women."

"I can't promise you that it'll be settled tomorrow, but I'll be glad to get this thing going so that we can start getting things settled. It doesn't matter where you are. We can still work on it and keep in touch. Any legal matters can be handled on the phone at your convenience. Just think about what I've said and keep in touch with me. That's what I'm here for. How much I can help is up to you, Rachel."

Julie started to open her mouth. Dave turned to her. "Now, if you want to help your friend, I advise you to just stand by her. Since this isn't your story, it's not your decision. I'm advising Rachel that it's in her best interest to let me handle this, and she'll need your support in whatever she decides to do."

Rachel got up and grabbed Julie's arm. "Let's go, Julie. I'll consider filling out the complaint papers for now and we'll see what happens." Julie got up and the two girls walked toward the door.

Dave got up and stepped out of the office into the lobby behind the two young women. He instructed the receptionist to give Rachel the requested forms to be filled out and returned. Before they left, Dave took Rachel's phone number for the nurse.

Back in the lobby, Rachel was steaming. "I've never felt so irritated in my life. This is not like me at all. Even so, I didn't do anything wrong. I know this is going to look like it was my fault. Dave was being so matter of fact. He just seemed so cold in spite of what he said. This could take months. In the meantime, I've got to worry about running into Brent."

Julie put her arm around her. "I know, Rachel, but we just have to deal with this in the moment. This kind of thing happens every day across the country in almost every college and very little is done about it."

"That's just it, Julie. Why should something like this be happening every day? Why isn't something being done to stop it? No! This time it's not going to be swept under the rug! I'm going to have to take a leap outside my religion, at the risk of disappointing my parents. I owe it to other women, if not to myself." Rachel's green eyes were flashing with fire.

"Now that's the fire that I wanted to see in you. So what are you going to do, lie down on an altar and martyr yourself and continue to worry about what your parents are going to do, or are you going to take some positive action with strength?" Julie retracted her arm and made a gesture to the graying sky.

Rachel suddenly put her hand over her mouth and headed for the ladies restroom door. Following her, Julie stood in the alcove as she listened to the retching inside the toilet stall.

When Rachel emerged, she was sweating profusely, and walked a bit wobbly. Julie guided her to the sink. She took a paper towel, wet it, and handed it to Rachel.

After Rachel was washed up, Julie guided her to the settee in the lounge. "Rachel, do you want to go on over to the clinic?"

"No, I'm fine now. My headache's starting to subside as well." Rachel looked around her. 'Where am I? I don't recognize any of this. It's so foggy in here." She followed Julie as she headed for the lobby doors.

Julie noted the lost look and the glazed expression on Rachel's face. "Are you sure that you're o.k. Rachel? You look a bit peaked and you're talking crazy."

"Sure."

"Well then...come on, let's get your camera and take pictures of your scratches and bruises. Then if the nurse doesn't call first, I'm going to take you to the clinic."

Julie stayed slightly behind her friend and guided her back to the dormitory. Several times Rachel started walking in the opposite direction.

Julie prompted her. "Rachel, where're you going?

Rachel sat down on her bed when she entered the room and leaned over on her side. Julie went to her and propped her up straight. "Rachel, don't be trying to go to sleep just yet.

I've heard and read that sleeping after a head injury's a dangerous thing."

Julie took her camera out of her drawer. "Ok, Rachel, look up at me." She flashed a picture. Rachel covered her face. "Ow, that hurt."

Julie had Rachel disrobe and took the evidence pictures. Rachel leaned back on the bed and became quiet. Rachel's phone rang and Julie grabbed it from the purse. "Come Rachel, get dressed, that was the nurse practitioner calling back. Let's get over to the clinic."

Nurse Practitioner Edna Graves made no comment as she treated Rachel's scratches and listened to the story. "Is there any reason that I need to check for rape, Ms. Brooks?"

"No. He didn't get that far, but I've got to do something to keep him from succeeding with other victims. If word gets around about this jerk, maybe his other targets will stay away from him." Rachel's voice conveyed the fury she felt inside.

The nurse, Edna, touched stains on Rachel's blouse and then looked into her eyes. "Ms. Brooks, I have to ask this. Have you been drinking?"

"No Mama, I mean, I took one sip. I remember wine all over. Brent was trying to force me. I don't drink."

Edna checked her vitals, examined her arms, and checked the reflexes in her knees. "Nothing feels broken, but let me know if you have problems breathing. Let me know if you have any pain or discomfort anywhere."

"I have a slight headache, but it's better than it was. I took some aspirin and now it's just a low ache."

"Did you sustain a hit on the head?"

"Oh, I bumped it a little, but no big deal."

Edna parted Rachel's hair where Rachel indicated and examined the scalp. "No bump there. It's pretty red." She stepped back to the counter and wrote a note on Rachel's clip file.

"I think that you need to go into the emergency room at the hospital and get x-rays, Rachel. If you hit your head hard enough to get a headache, you need to get it checked out. There may be trauma there that we can't see."

"Oh, no, it's just the stress of everything that has gone on. I'll be fine."

"Here, let me look at your eyes again." Edna peered into her eyes with her light. "Your pupils are a bit dilated, Rachel. I wish you'd consider having this checked out further."

"No. Thank you for your concern. But, no, I'll be fine."

"Edna, Rachel's not maneuvering very well."

"I'm fine, Julie. It was a dramatic event, but I'll get over it." Edna turned to Julie. "Keep an eye on your friend. Let me know what's going on."

"Rachel, let me know if your headache continues."

Edna finished off the last of her examination and handed Rachel a medical form. Leave this at the front office and they'll bill your insurance company and your parents."

Rachel turned pale. "Oh, I can pay cash. There's no need for paperwork to be sent to my parents. But I need records of treatment."

"We'll be sending medical record copies along with the privacy policy you signed to the security office. We'll send you copies of everything." She paused. "I see here on your paperwork that you're not quite eighteen, Rachel. But regardless of your age, as long you're over sixteen, I don't need to send this work to your parents unless we file with your parent's insurance company."

"Please, don't claim this on the insurance company. I'll pay for it up front." Rachel was tearful as she spoke. "Then just let them know that at the front desk."

Julie gave Rachel a strange look. On the way out, Rachel asked the medical secretary for the paperwork and settled her bill.

Julie had been quiet on the way out. "You realize that if you file all those assault charge papers, your parents will definitely be finding out sooner or later."

"Yeah, well. I guess later is better than now."

Julie sighed. "It's just so unfair that you've got to pay for medical bills when you're the victim. You should be compensated for this if it goes to court."

"Do you know what my parents will say, if and when they do find out? They'll say that it was my choice to be on that mountain and my choice to run down the trail."

"Your parents don't sound very supportive of you."

"They are when I make the right decisions. However, when I don't, they expect me to work it out. However, you see, I begged to come to this college. They wanted me to choose a Christian college, but the other institutions didn't offer the curriculum that I wanted to study. So this episode will just give them an excuse for them to take me out and send me to a college of their choice."

Back at the dorm, Rachel noticed that the van had been moved to a parking space in front of the office.

"Oh. No. I'll bet he's back." Her heart rate quickened. She stopped walking and grabbed Julie by the arm. She motioned toward the van. "Let's take a detour around the fountain. Brent can't be too far away."

Rachel glanced back toward the security office and caught her breath. There he was; leaning against the van and staring back at her with cigarette smoke swirling around his head. She started running and didn't stop until she entered the safety of the dorm room. Julie was right behind her. Rachel turned and locked the door behind them.

Chapter Five

"Rachel. You're really scared!" Julie said between breaths. You need to get something to eat. We've been so busy that you barely ate any of that sandwich for lunch."
"I've just got to rest. I've still got a dull aching head. I'd choke if I tried to eat. Do you mind if I just bathe and go to bed? We'll talk in the morning."
After a long, hot shower, Rachel curled under her comforter and tried to relax. The thoughts kept coming. O.K. Toes relax, legs relax...body relax...Why should I feel so guilty about anything. I was the victim...Aarr...Go away bad thoughts. O.K. Maybe doing it the way I've always been taught will help. Our father which art in heaven...Gees, I wish this headache would go away. Maybe I should take another pain pill...when did I take the last one?'
Rachel stuck her leg out of bed and sat up. I'm sure that it's been long enough. She leaned over to the chair where her coat was hanging and retrieved the prescription bottle. Grabbing the glass of water on her stand, she downed a pill.
"I wish I could talk to Mama about all this. Not a chance…Mama and Daddy would come down hard. I'm not ready to challenge them on my right to stay here.'
She lay back down. Staring straight at the ceiling, she tried the meditation again. 'O.K. This time I'm affirming. I affirm that all is well. I'm denying my headache.'
She took a deep breath and spoke out loud. "Who am I kidding?" That affirming stuff had never worked all the years that she was growing up. She pictured her mom, kneeling, affirming that God was healing her of whatever affliction she had at the time. That stuff nev...Rachel was asleep. The dreams started. First Brent's face loomed up in her mind, then the face of the woman.
'Why do I feel so dreadfully guilty and ashamed?' She verbalized in garbled grunts. The woman was chasing her. No, that's not a woman, that's a man. Rachel was running backwards. What a strange, dreadful feeling.

A voice in her dream, her own voice, or was the voice of the woman kept saying, you shouldn't have been there, you shouldn't have led him on, it's your fault. Rachel woke and slept sporadically and fitfully.
She got up in the early dawn and took another pill. This time, she fell into a deep sleep without dreams.
 The light seeping through the cracks around the window blind hit Rachel's face. She turned toward the wall and tried to open her burning eyes. I feel fried. I think I'll just stay here all day. After all, what've I got to get up for? Prying her eyes open, she looked around the empty room. "Julie... Julie?"
Rachel got up and checked the door lock.
Everything's o.k.
What day is it? She slipped back into bed. That headache. Maybe I need another pill. She rolled out of the bed and grabbed the bottle. No, I think I may be taking too many of these things. I should get up and get dressed.
 She rolled to her side, got up and walked over to the desk calendar. Must be Sunday. Yeah, yesterday was Saturday. I don't want to remember yesterday or think about that day ever again. Ah, if only these pills I've been taking could just erase everything depressing.'
Rachel peeked through the blinds. Ouch, the light...She pulled her hand away and put it over her eyes as she sat down on her bed. Not too many people on campus. Maybe I won't leave the room today.
Brent's face flashed through her mind. What if I run into him? Monday. Tomorrow will be a good day to get out. She glanced over to her term paper notebook on the desk. I should finish it...Oh, no. I forgot my research notebook and the library books. I left them on Starlight Plateau. She scolded herself.
She jumped up and started pulling on her jeans. Maybe Julie will go out with me to find them. She looked into the mirror at her scratched face.
'How can I go back there?'

She panicked as she heard a key turn in the door. Julie stepped inside. Rachel sat down on the side of the bed holding her hand to her chest, catching her breath. Julie came over and sat down on the bed beside her.
"Hey, Rachel, calm down."
"How about two knocks before you put the key in the door?"
"Sounds good."
"Julie, would you drive me up to Starlight Point? I left my books up there."
"Brent left the books in the office, Rachel. I saw Dave and he wants to talk to you about something. The talk around campus is that Brent is claiming that you went nuts for no reason and stole his van. Dave won't deny or confirm that with me."
"Oh, good one! How can he explain the bruises and scratches?"
"Judy Cramer said that Brent said you tripped and fell running off the trail into the brush."
"He's lying about my falling down. I ran into a lot of brush. But I was afraid for my life."
"It seems to me that if he'd filed a report, the police would've been questioning you about all this. It's your word against his. I hate to say this, Rachel, but you may have to drop this, after all.
He's probably found a way to trump your Ace."
"You're probably right. But if I make waves, maybe some girl out there will believe me who would otherwise be his victim."
Rachel was still sputtering when Julie pulled her out into the cool air.
"You're all over the place, Rachel. First, you want to fight, and then you want to hide. Just stop worrying and let's just get your books."
Julie stopped and threw up her hands. "I just remembered I need to go to the book store before it closes. " Are you going to be o.k. Rachel?"

"I'm fine. I'll just get my books and go do my research. I need to check out a few more articles."
"You need to talk to Dave first and find out why he wants to see you. You should get this out of the way."
"I will, I will." Rachel rubbed her head.
"Is that place on your head still sore?"
"Yeah, but the pain is bearable now or maybe I'm just getting used to it."
The front room of the security office was empty. The books were on the receptionist desk. She stepped in to peek into Dave's office, but he was not there. Rachel retrieved the books and headed for the library.
In the building, she thought she saw a familiar figure disappear into the study area. I'm being paranoid. She thought.
She put her hand to her heart and took a deep breath. The nauseated feeling in the pit of her stomach rose to her head and she leaned against a wall. Recovering, she worked her way through the aisles of the library, carefully trying to avoid the open spaces while she searched for her research books. All the while, Rachel watched for any sign that she was being approached. Finishing her choice of books, she peered out from her aisle. Spotting the table near 'Aisle History European', Rachel started to walk. Then she saw them. Shivers ran up her spine. 'Ah, Brent Morse is on the move again. This time his target is that red head with big, blue eyes and a rose bud mouth. She looks so innocent.' Rachel rubbed her head. 'I don't know what to do. I wish I could just take my aching head back to bed. I'd like to punch somebody out. To be exact,
Brent. So, now, o.k. my fuse is lit.'
Forcing her legs to move, she walked up to Brent. Smiling as sarcastically as she could, she looked straight into his eyes. To blazes with not looking the mad dog in the eyes. "Is this your next victim, Brent?" Brent stepped back and turned to the little redhead. "This woman's crazy. But the

police will have her in lockup as soon as I get my report filed."

Rachel flinched, but not to be undone, she kept her eyes on the redhead, as she charged back with, "Don't be alone with him. He's dangerous." Brent hurried his quarry out the door.

The redhead's innocence turned to sarcasm as she grinned at Rachel. "What do ya have here? Brent? A virgin?"

Brent laughed loudly. The librarian quickly walked up and looked down her nose at Rachel. Feeling numb, Rachel turned to the nearest table and pulled up a chair. I can't believe what I just did or what I just heard. She looked blankly around her. Oh great. Everyone is staring at me. She walked awkwardly to a table with her books. Do I really care? She sat down. 'Now I'll be known throughout the campus as that crazy woman, but I don't care.

Rachel put her elbows down over her open book. 'I do care what happens to the red head, though. I do not know why I care. She could be either a slut or just playing along with Brent's little game to make herself popular. If she's innocent, I really want to help her...but I just don't know what to do about it.

Someone had left a magazine on the table and she thumbed through it. A title jumped-out from a page at her: "College Campus Rapes."

She read account after account about rapes that had been hushed up by campus police to save the college image. She wrote the name of the magazine and notes from the article in her notebook and stepped up to the checkout counter to check out the books. She muttered to herself. There in the open atrium, locked in an embrace was Brent and his new target. At least I didn't wrap myself up into that kind of intimate display. Rachel thought.

Suddenly from behind her, a voice interrupted her thoughts. "I see that you're carrying some pretty hefty books. Can I carry some of them for you?" Rachel turned to stare up at the lanky sophomore who had befriended her on her first day of school. Jerrod Showalter wasn't a classically handsome character, but he wasn't hard to look at, either.

Rachel had hardly given Jerrod a thought since that first day. Nevertheless, he always seemed to be around, smiling at her. He seems innocent enough, but I can't be too careful. He makes me feel skittish. After all Brent seemed harmless too. Maybe I'll never trust again.' She thought.

"Thank you. Perhaps you can carry the big ones," she answered.

She thought, 'With any luck, you'll shield me as I pass the clutching couple in the center of the atrium.'

"That is, if you are you going anywhere near Zephyr Hall," she added as Jerrod took the larger books from her.

"Sure. No problem. In fact, some of these books are ones that I just turned back in yesterday. If I can help you with the research, let me know," he added.

They reached her dorm and Rachel turned to take the books from Jerrod. 'Gees, I feel guilty using Jerrod. He really helped me get past a rough time, but I've got to find a way to dismiss him gracefully. I just can't handle a relationship.'

"Thank you for your help. I don't know how I thought I was going to get all these up the hill steps."

"That's o.k. Are you sure you don't want me to take these in for you?"

"Oh, certainly not, thank you for asking. I think that I'll study at the atrium table. You can just leave them there for me."

Jerrod followed her and sat the books down. He lingered as Rachel awkwardly sat down on a chair and opened a book.

'Now what do I do?' She asked herself.

"Thanks again," she said, looking up in a dismissal.

Jerrod grinned. "No problem. Uh...Would you like to go out for a movie tonight with me?"

"Oh, I'm sorry, Jerrod. I have way too much to do."

"Well, perhaps, we could just hang out sometime? Just let me know."

He pulled his backpack off and taking out a pad and pencil from the outer pocket, he scribbled on a piece of paper. Handing it to her he said, "Call me anytime for any reason."
"Thanks, I appreciate that." She took the paper, put it into her jean pocket, and returned to her books.
Jerrod put his pack on his back and walked away.
As soon as he was gone and out of sight, Rachel picked up her books and headed outside and toward the dormitory doors.
Suddenly, she went into panic mode. Julie, who came up behind her almost ran into her when she stopped abruptly. Dave's van was parked in the parking lot and he was standing nonchalantly in front of it. The little red head stood next to him.
Rachel glanced at her and looked straight at Brent. Rachel stood in a locked stare with her tormentor. "Hey, Slut, look what you did to my van."
Rachel followed Brent's hand as he motioned toward a good size dent on the right hand side in the fender.
Julie came to Rachel's rescue. "That wasn't there yesterday."
"Oh, yes it was. My little squeeze here can testify that the dent wasn't there on Friday night when I took her to the movies." He pulled the red head tighter to him. "She knows how to treat a guy. You left me abandoned. I had to walk to the next farm to call her yesterday when I couldn't get a signal on my cell. Anyway, Angel noticed this dent before I did. You left the motor running and it was out of gas. So we had to run into town to pick up a can of fuel. Not only that, you screwed the starter up. I had a heck of a time getting the wires back together to get it started."
From somewhere deep inside, Rachel grabbed for her strength. She averted Brent's eyes and stared beyond him to the dent on the van fender.
The expression on Brent's face changed to a mirthful grin for a fleeting moment. Then he sobered. "We can just let the police handle this."

Rachel's blood was pulsating, rushing in her veins like wildfire. She thought the top of her head might blow off. On the other hand, she couldn't allow him to think that she was afraid or that he affected her in any way.

Julie squeezed Rachel more firmly and pushed her gently past Brent to the fender.

"What makes this dent so special, Brent?" Julie asked Brent. Julie felt the dent. "Is that rust on the edges of the dent?" Rachel reached out and ran her fingers over the other dents. They were rusted as well, and the metal was pitted and dull.

Brent stood on the sidewalk watching them. "Don't worry about it. I think I should go over to security and make a report. I've got no problem with them investigating the cause of this dent. They certainly should know about how the wiring got screwed up. I can't believe that an innocent freshman knows about how to hot-wire a car, Rachel. That should be a trait left up to criminals. Maybe you're not as squeaking clean as you claim, you with all your pious religious talk."

Julie wasn't backing down. She stopped examining the dent and then charged. "Yeah? Well, Brent. All these dents look ancient to me. I think you'd better think twice before you file a false report."

"Hey, all I have to do is to take pictures of the dents and that wiring mess under my dash and file the report. The cops are all going to take my side when they see all that." He turned towards Rachel. "Maybe the police will find out that you, Miss High and Mighty, have a rap sheet a mile long. Wouldn't surprise me at all."

Rachel backed away from the van. She turned and walked toward the dormitory building and Julie followed her.

In the foyer, a student stopped Julie to ask about an assignment that was due. Rachel continued walking toward the stairway. When the girl started to leave, she yelled back. "By the way, there was a hit and run accident up there on the mountain road. One of our teachers was found in a ditch this morning. Seems she was down getting her mail from the mailbox sometime yesterday and someone hit her and took off."

Julie yelled back at the student who was continuing down the hallway. "Yes, I heard about that. Wait up Rachel."

Rachel started to weave as they got to the bottom of the stairway. Julie put her arms around her and took the stack of books from Rachel, lowering them to the bottom stair step. "The fender, Julie, and the woman on the mountain...I just can't shake off the thoughts. I feel like I'm going to be sick."

She doubled over and sat down on the step above the books. Her inner voice yelled, but I have to be strong! The memory of her mother's crying spells and her nervous illnesses arose in her. She struggled to be like Dad, reserved with all emotions under control.

She broke out into a sweat and started shaking. The tears welled up, but she choked them back.

Julie sat down and put her arms around Rachel. "Come on; let's get upstairs to our room. Is the headache worse?"

Rachel got up, turned, and grabbed the step railing. "It seems so much farther up these steps than I thought. The fog is back."

In the room, she sat down on her desk chair.

"Am I still in my dream?"

Julie put the stack of books on the floor and handed Rachel the prescription bottle from the desk and a glass of water

She helped her back into bed. Rachel looked up at Julie and whispered, "I'll wake up and it will all be a dream."

"Yes, Rachel. Just a dream." Then Julie pulled the blankets up over her. "I'll go out and get us something to eat. I'll be right back."

Rachel pulled the blankets tight as she heard the door shut and the latch set. 'This has to be a bad dream.'

She threw the blankets off. She started to cry. "It was Ms. Bence." She cried out. "Last night's dreams were real."

She lost all control. The tears flowed uncontrollably. "Oh, Ms. Bence, I'm so sorry. Could I have killed you?" The vision of Ms. Bence face was so real.

Rachel stopped sobbing. The room cooled off.
She pulled the blankets back over her.
Her inner turmoil continued. 'No, that can't be. I talked to the woman. The woman talked to me. Ms. Bence, yes it was, Ms. Bence, invited me up to her house. She was alive.''
There was no sleep, just frantic and uncontrollable tears. Sometime in the night, she got up, peered out toward the shadows of the mountain range against the sky, and listened to the echo of the wolf spirits from Shady Mountain.

Chapter Six

Monday morning, Rachel woke slowly from dreams. Brent's chasing me...no it's Jerrod laughing. Why is he mocking me? That foggy ghost of a woman in the corner just smiled. Why did the woman start to cry?
The clock on the stand started to buzz. Why can't I feel my body? Arms, legs...they won't move. Am I paralyzed? Come on legs, move. Dreams, go away.
She turned to look through blurry eyes at the digital numbers on the clock. Her vision cleared.
Six o'clock.
Finally, she was able to pull herself up. She clung to her bed and cried softly.
'Brent chasing me...will I ever get rid of the memories?'
She wiped her tears on her pajama sleeve. 'I should have gone to church yesterday. Mother and Father would be so disappointed if they knew I skipped services.'
She stood up and stretched. She looked down at the styrofoam container on the table. Then she remembered. Julie must have left her dinner. She looked at the corner bunk where her roommate breathed evenly in silent slumber.
Her thoughts returned. The student body was holding vigils for Ms. Bench. 'I just can't bring myself to facing that.'
She made her way in the darkness across the room and entered the small toilet. 'Poor Ms. Bence. She must've been going to a mailbox across the road when I talked with her. That's why she disappeared. Ms. Bence must've walked behind the van. That's it. What else could happen in such a short period of time?'
She shivered. 'No, I won't think about it now.'
She turned on the toilet light. Rachel looked into the mirror at her shallow face. I look like I've been through a war. I need to get back to my faith. Mother says no one can help in this world, except with guidance from God. Mother and Father's faith has kept them sane and peaceful. Maybe they know best. Even when they've disagreed with me about my

choices, they've never raised their voices. Of course, they didn't have to. They'd verbally put the fear of God into me and I'd step in line. Their choice of words based on the scriptures and reciting actual scripture were enough to make me feel like I was going to go to hell if I didn't behave. There was that time when Stephan came home later than his curfew on Prom night. Stephan got angry and raised his voice. Mama started to cry. Father quoted scripture about disobedience and Stephan slithered up the stairway to his room. He came down later and apologized.'

Rachel finished brushing her teeth and returned to the main room. I had to manipulate Father and Mother to allow me to come to this college. I worked too hard to get them to see the advantages. On the other hand, I can't let all that slip through my fingers. I can't get the education I want anywhere else for the cost. But then, considering the mess I've gotten myself into, maybe they're right.'

Rachel lay back down on the bed. 'Perhaps if I meditate and try to find some connection with the spirit, I can find peace.' Julie stirred in her half bed. It was too early to turn on the room lights. Rachel got up and gathering her clothing from her little cubbyhole, she slipped out of the room, locked the door, and headed for the shower room.

Rachel could hear a shower running in another stall. She slipped out of her nightclothes and turned on the water. She watched the water running down the drain. Throwing back her head, she closed her eyes. Her headache subsided. The warmth flowed over her, and relief from the dreams, the hurt, and the troubles seemed to leave her body.

She looked down as the water took it all down the drain. If only I could make something positive happen out of all this. I'm not the only woman who's had to suffer from sexual coercion or rape.

The statistics in the magazine were staggering.'

She stepped out of the shower and started drying her hair with the towel. Suddenly, she stopped moving her arms and dropped them to her side. Ah, divine intervention. I know what I want to do. Somehow, I'll form an awareness and help group for date assault and date rape cases. If the college won't assist me, I'll take my case outside the campus. Perhaps there's a way to make this hurt have a positive result.

She left the shower stall while drying off and reached for her clothing. There was no clothing.

There was not a stitch, no blouse, or pants, not even her pajamas as she searched every hook, every stall and every wastebasket.

She yelled out, "O.K. this isn't funny." The echo of her voice jarred her head and the ache returned. She pulled out all the bath linens from the racks. Nothing. Giving up on looking for her garments, Rachel grabbed two large towels, wrapped them around her into a dress affect, and headed out into the hall.

As she rounded a corner and started up a stairway, she ran into the little red head coming out of her room with her arms folded.

Angela giggled and said, "Are you setting a new fashion trend, Rachel?" With that, a whole series of laughter vibrated down the hall. A whole group of girls was standing in the halls and in the doorways.

Rachel's irritation flared. She thought, 'Chick, I've got a skull that's exploding and you're going to hear my wrath.' She stood for a moment and let the laughter die down. Then she stared at the little red head and spoke as loudly as she could in spite of the burning in her brain. "It seems that someone else less fortunate than I needed to borrow my clothing this morning. I'm sure that they'll return them to me. And if they don't, I'm always eager to donate to the needy."

Angela's face lit up as brightly as her hair. The whole building echoed with the laughter from the hallway as Rachel turned and headed up the stairway.

Julie met Rachel at the door of their room. She looked at her attire and giggled.

"You know you could've gotten some clothing to take with you." Julie looked toward the stairway. "What's all that racket for? Were they laughing at you? They were, weren't they?"

"Oh, yeah. Mostly, they were laughing at the red head. I guess they were anyway." She started rummaging for another outfit to wear. "Oh, and if you're headed for the showers, make sure you keep your clothing where you can protect it."

"I'm headed for the showers, but I don't think anyone will pull that on me. I think it was the red head and she just wanted to pull something on you that she could brag to Brent about."

"Before you go down, I want to tell you my plans for a date rape group." After she finished, she asked, "Who do you think I should go to for help?"

"Well, first off, you need to get your own troubles taken care of, Rachel." Julie pointed out. "Do you realize how much time all of that organizing is going to take? That's if you can get the college to allow you to start a club like that."

Rachel's lips were set in determination. Her eyes were steady. "I'll find the time. It's worth it to warn naive women like I was to the red flags, and perhaps prevent assault or rape."

"Okay. If you can get the college board to approve of it, I'll help you with it."

Rachel sat down on her bed to put her shoes on. "You know, if Ms. Bence was alive, she'd be one of the first to help. I know that she would."

"Well, that's another thing. A lot of the classes are closed for today. A lot of the students came back to see the flags at half-staff and to find out about the accident. By the way, you'd better get your legal papers against Brent filled out and get them filed."

"I've got class this morning."

"English class, right? I think you will find out that class is closed and there will be a wreath on the door."

Rachel bent over holding her stomach.
"What is it?"
"I'm feeling sick to my stomach again."
Julie sat down in front to Rachel and looked up at her eyes. They had that glazed over look to them again.
Rachel shook her head as if to clear it. "I keep having flashback visions of the woman's face, the kind, sweet face of the teacher on the side of the road." She shivered and brought her arms up around herself, squeezing her shoulders. "I'm trying so hard to hang onto my resolve but…" She started to cry so hard that she could hardly sit up straight.
Julie sat down by her and put her arms around her. When Rachel calmed down, Julie went to the small refrigerator and brought back a bottle of water, opening it for Rachel.
Rachel sat, drank the water, and popped a couple of pain pills. She stared at the floor. "You know, Julie, I don't know what I'm feeling anymore. There's so many thoughts raging around in my head, I just wanted to shut them all down."
Finally, Julie spoke. "Rachel, I'm going to go downstairs and get the house mother. She can help you talk to a counselor."
Rachel smiled and said, "I'm o.k. I guess I'd better go to the library and work on the mid-term papers for history. And the library will have a posting of classes open or closed for today."
Rachel, the housemother will have the posting.
Come on and go with me."
Rachel looked at Julie who still had her P.J.'s on. "Julie, go take your shower. Don't you have any classes this morning? You should be worrying about yourself."
"No, I don't have class. Remember, we both have the same English class. Now come with me. I don't care if I am in my nightclothes. If you can run around the halls in a couple of towels, I can strut in my P.J.s. Now come on, let's go see what's going on with campus life."
Rachel got up and rolled her eyes. "O.K. But don't be surprised if we run into the little red head."

"Oh, I don't think we'll see her. She's probably blabbing to Brent about this morning's shower right about now."
Sadie O'Reilly was a very bubbly middle-aged woman who loved all the girls unconditionally. When Rachel walked into her office, she put her arms around her and hugged her.
"Rachel what's this that I hear about you having a hard time of it?"
Rachel looked at Julie, who looked sheepish.
"Oh, so my friend here has filled you in?"
"Better her than half the dormitory of gossipy little women. Now why don't you sit down here and tell me what's really going on."
Rachel sat down on big stuffed chair in front of the desk in the small scrunched up little room. She skipped over details and told Sadie about her idea for a women's help group.
"You know, there's a women's group already on campus. Let me check, but I think it meets sometime today."
"Oh, would you? Good. I'd really appreciate it if you could do that. It needs to be more widely publicized."
"Well, I'm sure they're looking for volunteers with that, too."
The phone rang and Sadie answered, leaving Rachel to look around the room. It was so small that one could hardly turn around in it, but it was amazingly organized and clean. Rachel looked at Sadie as she hung up the phone. Sadie was a small boned and short little woman with short-cropped brown hair. 'She's really quite pretty,' she thought.
"Rachel, that was Dean Johnson of Student Services. "
Sadie hesitated a little, looking down at her fingers as she entwined them and put them in front of her on the desk. Then she spoke again. "I want to talk to you before you make an appointment with him. I wouldn't want you to tell anyone that I'm telling you this, but I take care of you girls. Sometimes that means going above and beyond policies."
Rachel stayed silent. When she didn't answer, Sadie got up and closed the door. "I hope you're not claustrophobic, Rachel."
"I am, but I'll deal with it."

"It won't take long." Sadie sat on an ottoman in the corner by the file cabinet, putting her at a lower level than Rachel. "There have been some nasty rumors going on around the campus. Stories of several versions implicate you. I have a feeling that's why the dean is getting involved."

Rachel started to shake and Sadie leaned over and took both her hands in hers. "Rachel, you need to call your parents. They can get a lawyer for you."

"A lawyer?"

"You don't realize how serious this has gotten. Brent filled out a police report this morning about a dent on the fender of his van. He told the police that he found the dent after you stole it the other day. The whole thing's getting out of hand."

Rachel started to cry uncontrollably. Sadie let her cry as she moved over and hugged her until the crying stopped.

The phone rang and Sadie reached over her desk and picked it up.

"Yes, Dean. It just so happens that Rachel's in my office right now."

Sadie whispered in Rachel's ear, "Be strong." Then she handed her the phone.

The dean's voice was a deep baritone...like Brent's. "Hello Rachel."

Rachel put her hand on her chest. She gave Sadie a startled look and pulled the phone away from her ear. "Who did you say this was?" "It's Dean Johnson, Rachel." Sadie confirmed.

Rachel returned the phone to her ear. "Ms. Brooks, could I get you to come to my office? There are some things I need to discuss with you, immediately."

"Yes, Dean. What time?"

"As soon as you can get here. Ms. Brooks, your parents called me this morning. They couldn't reach you Saturday night and yesterday. We'll be doing a conference call with them after you get here."

Rachel's hand gripped the phone for a few seconds after the dean hung up. The buzz on the line was one long string of noise, and she stared at the butterfly motif on the wall, as if mesmerized by something ghostly.
Slowly, she put the phone on the cradle.
Sadie spoke. "Rachel, do you want me to walk you over to the dean's office?" Rachel broke the stare and looked at Sadie. She nodded her head. Sadie grabbed her jacket from the back of her chair.
Julie met Rachel and Sadie as they were going out the large front doors. Sadie quickly summarized. "The dean needs to talk with Rachel. She needs our support. Could you run up and get your jackets?" Rachel said nothing. Sadie felt a bit worried. It was as though Rachel were a zombie, helpless, like a puppet on a string. Sadie read her inner feelings well.
The dean's office was in the cluster of administration buildings on the outer campus side near the front entrance. It was starting to sprinkle a cold rain. The wind was still, but the fall chill hit them all full force as they walked across the campus.

    As they rounded the corner on the sidewalk side, Rachel stopped and stared. A city police car sat next to Brent's van. Sadie saw it too, and stopped in unison with Rachel. Julie had been walking with her head down. When the other two stopped, her eyes followed the direction of the target of their attention.
Rachel started to shiver uncontrollably. Sadie put her arms around her and pulled her inside to the lobby. Rachel started to go down, and Sadie supported her as she maneuvered her to a lounge couch. She turned to Julie and said, "Would you go to the dean's office and tell him that we need a doctor, the nurse practitioner with a wheelchair, and/or a school counselor here to speak with Rachel before the meeting? Make sure that he understands how serious this is."
Julie hurried up the stairs to the upper level.

Sadie looked at Rachel's ashen face. Rachel still had not stopped shaking. "Are you chilled through from the wind, Rachel?" Rachel stared at her, her eyes glassy and dilated.

Chapter Seven

Julie's voice shook a bit as she explained to the secretary in the outer office that she urgently needed to talk with the dean on the subject of Rachel Brooks. The secretary pushed the button to the dean's office and relayed the message.
Dean Johnson immediately appeared and closed his office door. "Julie, where is Rachel?"
Julie started to cry softly and tremble a bit. "Sadie's asking for Edna to get here as soon as possible. Rachel's in a terrible state, Dean. Sadie's with her downstairs in the lobby. I think she may be having a nervous breakdown or in shock or something. She's as ashen as a ghost and she's shaking uncontrollably. Her legs buckled out from under her. She just stares and doesn't respond."
Dean Johnson looked at Julie's troubled face and responded. "I'll get a counselor to go into the lobby. You need to go back there. I'll take care of things here."
Julie breathed a sigh of relief and headed back downstairs.
Dean Johnson stepped back into his office. He faced Detective Lieutenant Yoder and Dave Taylor, the school security officer, and Brent Morse.
"Brent, I need you to wait in another office for me while I speak with Lieutenant Yoder and Dave."
Brent got up and followed the dean to another room on the other side of the secretary's window office.
Back in his own office, the dean explained the situation to Yoder and Dave. He turned to Dave. "Would you be able to wait a little longer while my staff and I assess Ms. Brooks' condition and her stability to answer questions?"
"Of course, unless you'd like us to come back in an hour?" Yoder said. "We've already got Brent Morse's statement, and we have the reports from Dave here, so we could let Brent wait in his dormitory until after we talk with Ms. Brooks."

"That would be an excellent idea. Considering the situation downstairs, Dave, I need you to escort Brent out down my back stairs to keep him from running into anyone from the Brooks' side of this controversy. I need to make a phone call while you men handle the situation with Brent."

Dave nodded and left. Yoder followed him where Brent sat reading a magazine and watching a TV program in the small waiting room.

Brent's face showed confusion and disappointment when the detective explained to him that he had all the information he needed from him for now.

"I do have one more question for you." Yoder poised his pencil above his writing pad. "Why did you wait until this morning to report all this?"

Brent's face was beet red. His voice turned raspy and developed a high pitch as he spoke. "I reported it to security." He turned to the security officer. "Dave, you know that. You gave me complaint papers to fill out. You told me to go down town and file charges for the stolen vehicle, but I figured that since it was the weekend, the downtown office wouldn't be open and I got my car back. So... it's no big hurry, right?"

Dave spoke up. "Brent, I asked you if you wanted me to get the downtown officers to come out and investigate and question Ms. Brooks. I also told you that Ms. Brooks had forms to file and asked you if you wanted to fill out forms to counter her claims. You told me that you'd just file the papers for now and that since you had your car back, you wouldn't report it as stolen."

Yoder looked in disbelief at Dave. He looked back at Brent. "Even if you didn't have the expert advice and help from Officer Taylor, all you had to do was to call 911 and we would have been here in a shot. We are always open."

Yoder cleared his throat. "Why did you change your mind and decide to report the vehicle stolen?"

"Well, after I found out about Ms. Bence, I figured that it was a suspicious coincidence that my van was on that mountain road at about that time, and when I got it back it had a dent in the fender. That's all I'm saying."

"Well, yes, I see what you're saying. In fact, I've been working on the Bence accident report from the investigating police officers at that scene. Anything you have to offer may shed some light on it all."

Yoder cleared his throat and continued. "By the way, when you came down the mountain road with your friend, who picked you up, did you see anything suspicious, like tire tracks, or anything?"

"Well, we did notice tire marks, but sometimes the guys go up there and burn rubber. So we didn't think anything about it at the time."

"You didn't see clothing or anything to indicate a person laying in the ditch?"

"No sir."

Yoder looked down at his pad. "And. let's see. You said in our earlier interview that your friend's name is Angela Pike. Is that right?"

Brent nodded his head. "Yes Sir." Yoder's pen moved on his pad.

"Thank you for bringing this to our attention. We have all the information that we need from you right now. We'd like for you to stay where we can reach you if we need anything further." Yoder explained.

Dave added. "Do you have any classes this afternoon, Brent?"

Brent stuttered, "Ye...Yeah. Well, not really. I mean, I don't know if that class is open today because of...you know, because of Ms. Bence."

Yoder spoke again as he was turning to leave the room. "Oh and by the way, Brent, it would help this case develop properly if you didn't speak of this to anyone else outside of this room, unless you're asked questions by the police department, the courts, or the school officers. So whatever information or suspicions you have, keep them..."

Brent interrupted. "I understand. I've a talent for being discreet."

The detective hesitated at the door, then added when he saw Brent's flushed face, "I'm not scolding you. But you need to trust us when we say that gossip has ruined more cases than you can imagine. Someone can take what you say and give a defense lawyer the meat to throw everything out of court. So just help us out and keep your information within our circle."

Brent smiled, his chest pumped up and he reached out and shook the detective's hand. "You can count on me, Sir." He said with a militaristic air.

Yoder continued. "Dave will walk you down the back stairs to protect you from anyone who might see and want to question you. We don't want you to have to face that right now."

Brent flashed a confident smile and followed Dave down the back hall.

The sound of the canine echo from the mountain sent chills up Dave's spine as the pair passed an open window. He thought he would never acclimate to that sound.

School Counselor Joanna Scholz had walked from her office when she got the call from the Dean of Student Services office. Dean Johnson filled her in completely and she thought she was prepared for the situation she found in the lobby.

She wasn't.

Rachel Brooks had gone into a world of her own. She was as limp as a rag doll, breathing shallow and totally unresponsive. After trying to focus through her glassy, tunnel vision, Rachel closed her eyes.

Joanna looked at Sadie. "How long has she been like this?"

"It's been building up since I saw her this morning and probably before that." She turned to Julie. "Julie?"

"She's been building all this up since Saturday morning when all of this started." Julie was visibly shaken.

"All of what started? Do you mean about Ms. Bence." Joanna asked.

Sadie looked at the counselor. "It's more than that. You haven't heard the gossip, have you?"

"No, I was out of town this weekend and heard about Ms. Bence on the news. But that's all I heard."

"I'm surprised that the media didn't pick up on what's been said about it around campus. Of course, they probably just know what the administration told them in a phone interview."

While they talked, Joanna had been rubbing Rachel's limp hands. She took her pulse both in the wrist and on the neck. Joanna took out her cell phone. "I'm going to call the nurse practitioner over here to check her out."

She stepped away to make her call.

Yoder and Dave were coming down the stairway as Joanna was conversing with the nurse practitioner on her cell phone. When the men reached the lobby floor, she turned to them.

"I believe we have a serious situation here, Dean Johnson. Ms. Brooks is like a zombie. I have never seen anything like this on a campus. I have Edna Graves coming over here to check her out."

"I see. However, I think it would be safer to have Ms. Brooks brought up to my office. There haven't been any other students in this lobby today, but it's about ten o'clock and we may be getting some traffic pretty soon."

"No, all the students have been over in the counseling offices and waiting rooms today. The trauma of Ms. Bence has brought them in by droves. The counselors on duty this weekend had their hands full."

"Yes, I've been told that. We need to get her upstairs. We can leave someone here to wait for Edna to get across campus from the clinic."

Joanna looked through the windows at the figure hurrying toward the building. "I see Edna coming with a wheelchair." Joanna stated. "We will have to take Rachel up the elevator. She doesn't have any balance."

Dean Johnson started toward the lounge area. Yoder and Joanna followed. Yoder knelt down in front of Rachel. "Ms. Brooks, my name is
Lieutenant Yoder. How are you today?"
The detective looked straight into Rachel's eyes. She did not respond, flinch, or make any eye movement.
He rose and looked at Joanna. He spoke, "Her pupils are dilated. We need to be getting this girl to the hospital. Rachel needs more care than she can get here." Joanna turned and looked at the dean.
"What do you think, Dean Johnson?"
Dean Johnson nodded his head. "I'm in total agreement. Let's see what the nurse practitioner says."
Yoder stepped away toward the large atrium windows as he called for an ambulance. At the same time, Edna pulled the wheelchair through the atrium doors and up to Rachel's chair. She immediately parted Rachel's hair on the left side of her head. She looked down through the part more intently.
Then she turned to the group. "Rachel had a blow to her head this weekend. It didn't seem like much then, although she said she had a headache. The bump's really quite swollen right now. I told her to report to me if the headache didn't stop. She refused to go to the emergency room, stating that she only received a light bump."
"Did she tell you how she received the bump?" Yoder asked
"No." Edna turned to Julie who was sitting on one side of Rachel. "Did she tell you how it happened?"
"No, she said that she didn't fall when she was running down the mountain. But she never explained the bump. She's had the headache, she's been moody, and she's been emotional ever since. When she was dreaming, she mentioned something about talking to a woman on the road." Julie looked up at Yoder and realized that she may have said too much.

Yoder and Dave looked at each other but said nothing. The ambulance pulled in without sirens. The paramedics came in with a stretcher and went directly to Rachel. Edna filled them in as they worked. They got Rachel on a stretcher and Edna and Sadie followed them with Julie right behind.

Sadie turned to Julie at the door. "Edna will go with Rachel in the ambulance. I'll get my car and meet them there. Do you want to ride with me? Julie?"

Yoder stepped up to Julie. "I'd like to talk with you first. I can drive you down to the hospital."

"That's o.k. I have my own car. I can walk back to the hall and get it later."

After permission from Dean Johnson to use his office again, Yoder led Julie up the open stairway.

Julie started to lose her resolve and she wiped her eyes on her sleeve. Her mind was busily sorting out what had been said by Rachel over the last days. She did not want to make her situation even more precarious than it was.

Yoder sat down on a chair away from Dean Johnson's desk and Julie sat beside him. He pulled his chair out so that he was looking at Julie.

"I'm Detective Lieutenant Yoder and your name is?"

"I'm Julie Thompson."

"O.K. Ms. Thompson. I'm recording our conversation. It helps me to keep things sorted out."

"O.K."

"And you're a friend of Rachel Brooks, is that correct?"

"I'm her roommate and her friend, yes."

"Now, Ms. Thompson. I'd like you to relate to me what you know about what happened to Ms. Brooks this weekend. I realize that this is hearsay, but we need to have as much first-hand knowledge as possible of what's been said by the people involved."

Julie thought a moment, trying to be careful about what she said; she related what happened when she met Rachel at the van on Saturday, all the events of meeting with Dave and

Edna, how Rachel was acting, her trauma and her headaches. She completely avoided conversation with Brent and his accusations to Rachel of theft and damage to his van.
When she finished, Lieutenant Yoder waited a moment, then said. "You started to say something earlier about Ms. Brooks talking in her sleep about a conversation with a woman on the mountain road. Could you tell me, as close as you can, what she said?"
Julie bit her lower lip.
"Ms. Thompson, in order to help Ms. Brooks, we need to find out what she's been going through."
"What she was saying was garbled. It was as if she was talking to someone. She said something like, 'I talked with you...on the mountain...you asked me to come in.'
That's about all I can tell you."
Yoder wrote something on his pad and turned to Julie again. "Did she indicate in any way that it was a woman?"
Julie looked down at her hands. "I think she did say something about a woman and teacher, but I can't swear to it. In her dreams she said, 'Ms.' but her voice trailed off and the rest was garbled."
"Was this before or after the two of you knew about Ms. Bence?"
"That was after we heard about the accident. I think she was just confused."
"Changing the subject, were you there when Brent Morse accused Rachel of putting the dent in his fender"
Julie drew in a big breath. "Brent Morse met us outside Zephyr Hall, that's our dormitory. He had his van in front of the dorm. Rachel and I were walking out. He accused Rachel of stealing the van, and he accused her of putting a large dent in the fender. Rachel just went into shock at that accusation. Besides, I pointed out to Brent that there were other dents in his van and that they all, including the one he said Rachel made, were rusted. They were all old dents."
Yoder made some notes on his writing pad. He thought that those dents looked strange when they examined them outside

the door earlier, especially the big one. It looked as if the edges of the big dent had been sanded recently, and despite some shiny spots, bits of the metal beneath was pitted and corroded. He said nothing. He and his partner had taken pictures of the damage and he would get the report from the insurance company. Maybe he would just call the insurance company and have them send an adjuster right away.

"Did this happen before or after you heard about the accident involving Ms. Bence?"

"This happened before we heard about it."

Yoder was fully aware that Julie was being cautious and that she might even be covering for her friend. He gave no indication of it to Julie.

"O.K. Ms. Thompson. Is there anything else that you can remember?"

"No." Julie lied. If he didn't ask her about the red head and the disappearance of Rachel's clothing, she wasn't going to offer it up. Besides, it had nothing to do with the accident or anything else.

Dean Johnson met the group in the lobby. "Julie, I called Rachel's parents back. They're going to fly in on their church private plane, so they'll probably be at the hospital in about three hours. I'll try to be there to meet them, but could you be sure to watch for them?"

"Sure." She turned and started walking toward the double doors. Julie knew that Rachel would be livid if she could comprehend that her parents knew anything about any of these events, but..." she wondered if the dean had told them any of it. She really wanted to know before she went to the hospital.

She turned around and walked back toward where Yoder, Dave, and Dean Johnson were talking. As she got close to the group, she overheard the Lieutenant say, "I need to talk with this friend, Angela Pike. Could you get her here within the hour, Dean Johnson?" Yoder paced back and forth on the Student Services lobby floor. Several students passed by. Some went on down the hall on the lower floor and others went up the stairway. He greeted each of them. He didn't recognize any of the faces, even though he had become acquainted with many of the older ones over the years.

Brent Morse had been an elusive one. He was into his fourth year, but Yoder could count on one hand the times that he had a conversation with him. Today's encounter was the first time he'd ever had to question him about any incident. His record was clear. Most of the students had a clean record. It was a good college with a great student body. Brent had been no exception. He was just barely above average in grades, according to Dean Johnson, just enough to keep him on the football team. There was always a write up and pictures of him in the local paper after a football game. Yoder was one of his fans at every game. However, there was a barrier when he would meet him face to face. He just couldn't put his finger on it. Something about that kid just didn't add up. He certainly didn't like his attitude today.

Yoder was standing in the middle of the lobby when he looked up to see Dean Johnson coming down the stairway.

"Lieutenant, Dave just called. He can't find Angela Pike or Brent Morse anywhere on campus. Brent was supposed to stay in his room or close by."

"Would they be in town for a wake for Ms. Bence, by any chance?"

"No, her body was sent home to her sisters in Illinois. The Student Body will be holding a memorial service in our chapel in unison with her funeral. That'll be held on Friday."

"Well, I can't wait any longer. It has been an hour since you sent Dave to find Angela Pike. I need to get back to headquarters. Have you heard from the hospital about Ms. Brooks?"

"Nothing about her, except to say that it was imperative that they speak with the parents."

Yoder shook his head. "Well, it sounds like I won't be questioning her tonight either."

He turned toward the door as he waved. "Keep me informed." He called back as he left the building.

Chapter Eight

Dusk brought out the wolves on Shady Mountain. The existence of the wolves had been denied by the park service for many years. How they came to the Alleghenies was a mystery. Some said that a pair had escaped from a zoo. Others said they had migrated from Canada. Many of the natives believed the handed down superstitious folk lore about wolf spirits. Joe just accepted that they were there long before the park service would acknowledge the illusive animals.

Joseph (Joe) Hardigan had just finished chopping wood out back in the clearing and hurried in while it was still daylight. He didn't want to deal with a hungry animal after dark. He stepped inside and listened to them howling. His German Shepherd mix met him at the door. The old dog lowered his head and whimpered.

Joe walked to the stove, not yet acknowledging the animal. Then he turned and walked back to the dog still standing at the door. "Yeah, you old coward. You'd best make sure you stay close to the house when you go out to do your job. Those canine relatives of yours would make mincemeat of you."

Any other dog would have been howling right along with the wolves, but this old mutt that he found on the side of the road ten years ago thought he was human. That was a lucky day for Joe. He sure was a ragged mess. He had taken him straight to the vet in Jasper, a small town beyond the mountain community. The vet had shaved his body down so that he just had hair on his head, his tail and on his feet. Lord, he looked funny. However, it had to be done. The poor dog had mange, and there was only one way to treat it, keep the hair clear, his body clean, force the medicine down him and keep the salve on the sores. It was an uphill battle for a while, but Dog was worth it.

The vet asked him one time why he named the animal, "Dog." He said, "Because there's no other dogs to compete with, so he's just "Dog". That was good enough for the both of them.

There was something different about the way the sound echoing down the mountain tonight. He looked out the front window rubbing his white beard. A large red van passed by on the road. He couldn't make out the model in the dusk, but it looked like one he'd seen before. He couldn't recall where. All of his neighbors had trucks or jeeps and were in early. No one up here liked to get caught on the mountain roads too late in the evening, and the sun had set about a half hour ago. "Fools," he told his dog.

His one room cabin with an upstairs loft area was just right for him and his mutt. The old fireplace kept him and Dog warm in the fall and through the winter. It was going to be a nippy night. He was glad that he had brought in plenty of wood. He put a few more chunks of wood on the fire and patted Dog on the head as the old mutt lay on the old rug in front of the hearth.

Joe leaned back in his old stuffed chair and day dreamed while he listened to bluegrass on the radio for a good long time. He thought about Carrie. Seems like yesterday, he thought. That was thirty years ago. His baby girl had left the mountain to go to college in the valley. She went to live with Eliza and Eliza was taking college classes, too. Then Eliza took off and went to Illinois. That's the last he heard of either of his daughters. He felt that they disowned him because he wouldn't move off this mountain. Life was too crowded in the valley. On the other hand, maybe it was because he didn't make the effort to come down to visit with them. Whatever the reason, the Irish that ran in the blood of the Hardigan's was stubborn and proud. Too late now to worry about it. That was then and this was now. All the same, the cabin still rang with the echoes of the voices and presence of his girls. They were all that was left after Jessie died. Carrie and Eliza slept in the loft. It was like camping out every day. Life was simple and fun. He and Jessie had come here from Virginia before the children were born. His commission as a Forest Ranger brought him to this spot where he built this little cabin.

The girls went to grade school in the community. It wasn't until after they started riding the bus to high school in the college town that things got a lot more complicated. Eliza started wanting to be like all the other teenagers. Then Jessie got sick and died. He had to rely on Eliza to do the household chores and help with Carrie. Eliza left and went to work at a restaurant in the college town and then after Carrie graduated from High School, she moved in with Eliza. She may as well have…Carrie stayed with Eliza a lot anyway. He lost track of them after they moved beyond the blue mist." He sighed. It was water over the dam and best forgotten.

No sense in dwelling on the past and ruining the best part of the day. The wolves were especially loud tonight, but otherwise, the popping of the fire and the sound of the crickets comforted him. An owl hooted nearby and he chuckled. "Well, Dog. That hooting owl was signaling me that it is time for bed."

He got up, stretched, and bent over to rub the soft, warm fur of Dog's back. Without shedding his clothing, Joe pulled back the quilts on the log bed in the corner and crawled in. Suddenly there was a scream from the wilderness. Joe sat up and Dog jumped on top of his lap. Trembling, Joe rubbed Dog's head. "What's the matter with us Dog? That's not a screech owl. That's for certain, but a panther scream shouldn't put us on that kind of an edge either." He pushed Dog off the bed. "Just go on now and lay down.

That panther isn't going to come near this cabin. You know how their screams carry across the mountains. That cat's probably clear over on the other side of the valley."

It was quiet again and the two companions fell asleep to the crackling sound of the fire.

About midnight, Joe heard a thumping on the door. He stirred and looked out through the window at the full moon dipping in and out of the clouds. Dog was scratching at the door from the inside and whining.

"What is it, Dog?"

The thumping started again. Dog jumped and whined even more. "Oh well, I guess I'd better get up and see what's going on. You don't normally put up a fuss to go out on a night when the wolves are howling, although they've been quiet for a little while. They must be prowling for food though."

Looking outside from the front bay window, he strained his old eyes. The clouds were covering the light of the moon. He rubbed his eyes and looked again. The clouds parted a little, letting the moonlight through a bit. He thought he could see the outline of what looked to be a human lying on the porch in front of the door. He turned around, picked up his glasses from the side table, and looked outside again. Dog kept whining and scratching the door. He talked low, almost in a whisper. "Yep, something's here." He hesitated to open the door. "You know, Dog, that may be a creature that the wolves attacked, or it could be a wolf. But then, I don't think you'd be scratching and whining if that was a wolf."

Grabbing his gun over the rack cabinet by the door, Joe pulled out a drawer beneath and dug out a shell. "Only one should do it." At least he hoped it would. He loaded the gun. He was sure that it was not a bear. Dog was too much of a coward to want to go out to face one of those hairy creatures.

With one hand, he unbolted the door and grabbing the handle, he pulled the door open just a crack. Sticking the barrel into the opening, he slowly pulled the door open. As he opened it wider, the light from the fireplace splattered out across the porch.

Dog was out like a light and sniffing the creature who lay sprawled on the boards. Joe put the gun back up on the rack and stepped out on the porch around to one side of the human form. Leaning down he picked the form up under the arms testing the weight.

"You don't hardly weigh nothing at all. And I can tell that you're a girl with all this hair. He put his arms up under her and stepped back inside. In the firelight, he could see the red locks cascading down his arm. He laid her on his bed, shut the door, and latched it.

He lit the kerosene lamp on the bedside stand. Going to the sink, he pumped the handle of the pitcher pump up until enough water ran in the basin beneath. Taking an old rag hanging there, he wet it. He knelt by the girl and tenderly washed the blood from her face.

"What have you got yourself into, girl? What're you doing out here in these mountains with the wolves running around? Did they get you girl, did the wolves maul you?"

The girl moaned and slowly opened her eyes.

She jumped and tried to raise her head.

"Now, now, it's o.k. I'm going to help you. I just don't know how bad hurt you are. Dog's right here by the bed. You see him. We're going to take care of you, we are. Now you just stay calm."

"Thank you." The girl's voice was just above a whisper.

"Now, tell me what happened to you."

"... a doctor."" The girl started to cry. "I've been beat up."

Joseph didn't hesitate. No need to ask how it happened. Another human needed help. There was no time to probe into the how or why.

"Well, that explains the bruises. I didn't think the wolves would put bruises on you like that. They might chew the blazes out of you, but they wouldn't beat you. Now tell me, do you feel like you could sit up in my old truck seat?"

Her weak voice sounded relieved as she nodded her head. "Yes... "

"Well now, we have an hour drive into town to the hospital, and a good part of it is mighty rough. There was a time that I could've got you to a country, mountain doctor that used to

do business at his house down the road. Now we have to drive all the way into that college town to the hospital."
"Please, let's just go. I can make it." The girl's voice was gaining more strength.
O.K. Now, I'll go out, get the truck, and get it as close to the house as I can. Dog will guard the door."
In his mind, he chuckled at the thought of Dog guarding anything. That would make the girl feel better. He, himself was feeling a little cowardly at the thought of going out where the wolves might be prowling. However, this needed to be done. That girl was hurt and she needed more help than he could give her. She might have broken ribs that could have punctured a lung. It was best if he moved as fast as he could. He did worry about the rough terrain. Even more reason to get started now.
All the way down the mountain, Joseph was as tense as he had ever been. It had been a long time since he had traveled this road. He didn't remember it being so far. He had always gotten his supplies at a general store in a little community on the other side of the mountain. However, there was no doctor over there. It seemed like it took a lot out of the girl just moving her from the bed to the truck. As careful as he was, she let out a cry ever so often. Every little bump caused her tears. Now that they were almost to the main road, she was asleep. He hoped she was just asleep. He had her strapped in and cushioned pretty good, but he couldn't stop the jostling she was getting.
As he passed cars with lights, he realized how deteriorated his eyes had become. The bright glare almost blinded him. He was glad he'd left his mutt behind. That would have been one more creature to worry about, if he put this truck over the mountain. Of course, if that happened, he most likely wouldn't be alive to worry about it. He had to leave Dog shut in the cabin. There had been no sense to bring him. It was against the law around the bigger towns to have a dog unleashed. He just didn't have time to bother with all that.

A sign loomed ahead, 'Python Curve'. Oh, how he remembered that one. Many a car had gone over. Of course, that was before they widened the road. He slowed down anyway. The impatient driver that came around him didn't feel the need to be cautious.

The glare of the lights of the oncoming car was the last thing Joe saw as his head hit against the steering wheel. The truck took a nosedive over the railing of the mountain and landed hard on the grassy incline.

Chapter Nine

Tuesday morning, Echo Valley General Hospital had been experiencing an unusual number of dramatic and traumatic cases. The last four days had been hectic. More staff than usual had to be called back in for extra hours to accommodate the added workload. The overworked staff members in ER were commenting on the events on Shady Mountain.

Cynthia, an RN was preparing for a shift change. "What's with that mountain anyway?" she asked the small group.

Dr. Harris replied, "Full moon last night. The wolves were going crazy on the mountain

A CNA, Stacy said, "The chaos started last Saturday morning with that teacher."

Dr. Harris chuckled, "I guess her ghost was just trying to warn us that things were going to escalate.

Upstairs in intensive care at five a.m., Dorothy Brooks stood by her daughter's hospital bed where she had been since one o'clock. She had held the limp little hand since Rachel had been brought back from surgery. Seeing her youngest child so helpless and so near death had been devastating. Rachel's once rosy lips were blended into a placid, white face.

Dorothy touched cheeks that had been tanned and glowing. No, she would not cry and break down. She must funnel her strength into her daughter's recovery. She must put her in God's hands. It was her duty to keep presence of mind to be able to pray. Without prayer, there'd be no hope.

The distraught mother had been unusually quiet and steadfast from the first phone call made to the Dean of Student Services. Normally, she was able to cry. However, this was her daughter, her baby and no amount of tears was going to make things right or change the circumstances. Now that she was here, heaven and earth would not be able to move her from this bedside.

"I feel your spirit, my love. I can feel that you are coming back to me."

Rachel's eyelids quivered.

"Come on, Rachel. Wake up."

The nurse came into the room to check Rachel's IV bags.

"She's waking up." Dorothy told her. "There, there it is again. She's trying so hard to come back."

"Could be," The nurse said, "And the eye movement could be in response to dreams. It's good that you're talking to her, but your voice is starting to sound hoarse. You need to go out and get some water. Could your husband take a turn here by the bed?"

"He's out in the waiting room watching for family to arrive."

"Maybe you should go out and join him. I'll let you know…"

Dorothy interrupted. "No, I'm fine."

The nurse left and Rachel's eyelids started to move again. This prompted Dorothy to start to talk to her daughter again as she had been doing all night.

"Rachel, pray with Mama. Our father, which art in heaven, hallowed be thy name...."

Rachel's brain reeled as troubled thought shot through her neurons. 'There's so many lights, so much noise, oh, my head. Where am I? Why won't they answer me? My voice is lost.'

Rachel's brain was hot. Her thoughts raced in a semi-comatose dream, a myriad of rational thought and foggy mirages. 'Bence praying? I see her shadow. Why is she looking at me like that? I didn't kill her. How can I tell her that I did not kill her? Where's my voice. My arms and legs won't move. Oh, my head...'

Dorothy jumped as her husband laid a hand on her shoulder. "Sweetheart, you need to get something to eat and some rest. You're going to be no good to her or anyone else at this rate. Do you want to end up in a bed next to her?"

"I'm not leaving her, David. The staff told me to keep talking to her. She's going to wake up any minute. I can see her eyelids moving. The nurse said that it could be rapid eye movement in response to dreams. Nevertheless, I know that she is trying to wake up. I want to be here when she opens her eyes."

The bed was elevated to standing height, so that staff could quickly work on the patient, and Dorothy hadn't sat down since she had been moved to ICU.

"Well, you're most likely going to be on the floor from exhaustion and hunger. Let me stand watch for a while. I can keep talking to her. If anything more happens, I'll page you. Just go to the waiting room and sit down for a while. They've got juice and cookies out there."

Dorothy's only response was, "Have Stephan and Dianna arrived yet?"

"Not yet. I'll send them in one at a time when they get here. I'll go out to the lobby and call them on the cell phone to see where they're at right now.

They should be getting into town soon."

David gave his daughter one last pat on the hand and kissed his wife's forehead. Picking up a long stray hair, he pulled it back over her ear toward her bun.

"You're looking a bit tattered and I don't think
I've seen you use the toilet once."

Dorothy brushed her hands on her long skirt and checked the pins in her cap. "I haven't been drinking and I don't need a toilet. I'm not worried about how I look. God doesn't want fancy. He wants plain and simple. Besides, you need to look in the mirror. That tie could use a bit of straightening and your shirt's quite mussed."

David sighed. "I don't think any of that matters now. Does it?"

"No, Sweetheart. It doesn't."

David turned to walk through the double glass doors when Rachel started gasping. Her head went back, her mouth opened. Dorothy started screaming as Rachel stopped breathing. The monitor started beeping loudly. The nurse rushed in immediately from the monitoring station. A code blue went out as the nurse moved Dorothy gently aside to the arms of her husband. Dorothy resisted leaving, but soon there were several white coats filling the small room leaving David and Dorothy standing against the monitoring counter. The nurses and attendants started working in a frenzy. Rachel's spirit floated above. Oh wow, what's that high feeling clear to the top of my brain? Her spirit lifted, and suddenly she felt the air beneath her and she was flying. Don't cry Mother, I'm so happy to be free of the pain. I feel so wonderfully free.

She floated away and into the lobby. Looking down, she could see Jerrod. Jerrod leaning against the hallway wall, bent with his hand on his forehead. He's in pain. I can feel that he's hurting deeply and there's Julie, sitting in a lounge chair with Sadie. They seem so worried.

There is another presence here. The red head...she's touching me. Rachel's spirit settled in the hall. She turned to face the mist.

"What's your name?"

"I'm Angela Pike and I know that you're Rachel Brooks."

"But aren't our bodies dead?"

"I don't think so."

"We have some unfinished business. Go back."

Rachel's voice groaned and her body started to move erratically.

A strange voice said. "She's back."

The attendants kept calling Rachel's name as the doctor checked her pulse. "We need to get her back down for an MRI and CT scan to make sure there's no more leakage and to determine the swelling situation."

The attending nurse turned and walked to put her arms around David and Dorothy. Dorothy tried to move back to the bed. The nurse held her. "It's o.k. now. She's back and she's stable. But the doctors need to check her out a little more." An attendant pulled the curtains around the perimeter of the bed. Dorothy tried to go in. "No, I need to be able to see her."

The nurse held on. "Mrs. Brooks. Please. Your health is in danger right now as well. You need to leave this all in our hands." " No, we need to leave it in God's hands." Dorothy said, as she struggled toward the bed.

David stepped forward. "That's right, Dorothy. Do you hear what you just said? We need to leave this in God's hands. But we need to trust God to work through the hospital staff to get Rachel through this."

Dorothy started to shake and cry. David put his arms around her and she collapsed in his arms.

"Come on love. Let's go to the chapel to pray."

Rachel moaned. 'Oh my God, the pain...'

The doctor turned to the attending nurse, "Give her some more morphine. I think one more IV bag should help keep her comatose for faster healing and keep the swelling down. Then let's get her down for test."

In the lobby, David and Dorothy were greeted by Rachel's older siblings. When the hugging was over, they gathered in the waiting room. David and Dorothy filled Stephan and Dianna in on the latest developments while the friends listened in.

"How could a tiny bump on the head cause such a tragic outcome?" asked Dianna.

David answered, "The doctor explained that Rachel must have hit her head hard enough and at just the right angle to cause a small contusion injury that stayed between the skull and the brain cavity in a protective shield. There was a pinhole in the outer cortex shield. This caused a minute amount of blood to start to leak into the brain area. If the staff hadn't been able to draw the blood back, and off the brain, there would've been nothing they could've done for her at this hospital. As it was, the brain sustained a great deal of swelling and inflammation."

"So what was the code blue about?"

"We don't know. The doctor will talk with us after more test. He said that she's lucky that the brain didn't swell more rapidly. He said that usually this type of injury can kill a person in just a few hours."

Dean Johnson came in and joined the friends, Julie, Sadie, and Jerrod.

"How is she?" he asked the parents, and the explanation started all over again. After they finished, Dean Johnson introduced Julie, Sadie, and Jerrod.

David realized that he had seen them all night. "Oh, my. Do you mean to tell me that you three have been here in vigil all night for Rachel? I saw you, but I just didn't realize." He stammered on

Stephan looked at Jerrod. "What's your name?"

"Jerrod." Jerrod was not sure that he liked the strained, angry look on Stephan's face.

Stephan let out a sigh. "Oh, I'm sorry. I thought you were..."

"No, my name's not Brent Morse."

"That's good, because I was going to..."

"Take me out?" Jerrod gave Stephan a crooked grin. "It's o.k., because I would like to be able to deal with Brent Morse myself."

Chapter Ten

The man with the Santa Claus beard inquired about Angela at the desk and found that she had been transferred from ICU. He was relieved about that and hurried up the elevator to the third floor. Finding the room, he peeked in. The bed near the door was empty, so he looked further into the room and spotted the familiar little face from a propped up position near the window.
The small bump that Joseph Hardigan had from the accident had resulted in a brief loss of consciousness. The ICU doctor was concerned about an irregular heartbeat, and wanted to keep him overnight. After some argument with him that he could walk the entire mountain without stopping for so much as a meal, he let them have their way and keep him for overnight observation. He proved his abilities to leave the next day, by walking faster than staff down the hallways. The doctor signed him out at three in the afternoon. His old head was too hard to damage; at least that's how he saw it. Never the less, the noggin' was a bit sore and he had heartburn to beat the band. The medical profession didn't have to know that and there wasn't a thing they could do that he couldn't do once he got home. His biggest worry was for his passenger, Angela Pike.
Angela smiled weakly as he walked toward her.
"How are you?"
Joseph laughed. "A little sore, but a lot better now that I see that you're on the mend. How are you feeling? You still look a bit pale."
"They have me on a lot of drugs for my pain and panic attacks. Thank you so much for all you did for me. I'm so sorry about what happened...I mean... your act as a good Samaritan turned into such a disaster."
"That's o.k. I'm not sorry about that at all. Things happen in life and the main thing is that you're here getting help."
Joseph couldn't shake the feeling that this little red headed girl was so like his Carrie. He wondered where Angela's

folks were, but he was afraid to ask too many personal questions. Her life and what happened that night was none of his business. Too many people involved in other people's lives just made things a lot more muddled.

Angela chuckled. "I don't even remember if you told me your name. What can I call my benefactor?"

"Just call me Joe."

"Well, thank you, Joe. What you did for me along with what happened to me on that mountain changed my attitude forever. I think I grew up a lot in these last two days."

Joe smiled a big smile. "If I helped in any way there, then I guess God was using me for his good."

Someone entered the room from behind and Joe turned expecting to see a nurse. The face he saw put him into a trance. The big blue eyes stared back at him.

Finally, the woman with the auburn hair spoke.

"Hello Daddy."

There was a long, uncomfortable silence. Joe sat down on the chair in the corner. Shocked, he tried to hold back the tears. Then he said, "Hello, Eliza. I thought I'd never see you again." He said just above a whisper.

Angela was watching, stunned with her eyes wide. Finally, she spoke. "Joe, are you my grandfather?"

Joe looked at her and then back at Eliza. "Is this your child?" He found his speaking voice... barely. At least, he felt like he had said the words.

"No, this is Carrie's daughter, Daddy. I raised her," Eliza said in a soothing voice. She noticed the pallor of her father's skin as he spoke in a whisper.

"Where's Carrie?"

Eliza hesitated and then spoke reverently. "Carrie passed away in childbirth seventeen years ago."

The tears came and he could not contain them. "Why didn't you get in touch with me.? You moved through the blue mist and never told me where you were going."

"I'm sorry, Daddy. You didn't act as if you wanted more to do with us, so I took Carrie and we moved to Chicago where

I could get an advanced law degree. I had half way expected that I would run into you after Angela enrolled in my alma mater, but ...this is her second year here...well I was just hoping to see you, but...I didn't. I regret that it had to happen with this ironic and stressful chain of events."

Eliza looked at Angela who was trying to get out of bed.

"It's o.k. Angela. Stay there." Then Eliza moved to Joe and wrapped her arms around him.

Joe finally got up still hugging Eliza. "I never stopped loving you girls. I missed you so much."

'I know Daddy."

They moved back to the bed and Joe leaned down and wrapped his arms around his granddaughter. Angela hugged him as tightly as she could and cried.

Then they broke and she looked at her aunt. "Why didn't you tell me about him all these years?"

"I promised your mother that I wouldn't tell you about any of it. She knew she wasn't going to make it and she asked me not to tell you." Eliza sighed.

Joe looked sad. "You mean that Carrie never forgave me?"

"I'm sorry, Daddy. She was afraid of your reaction to how she turned out. We can talk more about that later. I'm sure that she's up there with Mama and I know that she's looking down and loving you right now. Especially after what the dean of the college and the detective told me about your rescue of Angela."

Angela looked at Joe. "So the detective talked to you?"

"Yes, he questioned me this morning. I hope that I didn't break a confidence, but I told him that you were injured already when you came to my cabin. I also told him about the strange van that I had seen earlier."

"It's o.k. Grandpa." Angela said as she patted his hand. "That felt so good and strange at the same time. I'm so happy. It's like God sent me to your cabin."

Joe grinned and gazed at Angela though his watery eyes. "Living in nature helps me to believe in miracles. We're living a miracle right now."

Eliza spoke. "I was just coming in to tell you that I talked with the detective on the cell just before I came in here. When I gave him my last name, it became clear to him that...well, now he's clear now about the Hardigan name. He asked me if we were related, and of course, I told him that Joe Hardigan was Angela's grandfather. So now, he figures that's why the girl in the accident was with the old hermit on the mountain. I didn't fill him in on the coincidence."
She looked back at Angela. "The detective will be coming in to talk with you sometime today. Do you feel up to it?"
"I...It's time. It's time that the truth is known. I'll be o.k. with that." Angela's voice was shaking and Eliza knew that her niece was just trying to buck up as she had always taught her. Tough people always buck up and face life. Doesn't matter what happens. It's what you do about it that counts. Those words were the exact quote from the man who was standing across from her now, her father.
"Oh, by the way, Angela. I just found out that another student at the college is a patient here.
Rachel Brooks. Do you know her?"
Angela gasps. "Oh my God. What's next?" Then Angela started to shake a bit. "Was the name Brent Morse mentioned? I mean, I know she's accusing him of attacking her."
Eliza felt a tug of her heartstrings. She squeezed Angela's hand. "No, no one else was mentioned. I don't know what her story is." She continued. "A young man by the name of Jerrod told me that Rachel was here. He was with the dean in the cafeteria and we started talking. He didn't give me any other information. The dean said something about, "When it rains, it pours. But he didn't say anything else."
A knock came at the door. The group turned to see a nurse aide walk in. "I'm going to be shutting you in Angela," she said, grabbing the drape and pulling it around. "There's no need for visitors to move."
The nurse aide peeked from around the curtain at Angela. "You're getting a roommate. How do you like that?"

Angela asked, "Who is she?" She knew. I feel it…just like in ICU when I was under. She started connecting dots in her head. The visions I had of Rachel…what she said to me in my dreams…I'm not sure I'm ready to see her. I was such a little witch to her. I don't want to face the nightmares. I don't want to ask forgiveness. Maybe Rachel isn't ready to forgive me. She seemed friendly enough in my dreams. Maybe that's wishful thinking. The nurse aide had already gone, leaving Angela's question unanswered.

Eliza was watching Angela's face as it showed more stress. "Angela, you're looking paler than before. Are you alright?" On the window side of the bed, Joe moved in closer to her and started rubbing her head with his free hand. Angela gripped her grandfather's hand tighter as she looked up into his eyes. "We've got a lot of catching up to do, Grandpa." Eliza said, "The doctors want you to stay here for observation for a few more days, so you'll have plenty of time to visit with your grandpa."

"Aunt Eliza, I hadn't thought about leaving the hospital. I still have to go back to the dorm and to my classes...but what if..." Angela was starting to work up into a sweat.

Joe kissed her forehead. "I don't know all that happened to you, Baby, but I can guess. I'm not going to let that happen again. We'll figure it out later. Now just rest and get well." Eliza smiled at her father. If Carrie only knew how understanding and non-judgmental her father had become, she would not have been afraid to tell him about her rough life. 'Maybe Daddy and I can talk later. Carrie wouldn't object now. Joe kissed Angela's head again. But Angela kept crying until the tears were uncontrollable.'

Eliza brushed Angela's hair back with her hand. "Angela, do you want me to ask for more medication for you?"

Angela shook her head yes'. Eliza pressed the call button. The noise on the other side of the curtain indicated that a transfer bed was being pulled in. The attendants instructing each other and family dialog was heard as they moved the patient into the empty hospital bed. A nurse aide peeked her head around the corner.

"Do you need something, Angela?" She started and then noticed the tears. "Are you in pain or do you need something for your nerves?" "Both," Angela replied.

"Well, I don't think they can give you both all at one time, but I'll check with your nurse for the shift. She will check your chart. You may be due for one or the other. I'll get Elaine for you."

The curtain between the two patients remained closed while the attendants were doing vitals and charting on the newcomer. Judging by the conversation, it was apparent that the father and mother were there. Then a man said, "There's nothing we can do right now, dear. Let her sleep while we grab some lunch. I promise. We won't be long."

The nurse with the badge that read, 'Elaine', returned around the curtain with a pill. "You can have your sedative right now, Angela. You're not due for your pain med for another hour."

Angela took the pill and drank the water down to the bottom, at which time; she asked to go to the bathroom. Elaine took the empty cup and said, "I'll have Trixie come back in to help you."

Joe said, "Well, I'm going to scoot out of here. I have to go back to the cabin and attend to my dog. I'll be coming right back, little granddaughter. You're not too worry about that. We've got a lot of catching up to do."

"How're you going to get back to the mountain, Daddy? Isn't your truck out of commission?"

"Yeah, I could walk it. You know, I walk these mountains all the time. That's no big deal for me. But I need to get back to the dog as soon as I can so I'll get a taxi. I've got an old jeep that I drive a lot on the mountain roads. That'll do me until I get the truck fixed."

"Dad, let me drive you." She turned to Angela who had calmed down and was sitting on the side of the bed waiting for the help of the nurse aide, who had been summoned to get her to the bathroom.

"Now you've got to remember how bad that road is washed out up there. You'll have to watch the undercarriage of your car up. If we go the long way around, it'd add an hour on to the travel."

"No we can go the short way. I'll drive slowly. Do not worry, Daddy. I'm rather curious to see the old place again." Eliza turned to Angela.

"Angela, will you be o.k. until I get back? I'll wait until the aide gets in here."

"No problem. I'll be fine."

Eliza and Joe went to her in turn and hugged her.

"I'll be back, Rachel. Hang in there now."

"Grandpa." Rachel said as she clung to him. "I love you."

Joe's heart was overflowing and his eyes burned hot with impending tears. "I love you, too, my Grandbaby." Joe wiped his eyes with his pocket-handkerchief. "Now, you're going to have me crying, too."

Angela waved to her aunt and newly found grandpa as they disappeared around the closed curtain. Wiping her face, she suddenly was hit by the silence in the room and thought about Rachel in the next bed.

She started to push the call button, then stopped and swung her feet over the side of the bed.

The communal restroom was located in the center of the opposite wall from the beds. Angela was not able to see the other bed on the other side of the curtain when she went in. She closed the door and wondered who was behind the door on the other side of the restroom. As she washed her hands, a knock came at the door to the other patient room.

"Just a minute." She yelled as she unlocked the door for the knocker and opened her exit door.

Angela looked right into the wide eyes of her roommate as she lay in her bed. Rachel drew her blankets up closer around her neck.

Angela stepped back. She wanted to say, it's o.k. Rachel. I'm not going to hurt you. I've learned and I'm so sorry. She couldn't find her voice.

She sidestepped quickly and grabbed the back of her bed. Angela made her way around it and sat down on the other side, taking gasping breaths, and staring out the window. She laid down and curled up like a caterpillar in a cocoon under the blankets.

Angela's sedative was starting to work, but she fought it. Sleeping meant dreaming and she didn't want to dream. She wanted to forget...forget the horror. She tried to concentrate on the positive event of finding her grandfather.

She listened to the heavy breathing of her sleeping companion on the other side of the curtain.

She jumped when Trixie popped her head around the curtain. "Hey, it's time to take your vitals."

As she worked putting the BP cuff on Angela's arm, Trixie asked her. "Did Elaine give you anything for your pain or a sedative?"

"Yeah, the sedative."

"Hmmm... Not working yet, eh? Your arm is as stiff as a board."

"I'm sorry. I'll try to relax."

After Trixie finished, she stepped back to the curtain and grabbed it, jerking it back a little.

Angela started shaking her head, no, and put her hand up. "Please leave the curtain drawn. I don't want to disturb Rachel."

Trixie had just disappeared when the voices from the morning joined with a new male voice in the room. "It's good that you're back, Mr. and Mrs. Brooks, but Rachel is still sleeping. Could we talk in my office?"

The echoed voices of "Sure." Sure" Then they were gone. Angela felt drowsy and then nothing...

Rachel woke to the sounds of Dorothy and David. She looked up at her mother as the gray haired matriarch kissed her forehead. "How's our girl?"
Rachel smiled. "Fine Mama." She waved to her dad standing at the end of the bed. "Doctor says you can come home with us on Friday. That's only a couple more days."
Rachel's smile faded. "But I need to get back to classes."
Dorothy looked at David. "Rachel, as long as that boy's still at the college, that's not going to happen. We can't take a chance."
"What if they need I...I mean for the hit and run trial? Or what about the complaints I'm filing against Brent?"
"Darling, we need to let the Lord Jesus take care of any transgressions against us. That's his promise." Dorothy lamented.
David looked at the drawn curtain. He felt an urgency to change the subject. "How's your friend, Angela?"
"Angela? You mean the little red head?"
"Yes, dear. Your roommate."
Rachel's eyes followed her dad's stare at the curtain. "I thought that I'd been dreaming." She said.
Elaine, the shift nurse came into the door and peeked around the curtain.
"Angela? Good, you're awake. The doctor has ordered some more test for you. We'll take you down to the lab right now."
As Elaine pulled the wheelchair backward with Angela comfortably seated, Angela looked toward Rachel. The two girls gave each other blank stares as Angela left.
"What's she doing here?" Rachel asked as they disappeared.
Dorothy answered. "Honey, she'll be alright. She was in an accident. It's nothing for you to worry about."
Rachel looked at her mother. She thought. 'I know you well enough to know that you are covering something up.'
She looked at her father standing staunch with his arms crossed. He glanced at his wife in a way that told Rachel to

push the issue. "Daddy, do you know more than Mama about this?"
"I think you should talk with your friend about it when she returns." He said.
Julie peeked her little curly head in the door. Her large almond, brown eyes were twinkling as usual with the obvious hope of surprising her friend. "Rachel, hello." She brought in a bouquet of mountain floral in a vase of water tied with a large rose-colored bow.
"Hey, girlfriend. How're you doing?"
Rachel started smiling. "I'm mending, thank you. I hope you haven't given all my things to the gypsies yet."
"No way. You look so good."
Julie sat the bouquet down on the side table and handed her a get-well card. Rachel rolled her eyes. "You didn't have to do all this." She opened the card and started laughing at the funny depiction of a doctor with a larger than life syringe standing over a petrified patient.
"Well, Rachel we'll go now and let you visit with your friend." Dorothy and David almost talked over each other as they spoke pretty much in unison. They hugged their daughter.
As they left, Rachel and Julie were chattering away.
"Rachel, where's Angela? I thought she was in the room with you." She looked toward the curtain.
"Well apparently, that's her bed behind curtain number one right there, but she's out getting lab tests right now. Can you tell me what went on while I was in the O Zone? My parents aren't being straight with me. You know, they'll do anything to keep from gossiping."
Julie crossed her smooth brown arms and stood leaning to one side. "Well, you know me. I love a good piece of action. Especially when it's a story about paybacks."
"What in the world are you talking about? Sit down and tell me."
"She was attacked and raped according to the gossip. According to the news report, she was hurt in an accident.

As it turns out, the gentleman who was giving her a ride down the mountain went off the road to avoid a head on collision. According to school gossip, the old man was bringing her down from where the attack happened."
Rachel gasped. "I want to ask... how, who..."
"Well, that's all I know. The detective and the school are just having fits trying to put all the puzzle pieces together."
"Poor Angela." Rachel pulled herself up a bit.
"What do you mean, poor Angela? After what that girl's done to you?"
"Oh, you know. She just fell victim to the same guy I did. Of course, I feel sorry for her. She was more naive than I was." Rachel lay back on her pillow again. "It was Brent, wasn't it?"
"Nobody knows. But everybody's assuming that it was him. The police are still investigating it."
"It's pretty obvious, I think."
"I feel so badly for her. What a horrible experience that must've been."
"Well, there's another rumor going around. Rachel, did you hit Ms. Bence up there on that road? You know, the day you were trying to get away from Brent?"
"Do you mean the day all our nightmares started?" Rachel held back the tears. "I don't know...that part's still foggy. But no, I don't think that I did. I had some deep dreams when I was out of it. I saw Angela and felt like I was floating. You know, Julie. I felt like I was having an out of body experience. You know what I mean? I could see Mama and Daddy and then I could see Jerrod, you and Sadie. I saw Joanna and everyone."
"Oooo, spooky. O.K... So what was I wearing?
"You had on that blue sweater with the gold and the blue skirt with the black stockings."
"Oh man, Rachel. That's exactly what I was wearing. You went into a code blue in ICU. We were scared to death. Did you see a light?"

"Yes, as I was traveling around. I saw Jerrod leaning up against the wall in the hallway. He was looking down at the floor and he really looked scared. You, Sadie and Joanna were all in the waiting room. Then I saw Ms. Bence and followed her toward the light. Then I ran into the image of Angela. She and I had a talk, but I can't remember what it was about. However, we both agreed that we needed to go back. We just weren't done yet."

"Wow, Rachel. I don't think I'd recommend that you tell that story to many people. They'd think you were hallucinating from the drugs. Believe me, I'm from a culture in Kenya that believes in spirits and all that. The first year I was here in the states, I had a bad experience with the mountain people claiming I was a witch. It was all because of a revelation I told to one of the local girls."

"Yeah, I know about tribal ritual and storytelling. But if you say that I had a code blue and I saw everyone as they were during that time, don't you think that it's possible that..."

"Not just possible. I think you did have an out of body experience."

Rachel put out both arms and the two girls hugged each other. "I'm so glad I came back."

"Me too. Rachel. Me too."

That's how Dorothy and David found them when they returned to the room. David cleared his throat and the two girls broke their embrace. Rachel reached out one hand toward her mother. "Mom, Dad, this is Julie, my roommate from my dormitory.

"Ah," Dorothy said. "You're the girl that was in the waiting room all night when Rachel was in
I.C.U. and into the next day, I believe."

"Yes, that'd be me. Rachel and I've become just like sisters...except for our ancestral roots, no one would ever know that we're not."

"I'm so happy about that. Are you from Nigeria or Ethiopia? I detect a familiar accent." said David.

"I'm from Kenya. I've been here since I was twelve, long enough to sound American. I do have my U.S. citizenship now and so do my parents."

"That's wonderful. We're retired missionaries from Ethiopia."

Rachel's doctor knocked and entered the door. He nodded in recognition to David and Dorothy.

"Hello, Rachel, I need to have a word with you and I need to speak with your roommate. But I think that she's down getting lab test right now."

"What it boils down to is that I'm here to do an evaluation to see if you are ready to speak with the police on a matter that according to Lieutenant Yoder is common to both you and Angela. I talked with the police last night, but I couldn't reveal even a little bit of personal medical information without your permission. The detective's going to want to hear the details from you. The Lieutenant may want to talk with each of you alone, and I'd rather that you, Rachel, stay in bed for this."

Dorothy gripped Rachel's hand tighter. "What are you saying, Doctor? How's Rachel's problems related to Angela?"

"I can't say, Mrs. Brooks. All I know of the details is what the Lieutenant said. He said that the subject matter was related and that he would like to speak with each girl alone, and then the two girls together."

The doctor asked Dorothy, David, and Julie to step outside while he examined Rachel. A nurse came in to assist.

Julie moved toward Rachel. "Rachel, I'll say goodbye and get back to campus. Here, let me hug you."

Rachel hugged her friend tightly. "I can't thank you enough, Julie."

"Hey girl. What're friends for? Besides, Jerrod said to tell you that he's been working a lot of extra hours lately, plus trying to keep up with classes. But he said he'd be in to see you at the next opportunity." " Tell him I understand and thanks."

Julie waved and winked at her as she left.
As the doctor checked Rachel's eye movement, he continued to talk to her, asking her trivia.
Then she asked. "What exactly did you do to me in that operating room?"
"We drew excess blood from your brain and cauterized the veins that were damaged. You cracked the skull just slightly and we're going to have to do daily and extensive testing for a while to make sure that all that is healing as it should."
"So that must have happened when I conked my head on the windshield."
"Oh, you remember that?"
"Yeah, I do."
"Then you're healing."
He turned to the nurse. "I'm done here for now."
After the doctor left, the nurse came back to say that her parents had gone in to talk with the doctor in the floor office. Another nurse, Elaine, pulled back the curtain, and the aide, Trixie, pushed Angela into the room. The two girls stared at each other face to face.
Rachel spoke to Elaine. "Would you please pull the curtain all the way back to the wall? Angela and
I need to talk."
Angela got out of her wheelchair and as the medical team left the room, she sat down on her bed. Rachel put her blanket down and sat up in the bed straighter.
"Be careful Rachel. Should you be moving so much?" She said as she stared at Rachel's bandages on her head.
"I'm fine. Believe me; I'll scream if I hurt. I'm a baby."
"I don't believe that." Angela twisted her fingers together. Angela stopped, took a ragged breath, and then changed the subject. "Did Brent hit you in the head?"
"No, I hit my head on the van window when I swerved on the mountain."
"Do you remember anything about that?"
"It's all slowly coming back to me. As I was talking with the doctor just now, I remembered some things."

"Did you hit Ms. Bence?"
"No, the more I remember, the more I know that I didn't. I know that I didn't put any dents in
Brent's van."
"Rachel, I'm so sorry about being such a jerk."
Rachel put up her hand. "It's water over the dam. Can't get it back."
"I have your clothes in my room if you need them back."
"I've had more serious worries than that. I really have been in such stress about whether or not I hit
Ms. Bence up on that mountain road."
"So you really are sure that didn't happen?" Angela was sitting up cross-legged on her bed. She unfolded her legs and leaned forward toward Rachel's bed.
"I know that I didn't hit her. I was having these weird foggy episodes and I thought I must've been seeing Ms. Bence ghost when I talked to her, but I know now that it was just the head injury. I've thought of some other facts, too. When I talked with Ms. Bence, she was standing on the passenger side of the van. I talked with Jerrod when I was in ICU, just before they brought me in here.
According to the news reports, Jerrod said that Ms. Bence was found across the road by her mailbox, which meant that the van would have had to hit her with the fender on the driver's side. There were no dents on that fender."
"You know, Angela, we've both made mistakes. There's nothing we can do about what happened. Both of us made bad choices, but we can't take back our actions and reactions. By the way, when's your grandpa coming back? I'd really like to meet him."
"I don't know. Sometime this afternoon, I think."
Angela pulled some tissues from the side table wiped her eyes and handed one to her friend.
"You were right, Rachel, to be afraid of Brent. He can really be intimidating." Her eyes welled with tears.
Rachel wiped her face. "What happened to you, Angela?"

The little red head bent down and her fingers wiped her eyes. "I was raped, but I didn't see his face. I was walking downtown toward the Elfin. It's a student hangout that you haven't been introduced to yet."

Angela took a deep breath and continued. "I felt something over my nose. It put me out like a light. When I woke up I was black, blue, and bleeding, and I was in the woods up on the mountain. I had never been in that area before. I was so sore I couldn't move. Then I got up enough strength to pull myself to a cabin porch."

Angela wiped away tears and blew her nose.

"But you know something? Fate is crazy. The man who rescued me turned out to be my grandfather. I didn't even know I had one. Isn' t that the weirdest thing you ever heard."

Angela filled her in on the reunion. "I'll introduce you to him when he comes back today."

Rachel sat up a little more in her bed, fascinated by the story. Angela put out her hand and took Rachel's fingers.

"I'm really sorry for my part in those accusations, Rachel. I'm sorry for my snotty attitude. You haven't deserved to be treated that way."

"It's o.k. Angela. I was taken in by Brent Morse, too."

"Well you know, Rachel. I'm not blaming Brent for what happened to me. Truth is that I don't know who the culprit is."

Rachel pulled herself up out of bed and sat up facing Angela. She squeezed her hand. "Let's just forget about our differences."

Angela squeezed as tears ran down her face.

"You're such a compassionate, wonderful person, Rachel. I hope you can forgive me."

"You're forgiven. Now, let's just start again."

"Should you be sitting up yet?"

"I'm a little oozy, but I need to get up. That bed is making me sore."

They both turned toward the door as Dorothy and David returned to the room. The parents smiled at the new girl in a hospital gown. They stood looking at the two girls.
David cleared his throat. Rachel reached out one hand toward her mother. "Mom, Dad, this is Angela. We live in the same dormitory."
"Ah," Dorothy said. "Are you the girl that was in the accident on the mountain?"
"Yes, that would be me. Isn't this all such a coincidence?"
"It sure is, and not a happy one." said David.
"But it's good that we are in the same room. We can help each other recover."
Rachel's doctor knocked and entered the door. He nodded in recognition to David and Dorothy. "Hello, Angela, I missed you when I was in to check Rachel. I need to do your check up now. Angela chuckled nervously. "We've got the same doctor, too. That's cool."
He walked over to the drape. "Is your aunt around the hospital, Angela?"
"She drove my Grandpa back up to the mountain."
"Oh, so you have relatives on the mountain?"
"Just Joe Hardigan. I just found out this morning that he was my Grandpa. It was such a big coincidence. I just happened to crawl up on his porch after my ordeal. Isn't that weird?"
"He was the driver of the truck you were in when First Response brought you in here?
"Yep, but I didn't know that he was my Grandfather until Aunt Eliza came in while he was visiting. It was quite a shock."
Rachel and her parents had been taking all of the conversation in with interest. Rachel held her silence with what she had already heard from Julie.
The doctor finished drawing the curtain as Angela waved a 'goodbye' sign at Rachel and pulled her legs back onto her bed. Elaine came in to assist.
The doctor's thoughts turned to Eliza and her father going back up that mountain. He couldn't help but wonder what

the story was for these people. The chain of events was surreal and never ending.

In all the years of his practice, he'd never heard of so much turmoil. He wondered if the cycle was finally broken. It was all folk lore, but he wondered what the legend of the wolf spirits had to do with all this.

Chapter Eleven

"Daddy, I forgot how beautiful these mountains are. This is really a nostalgic experience."

Joe had been studying his oldest daughter's face since they left the gas station. She was more like him, he thought. Carrie had been the spitting image of her mama, Jessie. His Jessie was fair, tall, and beautiful. She loved the mountains and the community near their cabin. She had a flair for organizing groups and worked once a week on quilts for homes and gifts for charity. Her main exercise was working in the community gardens and walking the trails. It seemed impossible that she could have ever been ill.

He sighed. "Yeah, your mama loved it, too. You know, when I saw Angela up there on my porch, it was almost like Carrie and your Ma had come back to me. Their red hair and blue eyes, and the shape of their faces...I can't get over how much they all resembled."

"I know Daddy. I was reminded of that fact every day of Angela's life."

"Did Carrie name Angela?"

"Yeah, she gave her the name Angela for Angel. It reminded her of the movies where her favorite actress played the angel. Remember when Carrie was the angel in the Christmas play?"

"Yes, Carrie always was a dramatic little soul." Joe remembered the times that Carrie had put on plays and come down the loft stairway pretending to be a Vaudeville girl. Eliza remembered too, and they laughed about some of Carrie's antics. "She always wanted my name. She begged you and Mama to switch the names because mine was more romantic and stage like to her."

"Why'd she die, Eliza? Do not spare me the details. What was her life like? Why was she ashamed to tell me? Why'd she make you promise not to tell?"

Eliza took a deep breath in and let it out again. He really needed to know all about Carrie, but this was going to be hard.

"Carrie tried to fit in at the college after she came down to live with me, but all she was interested in was the acting classes. Of course, there are only the small time theaters around here, but she couldn't seem to get the starring roles. Therefore, when I got a paralegal job offer in Chicago, she wanted to come with me. She had a few waitress jobs that didn't last for very long. I ended up supporting her while she ran around the city auditioning for first one role and then another. She had an agent that was less than reputable, promising her the moon. I tried to warn her, but she believed every lie that he told. She was so sure that he was going to take her to Hollywood."

Eliza hesitated. She glanced over at her father. His skin looked sallow today. "Are you sure that you want to hear all this, Daddy?"

Joe braced himself. "That bad, huh?" He waved his hand. "Keep talkin', I'm fine."

Eliza maneuvered another curve and began again. "The only contract she had was for a series of pornographic movies."

Joe put his hands to his face and wiped tears from his eyes. Immediately, Eliza wished that she had honored Carrie's wishes.

Eliza gave him another quick glance. "Dad, I think that's enough. It's too late to do anything about Carrie. So why don't we just let her rest in peace."

Finally he spoke. "I'm o.k. I'm just tired. Does Angela know about all this?"

"Some. I fed her just a little bit of information when she asked direct questions."

"I need to know more. Where's she buried?"

"She was cremated. I brought her ashes with me and I'll scatter them off the mountain. That was her wish."

"Her wish?"

"She knew she wasn't going to make it."

Joe sat quietly. Then he sighed and said, "When do you plan to do that?"

"When Angela is well enough to come up here with us." Eliza paused and glanced at her dad again. "I have her urn in the trunk, Daddy."

Joe sat silent a moment and then said. "Doesn't seem right that she's been having to ride in a trunk and we're up here all comfortable." Joe looked stalwartly ahead, but he took a quick, deep, involuntary breath, and exhaled slowly. Eliza could see the corner of his mouth twitch a bit.

"I think Carrie'd want me to know it all." He continued. "O.K. Well, during the time that Carrie was involved with the scumbag of an agent; she lived with him and married him, Cedric Pike. One day he beat her up when she didn't do the role right. She had some bruises and it was hard to cover up on camera so the agent husband became her pimp and she did some prostitution. When she got pregnant, the Scum Bag beat her up and left her on my doorstep. I came home to find her clinging to life. She didn't lose the baby, but she never quite recovered, in spite of all the medical help I got for her. When she was on bed rest, she became upset about how this child might grow up and find out about all the horrible things she'd done and especially about the porno videos.

By this time, I'd passed the bar exam and had a good position in a well-known practice. I hired a private detective friend of mine to look for all the video tapes that he could find so that they could be destroyed. We thought we'd done a good job of it, but one turned up, and one of Angela's high school friends found it. It was in his dad's old tape box. He brought it to a party that Angela attended. Anyway, when all the kids were gathered around a TV., watching a special movie, there it was and it didn't take long for Angela to figure out what was going on."

Eliza pulled over at the turn off to the rough ranger trail that wound up to the community road. She looked at her father. He was sitting with his fist clenched in his lap.

"Daddy, I'm so sorry. You wanted to hear it all. Now I'm not so sure that it was a good idea. Do you want me to get the urn out of the back? It's all packaged in a box, just the way it came from the crematory 17 years ago."

Joe just waved it off, like no big deal. All he said was. "I hope you have good tires on this fancy ride of yours. These ranger roads ain't improved at all since you were a kid."

Eliza didn't consider her four-year-old Ford Taurus a fancy car. She'd saved and skimped through her whole career to save for Angela's support and for her education. There was never enough for extras.

"Oh yes, I always keep good tires on my car and keep the maintenance up. I can't afford a new car every year."

"You're a lawyer and you can't afford a new car every year? Well, this one looks brand new, anyway. Just go easy. It wouldn't take much to bottom this thing out in some of these ruts."

Eliza started to continue the story, but Joe held up his hand. "Let's not talk until we get to the blacktop road. You're gonna need all your attention on this gulley washed cow path."

That was as good an excuse as any for a break from the knife blade that was digging deep into his heart. His arm felt numb and his chest felt heavy. It was all that he could do to keep from breaking down. However, men just didn't do that. Men sucked it up, but he'd been losing the ability to hold back tears since he found out he had a granddaughter.

He thought the road would never end.

Twenty minutes later, when she got to the top she said, "I don't remember this road being this bad when we rode the high school bus. That was a long time ago. And I can't believe you brought Angela down this road in your truck at night."

"Well, I didn't have any options. I had to get her to the hospital fast and it would have taken too long to go around. How that little girl took these bumps in her condition is beyond me. Anyway, she was all wrapped up in one of the old quilts that your mama made for Carrie's bed. I had her in there like a cocoon and strapped in with the seat belt. It was like Carrie and your mama was protecting her. I guess that's what saved her from further injury from the accident."

The small two-lane blacktop road was also in need of repair, but it was the freeway compared to the old ranger trail. Pulling into Daddy's rutted out driveway, Eliza could hear the muffled sound of his dog barking.

"Don't worry about Dog. He'll not hurt a flea. I suspect that he's madder than a hornet at me for leaving him in the cabin all night by himself. He's never been left alone at night before."

Eliza looked around the place as they exited her car. "So you just named him, Dog. So like you, Daddy. Mama had to name us because you suggested the names, Kid Number One and Kid Number Two."

"You remember Mama telling that story?" He chuckled. "Now you must know that Jessie made up that tale."

"No, I don't believe that she did, Daddy, because that was so like you."

"Well, I just liked to let your Mama have control over some things. Her thing was creating names. I figured that if she went to all the pain of having you, she should have the pleasure of naming you."

Joe hesitated by the car and then asked, "Eliza, why don't you bring Carrie into the house. You could leave her urn in your loft room until you and Angela come back for the ceremony. Don't you think she'd like that?"

Eliza smiled. "Yes, Daddy. She'd be pleased. She'd truly be home." She opened the trunk and brought out a medium size parcel box and she and her dad walked arm in arm toward the cabin.

Eliza breathed the mountain air in deep before stepping up on the porch. "The place hasn't changed at all, Daddy."

"Yeah, except to get old and worn out, like me. Right?"

"You're doing o.k. for your age, Daddy."

Joe felt the pressure in his chest again, but smiled. He needed to get inside and take some antacid tablets.

"Well, I hike at least once a week and I do a lot of work around here and for my neighbor down the way. That keeps this 87 year old body going in good shape."

Eliza could see the strain on her father's face as he turned and looked across the landscape in front of the cabin. He remembered the van that he had seen on the road the night that his granddaughter had been dumped on his porch. The detective had said that his testimony in court might just be an important piece of the evidence against Brent Morse.

"Daddy, are you alright?"

He turned and smiled at Eliza. "Oh, that hospital food has turned my stomach into a sour mess. I'll be alright after I get some antacids into me."

He took the door handle. "Now stand back and be prepared. Dog's probably gonna come at me with full force. Don't acknowledge him right away. It's like in a wolf pack. If you acknowledge an animal as soon as you enter the home, they'll consider themselves the leader or at least an equal. Wait for a while and then go back to them when they're settled down."

Joe opened the door and Dog flew out almost knocking his master over. Eliza leaned back against the door jam.

Joe chuckled. "Sorry about that. I've been meaning to build a doggy door. He fooled me. I thought he'd charge out of there like a bullet, but I didn't expect him to about knock me over." Joe said, breathing hard.

Joe left the door open and he and Eliza stood watching as Dog disappeared around the cabin. They stepped inside and Eliza stood looking around the rooms.

Joe stood watching her. "Has anything changed?"

"Not a thing, Daddy."

Dog came back in and ran up to Joe. Joe looked straight ahead. "Don't acknowledge him."

Dog looked up at Joe and Eliza and then dropped his head and went to the fireplace to lay down. Joe closed the door and then walked over and started patting the animal's head. The excited dog got up and started to walk toward Eliza. Joe said firmly, but quietly, "No, not yet." Dog laid down on the rug.

Eliza was impressed. I shouldn't be surprised. She thought. Daddy has always had a way with animals. He has always known them inside out. He has never hit an animal and he has never raised his voice to one. All the same, they've always known from the first encounter that he was the Alpha, the boss.

That was always how it was with Mama and with Carrie and her. They grew up knowing that if they disappointed Dad, they disappointed the leader of the pack. He never had to say a word. She knew that was why Carrie ended up the way she did; because she was never strong enough to take charge of her life and stop worrying about what Daddy thought.

Joe went to the counter and pumped some water into a glass. "Now before I give Dog his water, I have to drink a glass of water. Before I feed him, I have to take a bite of something. That's how it's done in the wild to establish dominance."

"Well, that's one thing that's different about the way things worked when we were growing up. You made sure that Mama, Carrie and I had something to eat before you ate."

"So I guess you three women were dominant over me, then."

"No, Daddy. You know that all you had to do was look at us and we melted."

"Well, then if you had it so good, why'd you two girls leave?"

"You know that things fell apart after Mama died. It was like she was the one that glued us all together."

Joe nodded his head. "That's the truth of it, that is. Yep, your mama was the wise one. She knew how to keep her family humming along."

Joe looked at the box in the crook of Eliza's arm. "Why don't you take off your coat and take the box upstairs. You can stay up there for a while if you like. The loft's just as you two girls left it. Nothing's been touched up there. " Eliza took two steps in one. "The climb to the loft doesn't seem near as long as it did when Carrie and I were kids." she yelled back at her dad.

At the top, she stood for a moment looking at the big open room with the vaulted ceiling. There had never been any walls there. It was plain with the logs still shiny and polished. Two half beds covered in Mama's homemade quilts sat across from each other. Rag rugs were on the plank flooring. Eliza walked over to the bed by the back dormer window and sat the box down next to the bonnet girl pattern. She sat on the edge of the bed and traced the blue piece that was the bonnet, then the pink head and along the arm.

Eliza stared out the back window at the majesty of the mountains. Even the surrounding fortress wall of the tree-topped hills couldn't protect the inhabitants of the valley below. Human kind certainly makes their own hell in paradise. Eliza sighed. Too bad things went so awry with Carrie. That was then and this is now. She turned and went back downstairs leaving the box with Carrie's remains on the bed she had slept on from the time she was two years old until she was fifteen.

As she came back down the stairs, Eliza noticed the cot in the corner. Well, that hadn't changed. She looked at the door to her right along the wall at the bottom of the stairs. The door had been locked right after they took Mama's body out and Daddy never went into it again. He slept in a cot in the living room from that day forward.

Dog finished lapping his water and Joe opened the door for him to go out. Then he opened up the wood stove door and chucked in some kindling wood. He lit it as he talked.

"After we eat, maybe we could do a trail."

"I'd love to walk a trail, Daddy, but I just can't take too much time here. It'll take an extra hour to get back down the mountain if I take the long way around, and I don't want to

leave Angela that long. The detective is supposed to talk to her today and I need to be there if she gets upset."
"Yeah, I promised to get back down there too. But I need something on my stomach before we go, and you do need something to eat as well."
Eliza contemplated how long it would take to get the stove hot and get something cooked. "You know, Daddy, if you can drive back in your jeep later, I think I'll just head back and grab something to eat at the hospital. Angela and I'll be back before we leave town."
"Did you say, "we leave town?"
"Actually, it all depends on how things go for Angela at the college. If they get that young man off the campus, then I'll feel safe in letting her stay. If not...I guess she'll just have to forego her tuition. Much will depend on Angela's mental health, as well."
"Did that young man rape her, too?"
"That's what the doctor said. Or at least there was DNA evidence left by a male."
Joe's eyes swelled up with the tears that he held there, mentally trying to refuse their release. He shook his head. "Are you pressing charges?"
"Yes, and that's another issue. It's a criminal case as well as a civil case, if we decide to seek damages."
"The world down there's a dangerous place."
"Is that why you tried to keep Carrie and me on this mountain, Daddy? Because I believe the danger has now come to your door."
"Yes, that's exactly why. You're right. My granddaughter was harmed here in the wild. But I long ago found out that a parents protection stops with the will of the child."
She looked over at her dad who was cramming a handful of anti-acid tablets into his mouth. She turned and walked to him. "Daddy, when was the last time you had a physical?"
"Oh, I don't need a doctor. Living in the mountains with nature is the only medicine I need. Why don't you wait until after we've eaten and I've arranged with my neighbor to take

care of things here? Then I'll follow you down the mountain. Or you could just leave the car here and we could both go in my jeep."

Eliza shook her head. "Thanks anyway, Daddy, but I need to have my car with me and I need to go now. I'll be fine. I'll see you at the hospital when you get there."

"Then take the left at the end of the drive and head toward the community. The new road to the highway comes off the other side of the mountain."

"I'll do that Daddy. That's got to be smoother than that stretch on the ranger road, even if it does take longer."

When you get to exit nine, turn off, follow that to the fork, and turn left. That's the mountain road past the college."

"I'd have to drive clear through town and it's still the long way around. I'll just stay on the highway and connect at exit 7. That looks like the fastest way to the hospital."

"Still as stubborn as ever. That'll keep you on that fast highway a lot longer."

"That's why I'm a lawyer, Daddy. I inherited your strong will."

Joe walked out to the car with Eliza. He had half wanted to ask her more about what happened to Carrie. On the other hand, he felt like he'd heard all he could handle for one day. Besides, he wanted to settle things here and get some clothing packed. He'd be better off staying at a motel in town for a few days. He'd get his friend, old Zeb Greenway to come stay at the cabin with Dog. He could bring his dog, Trek to keep company with Dog.

"I'll see you back at the hospital when I get things settled here. Tell Angela that I love her and
I'll see her soon." Eliza smiled at him from her car window. Then
Joe said something else. "I love you, too, Eliza."

"I love you, too, Daddy." For some reason that Joe could not explain, he started to cry as Eliza backed around and headed down the driveway. His chest felt like it was going to explode. Must be heartburn. Better get some grub into my belly. He rubbed down his arm again. 'Ah, these old body parts are trying to give way on me.'

Dog came bounding around the corner of the cabin and trotted back inside with Joe. The dutiful master felt like his dog couldn't wait for him to eat his grub first to establish dominance. He pulled out some sausage and put some into Dog's food dish. Then he put the rest in the skillet on the old wood stove and sat a pot of beans that he had cooked up two days before beside it. It would take a while to heat up and cook. Meantime, he needed to make some arrangements. Walking over to the ham radio, he turned up the dial and then spoke to the answering voice. "Hey, Zeb, I need you and your mutt to come and babysit Dog for me for a few days. Out."

"Hey, Joe, whar 'er ya off to? Out."

"It's a long story, Zeb. I'll tell you ..." Joe grabbed the explosion in his chest and his arms. Zeb yelled, "Joe, Joe," As the receiver button jammed on as it landed upside down on the desk.

Zeb could hear the barking of Dog as the animal panicked, jumping around his fallen master.

It took about twenty minutes for Zeb to get to the cabin. When he entered, Dog was laying on the floor beside his master, whimpering.

The dark gray ashen color of Joe's face as he lay on his back, told Zeb that his old buddy was gone. However, Zeb bent over his old friend and went through the process of CPR like he and Joe had been trained for as forest rangers so many years ago.

Finally, he walked over and took the burning food off the stove. Zeb sat shaking and crying in a chair for a few minutes. He dried his eyes and looked at Dog still laying by Joe and whimpering.

The howl of the wolf on the point brought Zeb to his feet. He walked to the window. There was only a shadow in the fog. The wolf howl reverberated again. Then the shadow slowly faded away. Zeb turned and went to the radio.

Chapter Twelve

The Detective Lieutenant Yoder took the call from the community constable. They would be bringing Joe Hardigan down the mountain in a hearse, and the responsibility to inform the next of kin fell heavily on Yoder's shoulders. How much more can this family take? He shook his head and another thought hit him. He picked up his phone. He left a message with the secretary on the other end to have the prosecuting attorney call him.
The witness that could testify about the van the night of Angela's assault was gone. He looked at his tape recorder. We still have the recording of his statement to me. He thought. It won't be as strong as the real thing...but..
The tall officer hunched his shoulders as he left the office reluctantly. This was the least favorite responsibility of his profession. Delivering the news was never easy, but this was going to be especially hard. He had learned that Eliza had just reunited with her dad and Angela had just found her grandfather.
In his car, he made a call to Eliza and found that she was at the hospital. He requested that she meet with him in the hospitality room. She said that she would ask that it be available.
Yoder was so engrossed in going over all the facts that he had learned about Eliza and Angela; he was in the visitor's parking lot before he realized it. He made his way to the third floor.
Eliza was already there. He made a half-hearted attempt at an unattached greeting, but just being in
Eliza's presence and knowing what he knew...realizing that he had to do this... What's the matter with you? It's not like you haven't done this before.'
Somehow, he choked the message out as Eliza stared across the table at him.
What's he saying? I don't understand.

The counselor from the college had been called into the lobby. Joanna was sitting next to her.
Why does she have her hand on mine?
"Eliza, I wanted Joanna to be here for you and for Angela. I just thought you should know first, and you could decide how we'd tell Angela."
Eliza started speaking without really hearing her own words. "Where'd they take the body?"
Yoder was taken aback by the seemingly cold statement. He stared back at Eliza's face. He had been awestruck from the time that he met her by how attractive she was. Add to that her strength...a single woman who'd given up her childbearing years to maintain a career and raise her dead sister's daughter…that strength was something that went far beyond physical beauty. On the other hand, this reaction was far more than strength. It was matte-of-fact and business-like. Her face had taken on a harsh, almost angry look.
Yoder spoke with a low voice. "The county morgue. His body needs to be identified and arrangements have to be made." There was a long silence.
My daddy at the county morgue...No, he should still be on his mountain. He never wanted to be anywhere else.
Yoder stared at the stalwart face. "Eliza, you'll have to identify the body so that the officials will know where to take him."
"Why the hell for? If they picked him up from his cabin and the neighbor was there, why do I need to do that?"
"You'll have to take care of arrangements."
Yoder said quietly "Isn't there any air conditioning in this place?" Eliza felt the lump in her throat. Her brain was on fire with fight or flight. I want to run from this room and find someplace to come unglued. I want to be on the mountain where I can scream my lungs out.
She spoke with a vague, far-a-way voice. "Daddy's hiked that mountain every day of his life. He is strong. He's...too strong to..."

Her hands twisted the Kleenex into a knot as she struggled with thought. 'Why do I feel so strange? My words...my voice, it's not me. I'm a seasoned lawyer. I'm never at a loss for words.'

Eliza turned to Joanna who was trying to put her arm around her. She spoke with authority. "I don't want to be rude, but would you please not touch me?"

Joanna pulled back and sat still in the chair. "I'm sorry. Would you like us to leave you alone for a while?"

Eliza shook her head yes. "Yes, I'm sorry to be so nasty. All the same, yes. I need some time to get my head around this."

"If you need me, I'll be somewhere in the hospital for a while. I won't tell Angela until you can be in the room with her. On the other hand, we can bring her in here if you'd like that better. Just have one of the nurses page me." Joanna reached into her bag, brought out a box of tissues, and left them on the table near Eliza.

Yoder got up from his chair and pushed it under the table. "I'll be leaving the grounds for a short time, but if you need me, have Joanna call me as well."

The door closed and Eliza stared at the wall for a while. 'I've got to think. How am I going to tell Angela? I've got to get myself together before I tear my little Angela's heart apart and add more hurt to her life. Oh God. When's it my turn to feel. I've been putting myself on the back burner all my life.'

The hurt and the rage came pouring out of her very pores. 'I want for once in my life to lose all control.'

"Damn you!" She yelled at the wall. Then the floodgates opened and she cried as she had never cried before. She put her head down on the table and for almost an hour, she cried, brought herself around, trying to gain control, and lost it again. Finally, after about twenty minutes of calm resolve, she felt spent and dried out.

It was time to come clean with Angela about all that happened in the past. That young woman has already had to grow up ten years at one huge leap; the night one man took her virginity from her in a criminal act. 'All those years, I've built a wall around her. As soon as I let her out into the world, Angela went wild. The tragedy is that the game she was trying to play was a losing one.'

Eliza stood up and faced the wall again. She closed her swollen eyes. Now she had to be strong. She turned around and opened the door to find Joanna standing outside the door.

"I used up all the tissues."

"Do you want more?" Joanna held up a new box of tissues.

"Might be a good idea. I'm all done crying, but now we have to get Angela in here." She wiped a few small drops from her face with a used tissue in her hand. "I don't want to go down the hall looking like this. Would you go and get Angela?"

She walked across the hall to the bathroom. She stared at the swollen face in the mirror... Oh, God. When did I get all these lines? I'm old. The years, where did they all go?' She turned on the cold water and pressed a wet towel into the creases.

When Eliza returned to the room, Angela was seated in the same chair that she had left. Joanna was sitting beside her. Joanna rose to her feet and faced her. "Do you want me to stay?"

"Yes, please."

Joanna moved to the other side of the table. Eliza sat down beside the bewildered Angela.

"You look like a mess, Aunt Eliza. What's the deal?"

"Oh, this is my no makeup look."

"I know better than that. You've always looked like a young chick."

"O.K. When was the last time they gave you a sedative?"

"Oh, about an hour ago."

"Have you had any more panic attacks today?"

"No, I haven't, I don't know if it's the sedatives or just having Rachel in the room with me." She smiled and continued. "Or maybe it's because I have a new grandpa. Isn't he the neatest guy, Aunt Eliza? He's my hero. I don't think I can ever trust another guy. But Grandpa...well, if I could find one like him...I guess there's still hope for me."

Eliza started to feel a panic attack herself. She looked at Joanna. 'Oh my God, help me to do this.'

The silence caused Angela to look with concern at Joanna's face and then she turned around half way in her seat toward her aunt. She touched her aunt's shoulder as she tried to get her to turn and face her. Eliza was staring straight ahead at the wall. The tears started to fall again. "I almost had my Daddy back."

Angela had been trying to look into Eliza's eyes as she talked. "What're you trying to say, Aunt?
Eliza? Is Grandpa mad at you for something?"

Eliza lost it. "Grandpa died about three hours ago of a heart attack," she sobbed.

Angela sat motionless for a second. That was a ton of bricks, she thought. Then she stood and with tears flowing down her cheeks, she leaned over to hug her aunt. "I'll never get to know Grandpa. " They sobbed together as Joanna pushed the tissues closer to them. Joanna got up and left the room.

Yoder heard the sobs as Joanna opened and shut the door behind her. He shook his head and folding his arms, he leaned back against the wall. "I came around to see how things are going. I guess I'd better wait until this crisis calms down before questioning Angela any more about the rape."

"Well, yes. Right now, they have a funeral to plan. Have you talked with Rachel?"

"I'm going in there now, but I need you to be with her in this. The family doctor stated that it was o.k. that I question her, if either you or Eliza is present. I think they're planning on retaining Eliza as Rachel's lawyer." He said. "I saw the family walking with Rachel down the hall as I came in."

Joanna looked back toward the door. "Eliza and Angela will be awhile. I'll go with you."

Yoder spoke quietly as they made their way down the hall. "I hate it when I have to talk to people in the hospital. The circumstances for these cases make it a doubly hard chore."
"I understand what you mean." Joanna stated just above whisper.
"I always make sure that I have the doctor's evaluation. In this case the questioning can't wait."
"Oh, I know. These young people need to get back to their college life, if that's possible."
"Yes, the dean and I agree that things have to get settled before either of the girls return to the campus, and the doctor won't release them until they have someplace to go."
"What's happening with Brent's case? I know that he's still attending classes."
"I can't expose the particulars yet. We're still tying things together. There're two, maybe three cases hinging on what these two girls have to say and all could be connected. It's the most tangled mess of events that I've ever seen."
Yoder thought, but didn't add, that with the death of one of his main witnesses, the bereavement factor was going to slow things down.
When he and Joanna reached the hospital room door, Dorothy and David were just coming off the elevator. Jerrod was with them.
"We were going down to dinner and look who we ran into." Dorothy said.
"Well, it's good to see all of you. I've come to question Rachel."
"Oh, well, maybe Jerrod would like to have dinner with us. Of course, Rachel may be getting her dinner tray soon as well."
"We won't keep her long. I wouldn't want to tire her out. She can make her statement quickly and we can let you know when we're finished."
At that moment, the light came on over the door down the hall, and Dorothy made the first move. She walked quickly and everyone else strolled along behind her.

A nurse aide got to the door at the same time. As the women entered the room, Dorothy was surprised to see an empty bed. Then her eyes were drawn quickly to the far right hand corner and she ran to hold Rachel.
The nurse aide took a quick look around and said, "Sir, you're going to have to leave or I'll have to get security."
The man stood firm at the end of Rachel's bed.
Jerrod stepped in behind the nurse and ran toward the man. Yoder walked in and almost ran into the nurse aide as she ran out. Jerrod was on top of someone across Angela's bed and Dorothy was trying to soothe her sobbing daughter.

Chapter Thirteen

Earlier, Rachel leaned over to get her water on the side table. She sensed that someone was in the room and looked to see legs in blue jeans.
"Hey, that was fast ser...."
"Oh, my God. Brent."
She jumped from the bed and backed into the corner.
"Hey, I'm not going to hurt you. I just came to see Angela. I heard that she was attacked and beaten up."
Don't look an assailant in the eyes. Don't provoke him.
"What about you? Are you doing o.k. after the surgery?"
There was no time to speak or act. The room exploded with people.
"Mother." Rachel hugged Dorothy tightly as she watched in horror as Jerrod lunged into Brent, knocking him down onto Angela's bed.
Yoder and Joanna walked in behind David. Yoder quickly surveyed the room, and walked over to the end of Angela's bed. He turned to Joanna. David stood holding the end of Rachel's bed. The detective addressed David and Joanna.
"Please take Rachel out to a safe place while I get to the bottom of this."
After David and the women left the room, he turned to Jerrod. "You can let him up now."
Jerrod got up and sat down on a chair on the other side of Rachel's bed.
Brent raised up, sat up slowly. "What the hell just happened? I was here to visit my girlfriend, Angela."
Yoder stared down at him, his hands on his hips and frowning. "Brent, I talked to you about staying away from the girls when I questioned you. Now, you see what happened."
Brent's voice was shaking. "I have the right to be here. I told you that I didn't do anything wrong. All I did was come in here to see Angela. I tell you... that Rachel is a sick

chick. She just comes all unglued over nothing. I was just asking how she was and she goes bananas." His voice became louder as he talked.

Yoder put his hand up. "I don't want to hear it. I'm going to escort you out and a patrol officer will follow you back to campus. If I find out you've tried to contact these girls again, I'll have to put you in jail for failing to comply. Don't even call them."

He stepped closer to the bed. "Come on, it'll go easier for you if you just follow my orders."

Brent was yelling. "I'm pressing charges against Jerrod Showalter. He attacked me. "

"Brent, you're not making any points with me with this behavior. Now, I'm going to advise you to comply. You're leaving now. If I have to tell you again, I'm going to cuff your hands and arrest you for non-compliance."

"O. K. I'm going." Brent headed for the door just ahead of Yoder.

Violet returned with the second shift nurse, Robin, and almost ran into Yoder as he walked out behind Brent. Robin peeked in the door. "Where are my patients?"

Jerrod got up from his chair. "I'm not sure where Angela is. I'll go and find Rachel." He walked out into the hall behind Robin. By this time, several staff members were in the hall watching as Yoder escorted Brent toward the stairway entrance. A security guard met them and opened the stairway door.

Jerrod spotted Rachel as he started to pass the waiting room window. She looked up and smiled nervously as he entered the room. *I misjudged him. He is so warm and protective.* Dorothy looked at her daughter's beaming face. She was pleased.

Jerrod kept his eyes on Rachel. "Are you o.k.?"

"Yes, I'm fine. Thanks for your help, but I hope that Brent doesn't cause you any legal problems."

"It's o.k. and I'm not worried. If I hadn't stopped Brent, Lieutenant Yoder would have."

Rachel said. "I'm just glad that Angela wasn't in the room when he came in. She and I had a good talk before she left the room to visit her aunt.'

Dorothy nodded her head. "David and I came back from lunch today and found out that the two girls had formed a strong bond. That was such a relief."

Rachel said, "We realized that we had too much in common. It was a burden lifted from the both of us."

Joanna spoke up. "That's so important to both of you in your healing process. You need each other."

"Yes we do."

The nurse said, "Well, it looks like everyone is fine here, and I've got to go attend my med rounds. Rachel, I think I hear the dinner cart. Maybe you'll want to get back to your room."

"Yes, for some reason, I'm starved. Angela may want to get back herself. She's been gone a long time."

"I'll go check on her." Joanna said as she got up and left the room. The counselor knew she had to let Angela give out the news of her loss. The trauma was never ending lately. Where were the days when this town was boring? She wished for them to be back.

Rachel got up and Jerrod helped her to the door. Rachel looked back at her parents. "Are you coming? "

David said, "No, I think that Jerrod can help you get back. Come on, Dorothy. I need to go to the hospital office to sign some insurance papers before the door closes and we need to do a little shopping. Jerrod, maybe we can meet later for dinner."

Jerrod turned to Rachel after he settled her in the room. He walked over beside her bed and offered his hand.

She took it and looked up at him, her eyes soft. "I really appreciate you, Jerrod. Thanks for being here."

Jerrod bent over and kissed Rachel's forehead, still holding her hand. "Get well, Rachel. I need to go now so that you can eat your dinner and take a rest. You need things to be quiet and calm now."

She looked up at him, her eyes soft. "I thought you were training to be a police officer. You're sounding like a doctor."

"Just worried about your health." He let go of her hand and turned toward the door. "I'll be back before you know it."

The room became extremely quiet after Jerrod left. Rachel sat and recalled the conversation that she and Angela had earlier.

Perhaps her friend's grandpa was back and that's what was keeping her from returning to the room so soon. The little red head deserved time with her family.

Rachel came back to the present as the aide brought in her dinner tray. She ate and listened carefully as two people in the other room got louder and louder. Straining to understand what they were saying, she got up and moved as fast as she could to the restroom and quietly sat on the bathroom stool.

On the other side of the door to the adjoining room, a female voice trembled and Rachel was sure of what she said.

"Sammy Ray, ah tolt you 'at you needed ta get 'at dent fixed out'a town. What if the cops trace...?"

A male voice spoke up..."Look, ah had ta' slip in here ta see you, 'cause you claimed ah beat you up. You was drunk as a skunk when yore mama brought you in. At's why you hit 'at woman up thar on 'at mountain road. Now yore bitchin'' at me
'cause of whar I'm gettin' the car fixed."

    Rachel almost choked. The voice paused. "By the way, I've been up on 'at road a number a times tryin' to find the bumper. You must've drug it quite a ways away."

The room was silent a moment, then the male voice continued, "What fer you was up on 'at mountain with them wolf spirits is beyon' me."

The door to her room opened up as the second shift nurse aide looked inside. Violet started to speak and Rachel put her finger over her lips to shush her. The voices stopped. Violet quietly helped Rachel back to bed. "Sorry about the loud noise in the room next door. We called security to remove the man in there. He's not suppose to be in that room."

Back in bed, Rachel asked said. "Do you know when the detective is coming back in?"

"The what?" Violet looked at Rachel as though she was nuts.

Rachel spoke as softly as she could. "I know it sounds strange and Trixie probably didn't tell you this, but we've had quite a lot of activity here in this room. Haven't you heard all the news about the accident on the mountain and the teacher who had a hit and run accident?"

Violet threw her head back. "Oh-h-h. Yeah, I did hear about all that. But I just didn't connect any of that." She turned toward the door. "I'll check about the detective for you."

"I'm right here." Yoder said as he came in the door.

Rachel turned to look at him. "Oh, good. I need to talk with you right away."

"O.K. What is it that you want to talk about? Uh...can I record this?"

He pulled the small unit out of his coat pocket and turned it on.

"I was told that you needed either your lawyer or Joanna with you when I did the interview, so maybe by the time we get to that questioning,

Joanna will be back. Is that o.k. with you?"

"That's fine. I'll be o.k. whether Joanna's here or not."

Rachel related the dialog that she had heard from the other room. Yoder showed no emotion. When she finished he said, "Let me check something and I'll be right back." He darted out the door.

In the room the he darted into, the detective talked into his two way. "I've got a feeling that this is probably hallucinations from her head injury, but I don't want to discount it."

He returned while Rachel was still sipping her water.

After the meeting, Rachel relaxed against the bed. She breathed a sigh of relief. That wasn't so bad.

"I hope I wasn't too hard on you."

"No, not at all. It was easy talking to you."

"Well since I have the recordings from the interview with the school security officer, there's no need to go into great detail on your run in with Brent. But I really appreciate you filling me in on your encounter with Ms. Bence and what you heard in the next room."

He gathered his equipment and turned toward the door.

"Thank you for your co-operation, and I'm going to look into this right away. We'll get back in touch. Except that I hope that our next meeting will be at the college in the dean's office."

"Sounds good to me." Rachel waved goodbye to Yoder with a smile.

Rachel settled back and thought about Angela. 'She retreated this morning when I asked her if she wanted to talk about the rape. I hope that my friend will open up about it. Then, she just might not want to hear about it yet or ever. It is a terrible and private matter.'

Yoder thought about the interview with Rachel as he waited for the elevator. He wanted to check with the office about the report from his inquiry into the people in the next room to Rachel. The name that he had retrieved from the doorplate to that room should lead to the truth of the matter. Maybe it was in Rachel's imagination. If the woman next door was clean, her driver's license was clear, and her car showed no sign of damage, then he'd have to talk with Rachel's parents and her doctor. If she had delusions from the head injury, it was going to be harder to settle this case. Of one thing he was certain, the insurance report on the dents in Brent's van stated that all the dents were old ones. The big dent had recently been sanded. A police forensic expert combed the van over for any evidence of having been in a recent collision with a human body. Nothing was found. There was still the lingering doubt about the head injury that

Rachel sustained. Still, Rachel had been lucid and reasonable in her accounting of how she swerved on the road and stopped. She had sounded like a private investigator as she laid out the scene of where Ms. Bence was standing and where police and news reports said the body was. That could have been fabricated. She was right about one thing. The dent on Brent's fender was on the passenger's side and if Rachel was coming down the mountain, she would have had to hit her on the driver's side.

He decided that he would go up on the mountain road and take another look around later. For now, he had to get the report on Rachel's hospital neighbor.

He settled down in his police cruiser and picked up his radio. "Justus, do you have that report for me yet?"

"Yeah, just got it and you'll not believe the new twist in this case."

"Let me have it."

"Delilah Wray. She's a frequent visitor to our drunk tanks. Her car is a White 1999 Saturn S400, license plate number SZ 345, and Wray's driver's license is expired. Her mother, Eugenia Frye just bailed that car out of impound a week ago. Delilah made out a report last night that her boyfriend, Samuel Ray Taylor beat her up. We have an APB on him. Did you see it?"

"Yes, I was aware of it. Did you find the car yet?"

"No, it's not at her mother's place. The old woman uses a walker. She said that she was selling the car and that a potential buyer had it out driving it."

"Well, check every nook and cranny for it. It's probably in one of the suspected chop shops that we've been investigating. Try that route, too."

"Got the word out. We're looking. I'll let you know as soon as I find it."

O.K. Thanks. I'm going to go back up to the site and check it out again before it gets dark. Get a patrol car and a forensic team to meet me there. We may need to scour up and down that whole length. From the information I have,

there may be a bumper that was thrown off somewhere along the road."
"You got it."
Yoder gunned his vehicle and pulled it out into the traffic. He contemplated all the entanglements of this case. How everything could just come falling down like a house of cards, he didn't know, but he wasn't complaining. He just hoped that he'd find what he was looking for as easily.
The patrol car pulled in right behind his cruiser directly in front of the Bence farm property. Yoder directed the two officers to search ahead along the road and he would walk through the tall grasses on both sides of the property. It hadn't rained in the last three nights, and he figured that the ground beneath would be dry.
As he was searching, a big black police van pulled up and stopped on the road behind the patrol car. He waved to the two officers as they spotted him. He walked back to the van. "What are we looking for?" He filled them in and they joined the search.
Yoder was walking half way up to the farmhouse along the lawn. He was about ready to give up when he saw some grasses bent toward the farmhouse. He reached down with his gloved hand and parted the weeds. There it was… a white fiberglass piece with what looked like blood on it. He waved to forensic. He yelled to the officers.
"Got it. Get a camera."
As forensic properly secured the evidence, Yoder felt triumphant and happy that he'd be able to give Rachel some good news. "Fiberglass and I'd say that it came from a Saturn. It's not bent, because this type of fiberglass just bounces back or it cracks. I'd say that the fender has blood on it, too. The damage will most likely be broken fiberglass like this bumper. That is, if we get to it before a chop shop does."
Back in his car, Yoder picked up his radio speaker, "Justus, I've sent out units to that suspected chop shop. Forensic has

some great evidence bagged and in route. I'm headed to the hospital. I need to speak to Delilah Wray."

Chapter Fourteen

Eliza and Angela were completely unaware of the scene going on in the hospital room. Their world in the hospitality room was one of pain, loss, and disbelief.

With a tug of Angela's hand, Eliza turned in her chair until their knees touched. She patted Angela's bare legs. "You must do something about your wardrobe." Eliza thought. That was a completely stupid thing to say.

"I have a long speech, so listen. I've faced many adversities in my life, starting with the loss of my mother. I was just a teenager, almost 15 and in my first year of high school, when Mama became ill and your mother, Carrie was ten. Carrie could understand less than I could about why Mama stayed in bed all day and had to be waited on hand and foot.

Daddy brought her here for the chemicals that were dripped into her veins. The bottom floor of this building was a clinic at that time. Daddy wouldn't let her stay here for any more time than it took for her treatment. Of course, Mama didn't want to be away that long. She was always saying that she didn't want to die in the hospital. That on again vibrant and off again lethargic woman who had been a busy, talented organizer and homebody crafter was becoming less the mother that we had always known. When she had a bad day, we all had a bad day. She lost her hair and lost her strength a long time before she lost her life.

So there I was, big sister Eliza, getting up every morning to get breakfast on the table. Weekdays, I sent my little sister off to the community elementary school. Daddy hired an aide to come in while he was at work patrolling the park or sitting up in the tower. When he was home, he was always with Mama in her room.

I ended up playing the role as Carrie's mom and she resented me for it. At the same time, she formed a dependency on me, especially when she got into trouble in the outside world. Even when Mama had her good days, when she

could come out and walk the property or a short trail with Daddy, she no longer seemed like our mother.
Toward the end of Mama's life, four years later, Daddy was Mama's principal caregiver. He took a leave from his service and waited on her night and day. He slept very little. We lost so much of Daddy and Mama during the teen years."
The silence in the room was deafening. Then Angela spoke. "You gave up so much for the family, especially Mama and me...we've given you nothing but grief all these years. I just never understood when I was being rebellious that you were strict because you loved me."
"I'm proud of you for having compassion, but I didn't consciously give up anything. I made mistakes. I'm just sorry that I didn't tell you all this years ago about your granddaddy. You missed out on so much without him, but you see I never felt that I really had Daddy. I never got a chance to know him, even though we lived in the same house."
"You were just trying to protect me. Now I know why you insisted that I come to this college. It was what you thought was a safe place for me. I know it must have been safe when you were getting your degree, but the world has crept in."
"I would say that the world has blasted in, judging from the events of this past week. When I graduated from Echo Valley Community, it was about the size of the high school. It was only a two-year college then. The current administration building was the only structure here and there were only 60 students in the whole student body. The students were all local and well disciplined." Eliza gave Angela a knowing smile. "But there is one good thing out of all this. I see insight from you for the first time. You sound wiser and more grounded."
"Oh yeah." Angela started to cry again. "I just wish Grandpa could be around to share with."
"If there is a heaven, he and your grandma are up there looking down and smiling. They would be pleased with their daughter Carrie's little girl."

"My mother would be very pleased with her sister for putting up with her troublesome daughter. On the other hand, I think she would be sad to know that you gave up the chance to marry and have kids of your own. Why didn't you get married, Aunt Eliza?"

"Never had time and never met a man that I wanted."

"Do you like the detective?"

Eliza laughed. "Do you mean Lieutenant Yoder? What makes you think that I would be interested in him?"

"Oh, I don't know. I just think the two of you would make a great couple."

Eliza just shook her head. "Well, I think it's time to get back to your room. I need to get to the business of taking care of your granddad's remains." Eliza choked on the words, and then started again. "... and you need to get some rest. The doctor said something this morning about dismissing you if I had a place for you. Let's plan on staying at the cabin, at least until things are settled down."

"That would be great."

Angela and Eliza stood up just as Joanna came into the room and shut the door. "You two need to stay in here for a minute until things are settled in your room, Angela."

"Whatever for?" Eliza asked.

"Brent Morse showed up to see you, Angela. Or so he said. Anyway, he caused a real ruckus by turning up here against the detective's orders."

Angela sat down hard on her chair. "Has he left the hospital?"

Eliza sat back down and took both of Angela's hands. Joanna shook her head yes. "He just left the floor escorted by the detective but they should be out of the building shortly. It's best if we just hang out for a little while longer in here."

Tears ran down Angela's face. "Is Rachel o.k.?"

"She's fine. We brought her to the waiting room. Jerrod just took her back to her room. Angela, if Brent is the one who raped you, you need to tell the detective."

Eliza brushed a curl from Angela's forehead.

"That's right. Sweetheart. You girls can't go back onto campus until there is no danger to either of you."

"Aunt Eliza, I don't think Brent did it. He would not have had to put a knock out rag over my nose to get me to go to the mountain with him. I think it was a sick man."

"Then why do you get upset when Brent's name is mentioned?"

"I don't know. I guess because I don't want to face him after what has happened to me. I feel dirty, not worthy. I guess because I feel guilty about siding with Brent about Rachel. I am so mixed up. On one hand, I know that Brent's a jerk for the way he treated Rachel. But I also know that he's too much of ah...too self-serving...I don't know how to explain it. I guess he's just sneaky, but not someone who is capable of actually going through the act of assault and rape."

Eliza took a deep breath. "Let's not try to solve this problem right now. We've got to work through getting Daddy's affairs taken care of. Then we'll tackle the Brent issues."

Yoder stuck his head into the room. "May I speak to you, Eliza?"

"Sure, come on in."

He stepped inside and sat down across from Angela. "I just stationed a police officer outside of the girls' room. Brent Morse, in my opinion is a threat. In spite of the fact that he's been warned to stay away from the girls, he came up here on the floor anyway."

Angela looked at Eliza and then at the detective. "I don't think Brent meant any harm, Lieutenant Yoder. I don't think he was the one who assaulted me."

"Why's that?"

"As I told Aunt Eliza, he's a sneak and a jerk, but I can't think he's capable of actually hurting anyone."

"And what makes you think that?"

"It all adds up. I was downtown when I got assaulted and I was chloroformed. If Brent wanted to beat me up, he had plenty of opportunity to do so on our dates." Angela looked up quickly toward Eliza. She lowered her eyes and took a deep breath. "Let's just say that Brent had no reason to rape me. I'd always been willing...." She stopped and started to cry.

Eliza put her arm around her niece. She said, "It's o.k. You don't have to say any more about that. Nobody is going to judge you."

Yoder leaned forward, his hands folded on the table in front of him. "Do you think you can tell me what happened that night? We need to go after the creep who assaulted and raped you. Every day gives him the chance to get away."

Angela wiped her eyes and began. "I was walking along Shephard's Street. When I came to the alley by the club, I felt strong arms come around me. Then a cloth came over my face. I don't remember anything else, except some vague nightmare about something horrible happening to me and feeling the pain." Angela broke down and cried uncontrollably.

Yoder pushed the box of tissues across the table and said with a lowered and soft voice, "I think that's all I need for now on your case. We've been searching for your car, but we haven't found it yet. It may have been stolen. Anyway, we'll keep looking for it. We can also look for the rag that was used to knock you out. If any other memories come to mind, just contact us. But could you fill us in on what you might know about the Bence case?"

"I can't be of much help to you on that. I wasn't there when it happened and all I can tell you are the lies and rumors that have circulated the campus." Angela lowered her head and started fidgeting with her tissue. "I'm partly to blame for the gossip. I guess I need to tell you what happened in the parking lot, not that it'll be any help." She related the hearsay from Brent on the alleged attack on Rachel that started the whole thing. Then she confessed her part of the antagonism around campus, in front of the dormitory and even the shower room theft.

Yoder listened quietly not taking his eyes off Angela. When she finished, he said. "Thanks for being honest. Oh, I forgot to tell you that I flipped on my pocket recorder when I came into the room. Is that O.K.?"

"Sure. I have got nothing to hide. I just wish I had all the answers for you. As for the Bence case, I don't think Rachel did anything wrong."

"Well for your piece of mind, we have new evidence with a new suspect. The problem is that the suspect just came up among the missing. It'd be helpful if you could tell us anything about the cars that you saw in that area as you were driving up to get Brent and on your way back down. It may be that you were at the crime scene after all and without realizing it."

Angela sat in deep thought and said, "I recall seeing what could have been a drunk driver that morning. I almost called 911 on the cell. The driver was really driving crazy."

"Which direction were you going and about where were you when you saw the car?"

"Well, let's see. I was going up the mountain road about half way up to Starlight Plateau. It was before the mist started coming over the car. A car came barreling around my car out of the fog and swerved around into the uphill lane in front of me."

"Do you remember the color of the car or the model?"

"It was white like the fog. But I don't know much about models or anything else."

"Did you see a woman at a mailbox?"

"No, there might have been someone out there, but I was so focused on the car barreling around me, that I didn't think about it."

"Do you know where the Bence farmhouse is?"

"No, I don't."

"Just where on the road were you when you saw the car?"

"I was coming up on the Echo State Park road turn off. There's a curve there and I remember thinking that the crazy nut would not make it. But when I reached the curve, I didn't see anything of the car."

Silence engulfed the room. Yoder cleared his throat. "Anything else?"

"No, I can't think of anything."

"O.K. I guess that's all for now. If you think of anything else, have Eliza call me."

Yoder looked at Eliza and then back at Angela. "I'm really sorry that your sophomore year has started out so rotten. Do you want to set up visits to the Women's Shelter for consultation?"

Eliza stated, "I'm hiring a counselor for her and she's been talking with Joanna here." She stood up and reached her hand across the table. "We'll get in touch with you if we find anything else out. I'll be representing my niece on any legal issues."

"Have the Brooks contacted you about representing their daughter on any level?"

"No, I understand that they're opposed to retaliation against a transgressor. At least that's what I understood them to say."

"Have you met them yet?"

"Only briefly in the hall one day."

Eliza's cell phone rang and she checked the number ID with a puzzled look. "Just my Chicago office. I'll call them back."

Joanna asked Angela if she wanted her to take her back to her room. Angela noted the looks that had been going on between her aunt and the detective. She nodded, "yes,"

Yoder dismissed himself with a warm smile for Eliza and a firm handshake. He could see no reason to hang around since Delilah had suddenly decided to check herself out of the hospital and disappear. Security had looked into every nick and corner of the building after a nurse found that her bed was empty and her belongings had disappeared along with her.

Eliza looked into his deep brown eyes. "Thanks for your gentle handling of this case. I appreciate that you're so sensitive to my niece."

"And I admire you for all your support for the girl you raised. There're not many parents who've done such a great job in raising their children. I know. I see the bad parenting every day."

Eliza smiled and watched Yoder as he disappeared toward the elevator. She opened her phone and dialed the number to her office. Hearing Cook County Prosecuting Attorney Chad Wentworth's voice, she said. "Eliza here."

"Eliza, we got your letter of resignation. What's that all about?"

"Like the letter says, I've decided to set up practice here in Echo Valley. Not much else can be said."

"Could a hefty raise change your mind?"

"Not a red copper's worth. It's not about money, Chad."

"O.K. You have severance coming, you know. You'll need to contact Samantha about how you want all that handled." Silence, then he sighed. "Eliza, I wish you'd change your mind. The team's losing a lot in losing you."

"Can't Chad. Besides, you have a lot of juniors who'll do great in my shoes. I'll be glad to keep in correspondence on the few minor cases that I left hanging."

"I disagree that anyone else could fill your shoes in the literal sense..." Chad chuckled. "Your feet are big." He chuckled. "No, not true...but seriously, we need you...I...well, if you change your mind, the doors always open here."

"I know Chad. Goodbye and thanks."

Eliza walked back to Angela's room feeling that one burden had been lifted. She and Angela would be fine once everything was back to normal in their lives. She truly felt that she was home, in spite of everything. She thought about Yoder. 'I wonder what his given name is.'

Chapter Fifteen

Eliza walked into the hospital room and found Angela and Rachel sitting side by side on Rachel's bed hugging each other and crying. Rachel's arms were wrapped around Angela's shoulder and Angela's arms were wrapped around Rachel's waist.

Rachel broke away and looked up at Eliza. "I'm so sorry about your father. I was so looking forward to meeting him."

Eliza sat down on the bed beside Angela. "Thank you. We were all looking forward to more time with him. But he had just used up his life."

The girls looked at Eliza. Angela spoke first. "Aunt Eliza, could Rachel come and stay with us when she gets out of the hospital?"

Eliza sat down in the chair across from them.

She looked at Rachel. "What's up, Rachel?"

"Oh, nothing's really wrong. It's just that my mother and father want me to leave with them this Friday, and I don't want to leave school yet."

"I understand your parents need to protect you. In addition, you won't be allowed to go back onto campus until the Brent situation is resolved. I have plans for Angela and I have to stay on the mountain for a while. I'm going to talk with the college about having Angela finish the semester online. If you could finish online, it wouldn't matter where you lived. You could go with your parents and still finish both semesters, most likely."

Angela and Rachel looked at each other. They were silent for a moment.

Eliza was puzzled by their lack of response.

"Are there any legal reasons why you can't leave Echo Valley?"

Angela spoke. "We need some time to help each other heal, Aunt Eliza. I'm not saying that you wouldn't be able to help me, but Rachel and I have a bond and we're kind of in the

same boat, right now. Rachel's parents just don't understand what she's going through. They want to take her out of the country to Ethiopia."
"Well, let me talk to her parents. It could be that the prosecuting attorney will need Rachel's presence in the hit and run hearing in the Bence case, and your claim against Brent. You two girls both witnessed Ms. Bence on the road that day. If the P. A. wants to subpoena you girls to help prosecute the suspect they have, you need to be available."
Rachel sat up straight as Eliza talked. "You mean that they arrested someone for that accident? "
"I don't know the details. All I know is what Lieutenant Yoder told Angela and me a few minutes ago."
Angela took Rachel's left hand. "I'm sorry. I forgot to tell you."
Rachel squeezed Angela around her shoulders. "It's o.k. This entire heavy load about your Grandpa is more than enough for you to remember. What did you say your Grandpa's name was?"
"Joseph...Joe Hardigan."
Rachel's forehead furrowed up and then her eyes grew wide. "Joe. What did he look like?"
"White beard, jolly face. He was almost 88 years old, but he didn't look a day over 70. He…"

Rachel gasped. "Santa Claus. Oh, don't tell me. He had a dog that he called, Dog and he had a deep, gruffly voice, and kind blue eyes."
Eliza and Angela said in unison. "How did you know?"
"He befriended me on the mountain road when I took the wrong fork and drove down to the state park picnic tables."
Eliza chuckled. "What a coincidence. Daddy must have been hiking."
"Oh my goodness. You met my grandpa before
I did and you didn't even know it."

"Yes, and that explains why I didn't meet you on the road. You must have been lost on the park road when I was driving past it. "
"I thought that I was dreaming all of that or hallucinating. It all adds up now. Oh my, this is so weird. He was such a sweet guy. He came up to my window and I was just sitting there, confused and lost. I thought he looked like Santa Claus. He got into the van and guided me back to the fork of the road."
"That would be Daddy. Always looking out for everyone else."
Rachel hugged Angela and then Eliza. "Oh Gosh, Angela, Eliza. I feel your pain even more." Tears flowed down her face.
Eliza wiped her tears away. "I have never in my life heard of people's lives getting so entwined. It's like that mountain has tentacles that just keep winding in and out and around us."
"Well, at least there's someone else responsible in the Ms. Bence incident."
Eliza's cell phone rang. "Oops, I keep forgetting that I need to turn this phone off in the hospital rooms. I'll be right back." Food trays came in for Rachel and Angela.
Rachel rearranged herself in bed and leaned back. She felt a little weak from all the discussion, but was determined not to let it show.
"Friday's coming up fast." Angela said. "I hope that we can convince your parents to let you stay with us."
The nurse aide pulled Rachel's food tray across for her. "I know. We have one more day to convince them. They'll be leaving in just two weeks for an excursion through Ethiopia. They'll so determined to take me with them."
Two figures appeared in the door. "And yes, you're going with us." Dorothy declared.
Rachel felt a surge of power. "You know something, Mom? The doctor wouldn't be willing to release me for such a long overseas trip and besides my papers aren't in order. I'm

certainly not going to agree to that long series of shots in that short a time. "

The shocked look on Dorothy's face was only topped by the red strained muscle popping in David's neck.

"Young lady, since when do you use that tone with your mother? She's "Mother," not "Mom".

Angela looked puzzled at the two adults and then at Rachel. Rachel took a deep breath. There was something about her ordeal that made her feel stronger.

"Daddy, I love you and I love Mom, but..."

"Rachel, in this last year, you've started calling your mother and me, Daddy and Mom. You know that we don't like those terms. It's disrespectful.

We are Father and Mother."

Details, always details, especially when they don't want to face reality and the real issues.

Rachel became silent, and held her head. The headache had all but gone away. Now it was coming back.

"O.K. Rachel. We're sorry. Why don't you finish your meal and we'll come back." Dorothy stated.

'No, Mother. We might as well..."

Eliza came back in. "Hello, Mr. and Mrs.

Brooks. I met you in the hall the other day.

Remember? I'm Angela's aunt."

The Brooks turned. David ignored the hand held out from the tall, woman with the short, neatly dressed short hair.

"Yes, I understand that Rachel wants to stay with Angela and you. We've already made arrangements and she'll be leaving with us on Friday."

Eliza shot a look at Rachel's shocked face. "Mother, Father, I've never in my whole life known either of you to be rude. What's with you?" Dorothy sat down on the chair across from Rachel. She was crying. "Sweetheart. Don't tear your parent's heart out. You're our daughter, our family. We didn't raise you in order for you to go to strangers. We almost lost you once. We're not bad people or even angry people. We just want to protect you."

Rachel pulled herself back up in the bed and pushed away from the food tray. "Mom..." She shot her mother a warning look. "Mom, you're completely ignoring what you heard me say when you came in here. I'm not going to be strong enough to travel, especially in a plane overseas in two weeks. I'm sure the doctor's not going to approve of me getting all the shots required. And even if they did, I'm not going to have time to get my visa or passport ready by then."
"Sure you can. We'll talk to the doctor."
"You can talk to the doctor all you want, but I'm not going to go with you. That's final." David took a step back and threw his arms up. "Another rebellious child, Dorothy. It must come from your side of the family."
The nurse with the label, 'Dorothy' stepped into the room. "Is there something wrong in here?" She looked pointedly at David whose voice was getting loud enough to hear down the hall.
Dorothy Brooks stood up and looked at the nurse's lapel pin. "Oh, hello, Dorothy. My name is Dorothy, too. I'm sorry, but my husband gets a bit rambunctious ever so often."
The nurse smiled at her. "I understand, Dorothy. I've got one of that kind at home. Your hubby's name wouldn't be Tom, would it?"
"No, it's David."
The nurse turned toward David. "Oh...O.K. David. Just remember that this is a hospital." Rachel had pulled her sheet up over her head. The nurse Dorothy walked over and peeked under it. "Need a headache pill?"
"I need some knock out drops for my parents. Got any?"
"No, sorry. But I can check your chart and find out what to do for you."
As Nurse Dorothy passed by Rachel's parents, she nodded for them to follow her. In the hall, she stopped and turned to them.
"I don't know if you understand about what's going on with your daughter, but our charts show that she needs to be kept

as quiet as possible. Given all the excitement of the past few days, it's a wonder that she hasn't had a relapse. That would be more serious than what she has already been suffered. I'm the head nurse over all shifts and I was just informed that there's going to be a police guard placed at the door to that room. Now if there's any more loud noises or upset, I'll have to ban even her parents from the room."
Dorothy started to cry. "You don't understand. We almost lost her."
Nurse Dorothy put up her hand. "And you still could if we can't keep stress out of the room. I'm sorry if this is hard on the two of you, but she's my patient and I need to follow orders."
David had been listening quietly. "You have to understand that this is totally out of character for us. We're Christians and Missionaries and we never raise our voices. God spoke to us on this and he has shown us that we need to become stronger than our opposition. But we're faced with a difficult child, who refuses to let us protect her."
"How old is Rachel?"
"She'll only be 18 at the end of next month." Dorothy said.
"Do you realize that's six weeks away?" The parents were quiet.
"In six weeks, your daughter will be able to decide more things for herself, legally."
David spoke. "What kind of things? Our insurance is paying her bills in this hospital. We're also executers to her college trust fund. If this hospital wants to get paid, you'll all stay out of family affairs."
Nurse Dorothy shook her head. "Sir, as long as she's here, she's in my care. I know that you have to be caring parents, and in that respect, I'm sure that you want her to get well. The only way that we can insure that is to keep her quiet and safe right now."
David let out his breath as though he had been holding it. "Of course we want our daughter to get well. She wouldn't be in the predicament that she's in if she had listened to us

and had gone to one of the Christian colleges that we approved. But no, she comes here to this hick town and...." He grabbed his forehead and started rubbing it.

Dorothy took his arm and looked at the nurse. "Can we now go back in and say goodbye for the day to our daughter?" David walked forcibly toward the door. "We don't have to ask permission to see our daughter." Rachel looked up as the couple walked in. Angela, Eliza, and Rachel were all able to hear what had been said in the hall.

Rachel stared at the couple and said calmly. "I'm ashamed and shocked at the two of you. I don't even know you anymore. Father, you've always been so calm, the strong, silent one. Mother, you've been just as you are right now... paranoid and weepy. The last few days after I came out of surgery, you seemed so strong. Now you're right back to being the weak and weepy one. You heard what the nurse said and you still just ignored it. You just don't get it. I have a strong faith in God, but let me tell you something. My God is not to be feared. He's a God of Love. I'm not afraid of disappointing the two of you anymore. I respect you as my parents, but I'm going to live my life and take care of myself. If that means losing my college trust and insurance, so be it."

Dorothy and David stood stiff and silent. Eliza started to move for the first time. "Let me take the two of you to lunch." She said and moved them out of the room. She winked at Rachel as they left.

Eliza moved the shocked pair toward the elevator. Dorothy turned to Eliza as they reached the elevator. "I apologize for my daughter. She was never like this before the accident. Injuries to the head can really cause a lot of trauma."

Eliza still said nothing. David was quiet as well. They all stayed silent except to pick up their food from the vendors and Eliza picked up the tab. David said grace and Eliza went along with the ceremony. As they sat eating, the silence continued.

As they were finishing, Yoder walked up to the table with a cup of coffee. "Can I join you?" He asked.
They all nodded their heads yes and he sat down beside Eliza. "Have you gone to the morgue to I.D. your dad yet?
Dorothy and David shot each other a look and then looked at Eliza. David spoke. "We're so sorry,
Eliza. We didn't know that.... What happened?"
"He had a heart attack."
"Oh, dear Lord. We're so sorry."
Eliza smiled at them through teary eyes. "I'll be fine. Daddy had a good life. He was 87 years old."
"Did he know Jesus?"
"He knew more about God and his creation than any man alive, including the top theologian in the world."
"But was he saved?" David asked.
Eliza dug her nails into the underside of the table. She held her silence with difficulty. 'Why's that any of your business?' Her insides screamed.
Yoder put his hand on her shoulder. "Eliza, I wanted to tell you and Rachel's parents that the guard has just been stationed at the door. Her job will be to keep the chaos out of that room."
"Her? The guard is a woman?" David asked.
"Yes. One of the toughest police officers I have on the force."
Yoder shot David a challenging look.
Both he and Dorothy stayed silent, exchanging quiet, but nervous eye contact.
Eliza spoke. "I'm going to have to excuse myself. I need to go take care of my father's affairs." She rose and Yoder pushed both their chairs under the table.
David and Dorothy mumbled, "God bless you," toward the parting couple.
Then they rose from their chairs. Dorothy turned to her husband. "David, I need to go to the chapel to pray."

"I think we'd be more comfortable at the church of our faith. It's only a block from here. Perhaps we can find the minister to guide us."

"Maybe we should consider getting a lawyer as well, David. We've been listening to God's messages about getting stronger. Maybe he's trying to tell us to stand up and fight for our daughter now."

"Let's pray about that and get counsel from the ministry."

There was a drizzle of rain as the couple started out across the parking lot. In their haste, they almost ran in front of a black police car.

"Wasn't that the detective...Yoder?" Dorothy said after they stepped back to the curve.

"Yes, he didn't even see us. Looks like he was focused on Eliza. Must be he's driving her to the morgue."

"Well, it seems to me that even the police in this town aren't safe to be around. He should've been paying attention to where he was going."

"You're so right. We have even more reason for taking Rachel out of here. Their conversation was sure keeping them focused on each other rather than on the road."

The sound of the wolves drew their attention toward Shady Mountain. Dorothy squeezed her husband's arm as she leaned into him. "That's another good reason for getting our baby out of here. This place is evil."

Chapter Sixteen

"I have some news for you about Angela's car, but I didn't want to talk in front of the Brooks. They already have a warped and bad opinion of our town. Rachel doesn't need them to have any more fuel for their argument to take her out of college."
Eliza stared at Yoder. "You know, that car has been the last thing on my mind. What has happened to it that could have an impact on the
Brooks affairs?"
"They found it in a chop shop. Luckily most of it was still intact, which is unusual considering how fast these crooks work."
Eliza's mouth flew open. "So Angela was not just a victim of assault and rape, but of car theft, too?"
"Yes, but after forensic went over the car, they couldn't find any evidence that she was assaulted in the car. All the evidence was found on the mountain in a clearing near your father's place. There was bloody clothing, her shoes and an earring. The tire tracks up there have been lifted and they match up to the tires on Brent Morse's van that was in the college parking lot. So the car theft could be a separate incident from the assault and rape issue."
Eliza felt hot tears well into her eyes. The mention of Angela's bloody clothing made her shiver. "Oh my...well, tell me. Have you arrested?
Brent Morse yet?"
"No, we're looking for him for questioning again. He disappeared without his van. Evidently, he has ties to more people in this community than we thought he did. As it turns out, his uncle is one of the people connected to the Bence hit and run."
Eliza's mouth dropped open. "Not another tentacle..."
Yoder looked at her strangely, as he pulled up to a stop light. "What?"

"Tentacle. We were just talking today about how intertwined all these cases are. I don't know if that's because this is such a small community or what, but it just seems like the mountain has tentacles that connect to other tentacles." She cleared her throat. "I know that you're a good detective. You're definitely problem solving at a fast rate."
"Well, I can't take credit for everything. My team found Angela's car as they were looking for the suspect's vehicle in the Bence case. It turns out that both the cars were in the same shop. On the other hand, I should say, the parts of the car in the Bence case had been stripped and were in the process of being sold. How much evidence from that car will be viable to build the case is questionable."
"Did you find the engine intact with the VIN number?"
"The VIN numbers were probably the first thing they destroyed. I think there's enough of a link that we can solve this puzzle. We have a reputable garage with top notch mechanics helping us put things together."
"So you have the chop shop thieves under arrest."
"Yep, Angela's car helped us to make that case. We've been dogging that bunch before all the college problems. We've had an undercover agent acting as a buyer, who'd been gathering evidence. When Angela's car came in, he helped us nail them before they had a chance to take more than the fenders off."
"You have a great police force here."
Yoder pulled the car into the morgue parking lot. "Top notch. So what're you planning to do when Angela's released from the hospital?"
"Angela and I are going up to the cabin for a while to recuperate and regroup. I have her signed up for online classes and I'll tutor her as well.
"What about your practice back in Chicago?"
"I resigned. I'm opening up a practice here in Echo Valley. I plan on buying a house down here, so Angela never has to worry about going back to the campus."

Yoder parked the car with a smile. "Welcome back to Echo Valley." He said.

Eliza giggled. "Thank you." She felt nervous about entering the morgue. Maybe if I laugh about this situation, I'll be able to hold up.

Yoder sat and looked at her for a minute, then said, "Eliza, you don't have to physically identify if you don't want to. You can just sign the papers as to what funeral home you want him moved to."

"I'll look at him. I found his will in a lock box at the bank. He wants to be cremated and scattered on the mountain as Mama was. Angela and I'll have a private ceremony for Carrie and Daddy at the same time."

"Let me go in with you, then."

"I'd appreciate it." How can I do this with someone who goes by his last name?

"By the way, what's your first name?"

"Greg."

"Thanks, Greg."

The mortician met them at the door. Eliza looked into the clear blue eyes. 'He's not as stern and cold as what I imagined he'd be…maybe 40's…my age.' Then she found her mind distracted and drawn to the sharp lines of the face. "Ah, yes…an old school mate, right?" Sheldon Grimes greeted her. "Hello, Eliza.

Sorry to see you again in such a sad circumstance."

He was warmer than she first thought from his looks. He led them to a drawer in the back room. The room was white and cold. Their footsteps echoed in the high ceilinged room. Eliza

"Are you ready?" Sheldon said in a quiet voice. Eliza spoke calmly. "Yes." She looked up at Yoder until the drawer stopped moving. His eyes were so kind. She could see the compassion. Maybe she saw that love in his face.

She looked down at the body still draped over with a sheet. Sheldon pulled the sheet down from over his face.

Yoder pulled her close to him with his arm around her shoulder. Eliza let out a soft sigh.
"He looks so peaceful, almost smiling."
Sheldon spoke softly, "So you're identifying this body as that of your father, Joseph Hardigan?"
"Yes, this is my father's body. His soul's in heaven now." She bent and kissed the cold forehead. Then she looked toward the ceiling.
Turning toward Yoder, she looked deeply into his eyes. "Let's go, Greg."
Sheldon said. "I'll need you to make arrangements in the office."
Later back in the car, Eliza held the folder with all the paperwork needed for the cremation of her father's body. Memories of Mama and the memorial service held on the mountain flooded back to her. Tears flowed for the first time after arriving at the morgue.
Yoder started the car and backed out. "Eliza, what can I do to help you?"
"I don't know. I feel like I want to go back up on the mountain for the night. But I don't want to go without Angela."
"Do you have any relatives to notify?"
"I don't know who'd care. Daddy was born in the Blue Ridge in Virginia. He moved to Arlington and didn't stay in contact with relatives. We never knew our grandparents on that side of the family. I think they died young. Most of the ancestors had died of Black Lung disease from working in the coal mines. Other relatives scattered down through to the Smoky Mountains and beyond. I probably have relatives all over the United States."
"How about on your mother's side?"
"They disowned my mother when she married my dad. They felt that she married beneath her. I saw my grandparents once when I was very young. Mother took Carrie and me to a big mansion in
Raleigh, North Carolina. Grandmother Victoria

Henry Jaynes claimed to be a descendant of Patrick Henry. I always doubted that. She was the most pompous creature that I ever met. Grandmother thought it terrible that mother hadn't taught us all the etiquette and skills that she'd taught her only child. She marched us through rows of quilts and needlework that she had done. Meal time was extremely uncomfortable. She was belly aching the whole time we ate about our terrible table manners."

"What about your grandfather Jaynes?"

"He was ill at the time and Grandmother had nurses taking care of him. I remember that he was confused as to who my mother was. He certainly didn't know who we were. He died two weeks after we left, but we didn't go back for the funeral. Grandmother said there was no need, because there was nothing in the will for any of us."

"That's terrible. So I take it, your grandmother didn't see the need to come for your mother's funeral."

"She died a week before Mother found out she had cancer. You see, since Mother was an only child, there were no siblings to notify. Grandmother's estate was in trust to all kinds of charities. I imagine the lawyers got a good chunk of that."

Yoder pulled into the parking lot next to Eliza's car.

"So it's just you and Angela for the ceremony?" "Yes, it always has been just us for everything. We thought we had Daddy, but.... Anyway, I'd like to add Rachel to our family if her parents will just let go of her."

"How about me?" Yoder asked.

Eliza was taken back. She found her voice. "You're certainly welcome to the funeral as our friend. We would love to have you. Come to think of it, I'm sure Daddy would want his friend Zeb there, as well. Perhaps there'll be other friends that I don't know about. I guess he really wasn't as much a hermit as people thought he was." The radio beeped and a call came on.

"Lieutenant Yoder, we have Brent Morse."

"What's the story?" Never mind…I'm on my way."

Eliza grabbed the door handle. "I'll be on hospital grounds if you need me." She said as she got out of the car. "Thanks for the support today."
"Anytime Eliza." He said. "You can count on me."
Eliza felt warm and safe inside for the first time in her life. She watched the car leave the parking lot until it was out of sight around the corner. She smiled. In all of the tragedy, there's hope for a better future. Greg Yoder. That's a nice name.
Yoder thought about the young man that he was going to interrogate for the second time. In all the three preceding school years, Brent Morse had been a puzzle to him. He had never seen any of his relatives at the football games, even though he had been one of the star players. Now, he found out that Brent not only had relatives in town, but those relatives were now being investigated for all kinds of crimes. They are the same people that have repeatedly been in trouble with the law.
It looked as though Brent had every reason to keep his identity secret. 'I just hope for his sake that he's got a good explanation in Angela's case.'
Yoder took the file from the clerk and glanced over it. He was shaking his head as he walked into the interrogation room. Brent looked up at the detective. Yoder was shocked. The young man was black and blue with a gash over his eye.

Chapter Seventeen

"Who did this to you?"
Brent stared at Yoder with a puppy whipped look on his face.
"Hold on just a minute. I'll be right back."
Yoder stepped out and confronted the arresting officer, Doug Wentfield. "Who's responsible for the whipping that boy took?"
"He is."
"Is this all in the report I have here?" Yoder held up the folder.
"Sure is. He tried to run from us. We had a car chase through the east end of the city. He turned a stolen car over into the ditch headed up the exit ramp to the freeway. Didn't you hear it on your radio?"
"No, I turned my clip-on off at the morgue." He waved his hand at the officer who stood with his mouth open. "I know, I know. I'd be reaming any one of you for doing that." He cleared his throat.
"Has the suspect been seen by a doctor?"
"He refused medical treatment."
Yoder turned to go back into the interrogation room. "Does Morse have a lawyer?"
"No. He refused a court appointed."
Yoder entered the room. "Brent, I hear that you refused a court appointed lawyer."
"Yeah. I don't need one. I know the law."
"I still think you should have one. Two heads are better than one, you know."
"Yeah. Well, I need to make a phone call."
"Do you want to do that before we talk?"
"Yeah."
"There's the phone on the table by you. Just dial nine and the number. I'll wait outside."
"Is this phone bugged?"
"What?"

"Will anyone be able to hear what I have to say?"
"I'm sorry, but yes, I'm afraid that all our phone calls are recorded here. Even I don't have privacy in this building."
"I'd protest if I were you."
"So do you still want to make a call? I'll leave the room."
"Yeah." Brent reached for the phone and Yoder stepped outside closing the door.

Yoder sat on a stool in front of the glass window and listened as he flipped through Brent's folder and read the report. Morse still didn't have that much privacy, but then maybe he didn't deserve any. From the report, Yoder started to lose any empathy for the kid. It was sad that he had to have such a rotten family, but he certainly made a lot of bad choices on his own.

He listened to the one-way conversation on the speaker.
"Hey, it's Brent. I'm in jail. Can't say much. The phone's bugged." " No." "Yeah. I know you know." "You said you'd help if I needed it. Should I get a court appointed lawyer?" "Well, Grand maw has money." " O.K." " O.K."

Brent sat the phone down and Yoder returned to the room.
"Do you want a lawyer present?"
"Yeah. My family's getting a lawyer. I'm not answering any questions until he gets here."
"That's fine. But I'd like to go over some preliminaries with you." Yoder shifted in his seat and opened the folder. You are going to be 21 tomorrow. Is that correct?"
"Yeah, not a way to spend my birthday."
"Sure isn't. You're refusing medical treatment?"
"Yeah."
"Why's that?"
"I wanted my mug shot to show my injuries. I might need that in court."
"Why's that?"
"You'll hear all that when my lawyer shows up."
"I thought you and I trusted each other, Brent. I'm not going to ask you any questions that will hurt you in court. I don't

understand why you can't talk with me. You know that I've been fair with you."
"Yeah, well maybe. However, you are on the law's side. I have to be careful what I say to keep from making me look guilty."
"Guilty of what, Brent? Why do you think you're here?"
"I borrowed a car from my cousin and suddenly I'm being arrested for car theft."
"Why weren't you driving your van, Brent?"
"It had a funny noise in the engine, so I walked to my cousin's house and borrowed his car."
"Who's your cousin?"
"I'll tell you when my lawyer gets here, if he says it's o.k."
"O.K. Brent. The officer will escort you to the holding cell until your lawyer gets here."
"How long will that be?"
"I don't know. How long did they say it would be?"
"Who?"
"Whoever you called?"
"Listen to the tapes. You said I was being recorded."
"Yes. Everything's recorded in this building. I'm in the same boat, Brent. Therefore, nothing's sacred here and nobody's exempt. But I can't listen to the tapes without a court order."
"So get a court order. I'm feeling dizzy. I need to lay down."
"Let me get a doctor in here to look at you."
"No."
"Then you need to let us take you to the hospital for a checkup."
"Thought I couldn't go near the hospital."
"You're just banned from going near Rachel Brooks or Angela Pike and you'd be going with shackles on."
"You said you were fair. That's not fair. I haven't been charged yet. I'm not a flight risk."
"You haven't proven that to me yet. If you're not a flight risk, why were you running from the officers?"

Brent put up his hand. "After my lawyer gets here. Right now I wanna go lay down."

Yoder turned and opened the door. "Officer Gray. Take this suspect to the holding cell."

The last person Yoder wanted to see coming through that door was Herbert Snow. That country lawyer family had advocated for the bootleggers, moon shiners, child and wife abusers, thieves and other ne'er do wells since the beginning of time here in the mountains. Herbert Snow was the daddy to three other practicing lawyers in the county. Henry Snow and Robert "Bobby" Snow were equally crooked in finding loopholes for the rats that the county, township, and city police tried to bring to justice. Leo Snow practiced mostly as a chauvinistic men's divorce lawyer and defended crooks in other civil cases.

"Howdy doo to you, Yoder. What noble citizen are you trying to harass now?"

Yoder stayed at his desk and looked up at him as though he hadn't seen him coming through the large swinging doors in view of his glass office window. "Hello Herbert. Who is it that you're keeping out of reach of the criminal justice system this week?"

"How about a young man who hasn't even had a chance to graduate college yet? An innocent young man who has served this hick town well with his excellent skills on the football field."

"Oh, I've never seen you at any of the games, Herbert."

"Too busy trying to provide the hard working people of this county piece of mind from the tyrannical injustice of the overseeing Lords that rain terror down on them and their innocent families. But I read about the college and the glory that boy in there has bestowed on undeserving citizens such as yourself."

"Why Herbert. I didn't know that you set such store by reading."

"Law books, mostly, but yes, I do read newspapers to keep up on current events. I especially watch out for lies and in discrepancies. Every so often, I have to defend a citizen from slander. That's what I may have to do in this case. Now if you'll bring Brent Morse into the interrogation room, I need to confer with my client...and turn off the damn surveillance in that room."

Yoder pushed the intercom button. "Stella, have Officer Gray bring Brent Morse into the interrogation room for Attorney Snow, please."

He looked up at Herbert's glare. "And turn off surveillance for that room."

Without another word, Herbert turned to the door. Yoder watched his broad backside leave with disgust. Oh well, as soon as he could make his case with interrogation, investigation and reports, Herbert Snow and his client, Brent Morse would be in the hands of Prosecuting Attorney, April Donovan. That was one appointment that Herbert Snow and those like him tried to block. Why, the thought of a woman in any kind of office was unheard of. How April pulled it off was a mystery. There was nothing that April liked better than to tangle with that crooked lawyer bunch. Then she was young and naive. She had only been with the county for two years. So far, she hadn't managed to reign in the Snow Dynasty.

He thought of Eliza. D.A. April Donovan would love to have her working for the county. He thought there was an opening there. Wouldn't Herbert be seething if Eliza started working in the D. A.'s Office? Another woman with some kind of power. There had never even been a woman preacher in this town. Things were changing and the new generation was ousting the old power out bit by bit...not soon enough for him. Herbert stuck his head back in the door. "My God man. Why is my client not at the hospital? He looks like he's been run over by a truck."

"He refused the medics, Herbert. I had to encourage him to get a lawyer. He refused council at first, as well. Maybe you can convince him to accept medical attention."
"Which officers beat the shit out of him?"
"Herbert, did you read the charges?"
"I don't believe that crap. Your officers had no business running my client to the ground like that.
He's not a hardened criminal."
"You're welcome to convince him to get medical attention, Herbert, but I'm not going to waste time arguing about what did or did not happen out there on that road. We have the cruiser videos, the police call recordings and the speed tapes to back us up. Did you also note that the car he was driving was stolen?"
"Allegedly. Everything's alleged until he goes to court and is proven innocent." Herbert slammed back out of the room.
"Or guilty." Yoder said.
After an hour, Herbert poked his head in the door. "My client's ready to face up to you. But I have to use the toilet first."
Yoder dreaded the questioning as he did every time he had to deal with Herbert Snow, but this was going to be especially hard. He wanted Brent Morse to be innocent. This was the first time ever that a college student had been in this much trouble. College students were usually tagged as 'do-gooders' or 'nerds' by the troublemaking bunch his age. However, as a football star, they considered Brent a jock. To be a jock was honorable. "I'll be right there."
"Now don't you start without me."
"Wouldn't think of it, Herbert."
Stella looked up at him and shook her head as he passed her. Yes, everybody knew the Snow tribe and everyone on the right side of the law hated them.
Yoder waited until Herbert joined him and walked into the small room behind him.

Herbert sat down across from his client and Yoder sat down at the end of the table facing both of them. "Well, let's get started."

Yoder started. "For the sake of the record, everything that's said in this room's being recorded for the benefit of all parties. Is this agreeable?"

"My client understands. Get on with it."

"Also for the record, Brent, would you like to go to the hospital for medical attention before you're questioned?"

"No."

"Would you like to have a doctor come here to check on you before we question you?"

Herbert let air, and then coughed. "You heard my client. Get on with it."

"O.K. Brent Morse. Do you understand why you're being detained and questioned?"

The gas emitted from Herbert was beginning to choke Yoder. He cleared his throat, then said, (trying not to breathe in too much air), "Why don't you tell me. You ran from the police when they tried to stop you. It's all on tape and documented, Brent. Do you know why the officers were trying to stop you...chasing you?"

"No, I was just driving along, minding my own business. I wasn't speeding or anything."

"Who owns the car that you were driving?"

"I borrowed the car from my cousin. My van was making funny noises and I walked to his garage and he lent me that car."

"Are you aware that the car is a stolen vehicle?"

"Not until you told me."

"Who's your cousin, Brent?"

Brent looked at Snow. Snow shook his head,
'No.'

There was a chill of silence. Yoder said, "Excuse me a moment." Then he got up and opened the door with the pretense of speaking to an officer outside. A little fresh air to clear Herbert's cloud would make it easier to talk.

Yoder closed the door and sat back down. He rubbed his forehead. "So, you're refusing to answer that question?"
"What question?"
"Who's your cousin?"
"Which cousin?"
Yoder gave Brent a harsh look. "Brent you're a college student with passing grades. Don't try to 'snow' me."
Brent giggled and looked at Herbert. Herbert grimaced at him then said, "That pun was not necessary, Yoder. Just explain the question to my client and get on with it."
"You said that you borrowed a car from your cousin. Who's that cousin?"
"Yes...Well I meant I'm not answering the question."
"That's o.k. and easy enough to find out. Do you know whose name's on the title to that car, Brent?"
"My cousin's name, of course."
"And what name would be on that title?"
Brent looked at Herbert again. Herbert again shook his head, 'No.'
Brent said, "I'm not answering that question."
Yoder cleared his throat. "Did you see a title to that car, Brent?"
"No. I did not need to see a title. If my cousin says the car belongs to him, then it belongs to him."
"I see. Didn't you check for the registration in case you needed it?"
"No. I didn't have any reason to check for a registration."
"Well, for future reference, Brent, the next time you borrow a car, you need to know where that registration is to present to officers."
Brent hunched his shoulders in an 'oh, well, whatever' gesture.
"You need to cooperate with us, Brent. The facts are that you were resisting arrest when the officers asked you to pull over, and you took off in an attempt to outrun them. Add to that charges that you were driving a stolen vehicle. We have

two charges right there. That is enough to hold you in jail for a hearing in the morning. If you don't cooperate with the judge, you'll be held in contempt of court. So I think you need to advise your lawyer to find a way for you to be able to answer questions."

Herbert slapped his hand on the table. "Just so you know, I didn't go to the toilet in there a while ago. I was on the phone to the judge. I've got an immediate hearing tonight. Judge Harder Snow will most likely set bail. My client will be out on bail tonight."

Oh crap.' Harder Snow, a relative to Herbert and his sons was another thorn in Yoder's side. Nevertheless, he had been out of town for two months deferring his cases to a more balanced Judge Moffett. So that S.O.B. Harder Snow is back to rattle my cage. Rats. Well, I'll just have to work overtime and then some to make this case for the prosecutor. He wondered if April was aware that her 'favorite' judge would be sitting on the bench for this case.

Yoder got up from the table. "Do what you have to do, Herbert." He went to the door and motioned the guard, who stepped into the room. "Take Brent Morse back to his cell." Then Yoder left without speaking to Snow or Brent.

Stella watched as Yoder stepped back into his office. She knew her boss and she knew when he was about to explode. Herbert stepped out of the interrogation room behind his client who was being escorted in handcuffs down the hall. Yoder watched Herbert pass through the office and out the door through his office window. Herbert had his cell phone to his ear. He reached over and punched the intercom. "Stella, get April Donovan on the line for me."

Yoder shook his head. God, what an ass that man is.

Chapter Eighteen

Eliza walked through the waiting room door that read 'Prosecuting Attorney April Donovan.' At Greg Yoder's advice, she had spruced up her resume and called for an interview. He seemed really sure when he called last night that she had a chance of getting this job, even though she preferred to take a rest after taking Angela up to the mountain. The P.A. must really be in a hurry to get that appointment filled, because the office wasted no time in setting up the 1:00 p.m. interview for me.

Soon she found herself sitting across the big desk from none other than Prosecuting Attorney April Donovan. She looked at the tiny woman sitting in the big chair. It almost swallowed her. What a spitfire she must be to take on the likes of the Snow lawyers. Yoder had described them as hell's nightmare in the court room.

Their conversation was free flowing. It was as though Eliza had known this younger woman all her life. The more they talked, the more she knew that April was a good match for any tough lawyer. In addition, April was more than impressed at the experience, ethics, and straightforward attitude of Eliza Hardigan.

"Well, Eliza. What do you say? This county cannot boast of the many tough criminal cases that you've faced in Chicago, but we're starting to get our share. We truly need your help. Would you like to give us a try?"

"I would, but I'll need a few weeks to get my affairs settled."

"No problem. Welcome aboard." April stood up and Eliza had to keep from looking surprised at the small stature of the county's prosecuting attorney. She could not have been over five foot tall with wispy blonde hair tied back in a bun, big brown eyes, and freckles. Eliza had to reach down to shake hands with her.

Back on the street, Eliza was still in wonderment of the fast changes in her life. Her to do list was growing. Right now,

she had to call Angela. She'd be chomping at the bit to get out of that hospital room. She sat down in her car and dialed Angela's cell number. It took several tries to get a signal from the community's one cell tower. "Hey. Are you ready to check out of there?"
Angela lowered her voice, almost to a whisper and stepped out into the hall. "Yes, Aunt Eliza, I sure am. But Rachel has one more day to work on her parents."
"Let me talk to her."
There was silence and then Rachel was on the line.
"Hello Eliza."
"I checked the law books at the courthouse library for any legal steps that you can take or options that you have to get your parents to turn over the trust fund to the courts so that you can stay in the college of your choice."
"O.K." Rachel voice was a bit tense.
Eliza recognized the voices in the background.
"Are your parents in the room?"
"Yes."
"I'll talk to you later then. Sorry to put you on the spot."
"It's o.k."
Angela came back on the line. "Are you coming right away?"
"As soon as I can get there."
"Then I'll let the nurses know. Talk with you then."
Eliza made another call. "Hello Greg. I got the PA Assistant job!"
"Hey, that's great. What's your schedule right now?"
"The doctor said that Angela's ready to check out of the hospital. I'm on my way to pick her up. We'll be staying in the motel tonight and then we'll do some house hunting tomorrow. It's a long haul to the cabin and we need to be close to medical care, at least for a while."
"When are you going to go up to the mountain to do the ceremony?"

"Oh, the cremation process will take a couple of weeks. I'll contact everyone who wants to be there and we'll all gather for a service for both Carrie and Dad at the same time."
"What's happened to Joe's dog?"
"His friend Zeb has him in the cabin. I think we'll just let Zeb stay in the cabin for right now, at least until after the ceremony. If he takes Dog with him to his hut, the poor grieving mutt will just run away and go back to the cabin. Angela and I might as well wait until then to go up there. I guess we'll take things day by day."
"Oh, I just remembered that there's an old farmhouse for sale in my neighborhood out by the college. Do you and Angela want to have breakfast with me in the morning and go look at it?"
"Sounds great. Who's the realtor?"
"My mother."
"Your Mom?"
"Actually, it's a For Sale by Owner and Mom's the owner."
Eliza grinned. "So you're introducing me to the family and we haven't even had a date yet." She kidded.
"Well, just Mom. Dad's gone."
"Oh, I'm sorry."
"No problem. Mom's been a widow for ten years now."
"Where's your Mom going to live?"
"Well, she's moving in with me...sort of. I own a duplex and she'll live in the other apartment. There is a divider alcove, which makes it easy for me to keep an eye on her, and she can still have her privacy. I've also got a house on the lake. I've got plenty of room for mom to share."
What a guy. Thinking of his mother.
Eliza felt a warm feeling inside for this man with the deep, kind voice and the love for his mother.
If he treats his mother with this kind of respect, he's got to be the best catch in the world.
Eliza looked at her watch and spoke into her phone. "What a wonderful idea. But I've got to go pick Angela up now."
"Let me take you two out to dinner tonight."

"Thanks for the invitation, but I'm going to try to convince the Brooks to have a nice sit down meal at the Birches. That is, if I can get late reservations. With any kind of luck, I'll be able to persuade them to let Rachel stay with Angela and me without going through a legal process."
"That would be the best solution for that young woman, but it sounds like you have a lot of convincing to do."
"Hey, I'm a lawyer. I will find a way. And I don't give up easily."
"Neither do I."
"What?"
"If the Brooks don't take you up on that invitation, the offer is still open."
"Thanks."
Eliza pondered over every line of that conversation as she headed to the hospital, but forgot it as she turned into the parking lot. Her thoughts turned to Rachel's dilemma with her parents.
The girl has a lot of legal options, but I'm not sure that she's emotionally able to take a stand against her parents. I have to step lightly with the Brooks.
The guard was missing at the girl's room and then Eliza remembered that Brent Morse was in jail, so the threat from him was no longer valid. Even so, as she neared the door, she heard voices.
Dorothy and David Brooks were sitting in the chairs by the door and the doctor and two other people were standing at the end of Rachel's bed. Everyone stopped talking as Eliza entered the room.
Eliza stepped through. "Excuse me. I don't want to interrupt." She turned to the doctor. "I've come to pick Angela up. Is everything o.k. with her?"
"Oh yes, she's ready to go. I've given her a prescription and she has an appointment to see me next week. She said you'd still be around town."
Angela stood up from her chair. Her bags were packed on the bed. "All set, Aunt Eliza."

Eliza stepped toward Angela while still looking at the doctor. "Yes, we will stay at the hotel tonight. But I expect that we'll be living in a nice large home near the campus very soon."
"Really? " Angela clapped her hands.
"Yes, and I got the Assistant Attorney's job."
"That's fantastic."
Rachel put both thumbs up from her bed.
"Congratulations, Eliza."
The doctor held up his clipboard. "Yes. Well, I've got to move along. Rachel, the nurses will come and get you for those lab tests before dinner. I'll see you next week, Angela." He turned to the
Brooks. "I'll be talking with you soon."
To the other two people he said, "It's good to see you again." Then he was gone.
Dorothy and David had been sitting in grim silence. Neither of them smiled or greeted Eliza in any way. However, the two other younger people looked pleased.
Rachel said. "Oh, I'm sorry, Eliza. I forgot that you haven't met my brother, Stephan and my sister,
Dianna."
Stephan and Dianna stepped forward and shook their hands.
Dianna spoke first. "We've heard so many wonderful things about you, Eliza.
Congratulations on your new position. I know that Angela's proud of you."
Eliza put her arm around Angela. "Thank you.
I'm very proud of her, too. She's been through a lot. But hopefully, everything will be settled down soon."
Dianna said. "So you might live near campus?"
"It's possible. We'll go and look at the house tomorrow."
David spoke up. "Aren't you afraid to be near the campus with that boy there?"
Eliza squeezed Angela tighter. "Brent Morse has been arrested for driving a stolen car and running from the police.

He's been suspended from campus permanently and may be finishing his classes online from jail."

Angela turned a bit pale, but stood strong.

"They found your car, Angela. In the same chop shop that they found the car that was used to hit Ms. Bence."

Everyone in the room was making short comments. Rachel let out a sigh of relief. "That's great. The police in this town really have it going on."

"Yes, they're really solving the cases quickly. I'm very impressed with this little town. They only had one policeman when I went to college here."

Dorothy got up. "Well, we aren't impressed at all. David and I are taking Rachel out of here as soon as the doctor will let her go."

Rachel started to shake. She raised up in her bed and put her legs over the side. Sitting straight up, she glared at her parents. Dianna moved to her side and sat down on her bed. David stood up by his wife and Stephan moved closer to them. "As I was saying when we were so rudely interrupted earlier, this town is too stressful for Rachel. Look at her now. As I told the doctor, she needs to be in Ethiopia with all the cheerful people there."

Stephan cleared his throat. "Dad, Mom. We'll discuss this more tomorrow. I think we need to let Rachel rest now."

"I agree. However, you and Dianna need to come with us. Why you came here in the first place I don't know. You didn't need to leave your jobs to come all the way back here when there's nothing you can do."

Dianna hugged Rachel. "This girl needs our moral support and she's going to get it."

Rachel spoke. "Father, Mother. Dad, Mom...whatever the blazes you want me to call you. I called Stephan and Dianna to come help me with all this. Like I told you the other day, if you want to try to cut me out of my inheritance, go ahead and go for it. However, you'll have to spend the money to fight me in court. Because when I get out of here, I'm staying where I choose to stay. I'll finish college whether it's online or on campus. But that'll be my decision."

Dorothy moved toward the bed, but David put his hand on her arm and drew her back.

He spoke to his children. "She doesn't need you to coddle her, Dianna. You and Stephan made your choices to follow the world. You need to let God have at least one of our children and save her from the evils and unhappiness that worldliness brings."

Stephan threw up his hands. "Dad...Father, if you love peace so much, you and mother had better leave the room before I say what I've been wanting to say since I got here. Now, let's just discuss this tomorrow."

David drew his sobbing wife closer to the door. "Very well. Tomorrow. But I warn you Stephan and Dianna. Don't you two be filling up Rachel's head with any more destructive ideas. I'm still your father and it's still a sin to disobey me. You don't need to keep adding to the sins you need to confess to stay out of eternal damnation."

David turned to glare at Eliza. "We've hired a lawyer. The best there is around here. Even you, with your big city experience will not be able to beat him." With that, he left, pulling his wife down the hall with him.

Two nurse aids came into the room. "What was that all about?"

Stephan spoke. "Just a family thing. Everything's fine now."

"Well, we've got orders to keep Rachel calm and protected. Rachel, how're you doing?"

Rachel waved the nurse away. "I'd be doing just fine, if my father and mother would just stay out of this room." She looked up at her sister. "In one way it hurts to see them in so much pain, but on the other hand, I feel pretty proud of myself. Do you think I'll be going to hell for what I said?"

The siblings laughed. "No, don't feel bad, Rachel. Stephan and I've been going through this since we were born and we still can't keep from losing it."

"Now that's the truth." Stephan said.

"Well, I just wish I could stop feeling so bad about it..."

"That's just a part of life."

Then Stephan turned to Eliza and Angela. "I'm so sorry that you've seen our dirty family laundry, and I profusely apologize for my father's threat." Eliza spread out her hands and waved it off. "That's fine. Believe me, every family has dirty laundry, however, I've been threatened by adversaries that are more formidable. Angela and I are going to get out of here. I'd hoped to be able to invite your parents out to a fancy dinner and win them over. I guess that's out of the question." Dianna handed Stephan her business card. "Call me and let me know how I can help. If Rachel needs someplace to stay, we'd love to have her. And if you need legal advice, it's on the house."

Rachel got up from the bed and came toward Angela. The two girls hugged. "Angela, thanks so much."

"Thank you, Sister. Yep, you're my long lost sister. You've got my cell number, so you've got to call me."

"Don't worry about that. We're joined at the hip."

Eliza hugged them both. "Maybe the two of you will be living in the same house."

"That'd be great."

Eliza turned to Stephan and Dianna. "So what's going to happen if your Mom and Dad come back in here tomorrow to take Rachel with them."

"That's not a problem. We talked to the doctor before they got here. He's not releasing her to them to haul across the world. He's writing up orders that she's not to be in a car, train or plane for a long distance. And she needs to stay close to the hospital for at least a year."

Dianna said, "I've got counselors set up to meet with the whole family in the hospitality room when our parents show up tomorrow. We've included ministers from their faith and from ours. I hope that we can come to a non-legal compromise. But if we can't, then we'll be calling you."

"O.K. Well, we're out of here for now. We may be meeting again with this Brent Morse situation. I guess we have to take life day to day."

Rachel sat back on the bed and leaned her head against the pillow as her friend waved and followed her aunt out the door. The headache was back.

Dianna stepped over and wiped a wisp of hair off Rachel's forehead. "Too much excitement for one day, Rachel?"

"Yeah. Would the two of you mind if I took a nap?"

"Of course not. We'll go get some things taken care of and we'll be back."

The siblings hugged and Stephan and Dianna left the room. Rachel grabbed the remote. It was almost time for the news, and for her dinner, she thought as she rubbed her rumbling stomach and clicked the TV remote.

The dinner cart came almost on cue and Rachel was soon dining on the hospital's best meatloaf and mashed potatoes. Oh well. When you're starved...'

She almost choked when she saw Brent's mug shot on the screen. Then they shot to a courtroom scene of Brent standing next to a pompous looking man with jowls like an owl. "Brent Morse, a senior at Echo Valley College and an accomplished football player was arraigned tonight on charges of car theft and evading police. The car was two blocks away from this building..."

A picture came on of a garage with a big sign over the door, 'Taylor Auto Body Shop'.

"...that housed a chop shop for car thieves in the area. Another car, which police reports identified as belonging to the suspect, involved in the hit and run of Echo Valley, English professor, Ila Bence, was also found in the garage. In addition, a car that was stolen from a victim of an unrelated assault case was found intact in the building. According to police, neighbors near the suspect's garage complained of loud arguing and domestic violence. When police investigated, they found Delilah Wray, the suspect in the Bence case hiding in a basement of a house next door to the garage. When the police broke in, they also found her boyfriend, Samuel Ray Taylor. Wray is being held for a hearing tomorrow morning on alleged charges of hit and run, resulting in death. Taylor is being held on car theft charges and running an illegal business involving the trafficking of stolen vehicles."

'Poor Angela! I hope she's not seeing this. It's a lot more graphic on TV and seeing Brent like that...Wow.'

Chapter Nineteen

Jerrod walked in and stood looking up at the TV screen. Rachel looked up at his face and smiled. He didn't break his concentration on the news report.

"You look like a Cheshire Cat after eating a mouse." She said.

He didn't blink and kept his attention on the news. Rachel looked back at the screen. "If convicted, Morse could serve a maximum of ten years or a minimum of five years. He is also a suspect in a rape and assault case that is still under investigation."

Rachel looked back at Jerrod. "Hello Stranger. Where have you been for the last two days?"

Jerrod sat down on a chair and leaned back flexing against the wall. "Oh, just wrapping things up."

"Oh, you mean the midterms?"

"Yep. Among other things."

"I'll bet the campus is buzzing with all the news reports."

"Sure is."

"Have you run into my parents lately?"

"Nope."

Rachel made a face at him. "I'm sure they have missed you."

"Now what does that mean?"

"They think you're perfect. They'd be so happy if they had you as their offspring."

"Why's that?"

"Well, you fit into their idea of a perfect son."

"Well, the last time I talked to them, they were sizing me up as a son-in-law. I liked that idea."

Rachel blushed. "Oh, you did, eh? What changed your mind?"

"Who says I changed my mind?"

"Uh-hun. You're just foolin' with my head."

"Why? Do you like that idea, too?"

"I tell you what I'd like you to do. I'd like you to persuade them to fire that lawyer of theirs and not take me to court."

"What's that?" Jerrod shook his head in disbelief.
"Oh yeah. They're trying to force me to drop out of college and travel to Ethiopia with them."
"You're kidding. And here I thought you to stay here and hook-up with me."
"Not at all. They're willing to suspend my college inheritance fund and cancel my health insurance."
"I'll talk to them." Jerrod jumped up and started to leave.
"How do you know how to find them?"
"I'll find them."
Rachel kept staring at the door as Jerrod disappeared.
Stephan and Dianna stepped in.
Stephan spoke. "Jerrod just stopped us and asked where he could find Mom and Dad. What's he up to?"
"Oh, he thinks he can get through to them. I guess it's worth a try."
Dianna stepped up to the side of the bed. "I see you've eaten quite a bit for dinner. You must have been hungry."
"Yes, but I can't wait to get out of here and have a nice big shrimp salad."
"It won't be long, dear. But you can't have slept very long."
"No. Dinner came and then Jerrod walked in just as the news was announcing that Brent Morse was being indicted."
"Yes, we saw that downstairs."
"I feel so badly for Angela. She wants so much to believe that Brent is an innocent, misunderstood guy. She's convinced that he had nothing to do with her rape and assault. But I believe that he's as guilty as sin."
"We'll have to wait and see on that one. Lieutenant Yoder is one smart detective and they have a great investigative team here. It's been...what...not even four days yet and they've got all but Angela's case resolved. Considering everything that's been going on, I'd say that the big city cops should be calling them in to solve all their cases."
"That's for sure."
Their attention was suddenly drawn back to the newscast.
"Breaking news. Channel 6 has just confirmed a report that

Samuel Ray Taylor has been added to the suspect list in the assault and rape of an Echo Valley college student. Taylor's girlfriend, Delilah Wray, who was being questioned in the Bence hit and run, also confessed to helping Taylor in his words, "gas the girl and take her car keys." Then Taylor instructed her to drive the girl's car to Taylor's alleged chop shop. Taylor then threw the girl into a van that she borrowed from her cousin, Brent Morse and drove the girl to the mountains where he assaulted and raped her."

Everyone was stunned. Rachel pushed her tray away from the bed and sat up on the side of it. "Oh, my gosh. Oh, wow. I wonder if Angela is watching this report."

"My guess is that Lieutenant Yoder has called her and her sister Eliza by now." said Stephan.

"I wish I could talk to her. You know, she kept insisting that Brent was not the one who assaulted and raped her. He's guilty of a lot of things, but evidently, not rape." Rachel absentmindedly pushed the tray toward the nurse aide as she walked in.

The nurse aide, Violet, looked up at the screen. "You know, Rachel, that woman, Delilah Wray, was the one who was in the room next door to you. She's the one you heard talking about that Bence case with her boyfriend, Samuel Ray Taylor."

Rachel pointed her finger at Violet. "That's right. I think you thought I was crazy when I told you that I wanted to speak to the detect...."

Violet shook her head 'yes' and the two of them giggled. "They were sure noisy over there, but I couldn't figure out why you were in such a hurry to talk to the detective. I thought you were hallucinating because of your head injury."

Dianna and Stephan had been looking from one girl to the other. Then Stephan said, "Do you mean, Rachel, that you provided the information that got Lieutenant Yoder on track to finding the hit and run driver?"

Rachel nodded her head.

Violet spoke. "Yes. I helped Rachel back from the bathroom one day. She wanted to talk to the detective. I didn't hear anything and I had not seen Ray sneak in there, so I thought Delilah was alone until I heard all the noise. I never saw Ray come out either. I know who both of those people are, and I never knew either of them to do anything all that bad, so naturally, I thought Rachel was just being paranoid."

Violet threw up her hands. "Well, I apologize, Rachel, and I promise that I'll never disbelieve again. Anyway, Delilah disappeared that same day, not long after that happened. I went in to take her vitals and she was gone. Security looked everywhere for her. Then that detective came back and asked for her. He was disappointed to find she was gone. He got her description from all of us and started talking into his voice thing on his shoulder and I overheard him put out an APB on her. Lord, I don't know what this town is comin' to."

Violet took the tray and left, passing and smiling at Eliza and Angela who were coming in the door. Angela went immediately to hug Rachel.

"Did you see the news, Rachel?"

"Yes. It was just on. Where did you see it?"

"Lieutenant Yoder, Greg...he called Aunt Eliza this afternoon and had us meet him. He told us all about it before it could get into the media."

"Well, how are you feeling about the whole thing?"

"I'm trying not to think about what happened to me. If I did, I'd be up chukking. But if I didn't have Aunt Eliza..." she looked lovingly up at her aunt.

"...and you, I'd be crazy."

"Ohhhh..." Rachel hugged her friend tighter. "I'll always be around for you."

Angela broke away and looked at Rachel full on. "Do you think you'll be able to stay with Aunt Eliza and me?"

"I'm determined that I will. Even if I lose my inheritance...I'll apply for scholarships and get a job. Other students do it. I can do it, too."
"Great. By the way, we ran into Jerrod earlier today and he said he was going to be coming up to see you today. Has he been here?"
"Yes, he darted in and then went to look for my parents. He said he was going out to talk my parents out of trying to take me to court." " What a guy!" Angela giggled.
"Yeah, a regular Dudley Do Right."
"A what?"
"Oh, it was an old comic...just something my brother always says...I don't know." Rachel turned and winked at Stephan. "Anyway, how does it feel to be out of this place?"
"Oh, nothing like breathing the fresh mountain air. Although I do miss my view of the mountains from that window over there."
Both girls looked that way and everyone in the room laughed. Then Angela drew sober. "It's really sad the way people desecrate the beautiful, euphoric aura of the mountains with such evil."
Eliza came forward and hugged her niece. "It's o.k. if you cry about it, you know."
"No, I'm not going to cry. I can't do anything about the past, and I'm not blaming these mountains or the college or most of its people. "
Everyone became quiet and there was a strained electricity in the air. Rachel pulled her friend close to hug her again. Her heart said what she could not verbally express. 'I realize now that you are trying to hide behind a positive attitude. My heart breaks for you.'
Rachel said, "Well, I have another reason for hanging around this town now. We need to become part of that women's movement and straighten out the attitude of some the people here."
"Well, you haven't forgotten that plan of yours, have you Rachel?"

"Definitely not."
Dianna winked at Eliza. "I think that our girls have grown up."
"Yeah. I'm proud of them."
Another voice joined them. "So am I."
Rachel's smile became wider and her face beamed. "Hi Jerrod. I see that you've escaped the jaws of the lions."
Everyone laughed. Stephan held out his hand to Jerrod. "Well, did you tame those two?"
"I don't know what to think. I sat with them across the table at the diner on the corner. I did all the talking and they just kept staring at me. Then your dad said, 'We'll take what you've said into consideration, and we'll let you know after we speak to our lawyer.'"
Rachel leaned forward. "What did you say to them?"
"Among other things, I just told them that I wanted to get to know you more and that I wouldn't be able to do that if they took you off to Ethiopia. Then as I got up to leave the table, this big burley man who reeked of cigar smoke came in with another younger look-a-like and stood by the table. Your dad stood up and shook hands with them and then your dad introduced the two. A man named, Herbert and another man...I think his name was Henry...both their last names was Snow. I guess that Henry Snow mostly does the law suit cases."
Eliza and Angela glanced at each other. Eliza thought, 'Crap. That's the legal family that terrorizes the law abiding people of this county.'
Jerrod continued, "I wanted to hang around and listen, but I had already said my goodbyes, so we'll just have to wait and see what happens."
Rachel held up her hand. "It's o.k. Jerrod. You did a good job. Thanks."
Stephan turned to Dianna. "You know. I can't stand it. I've got to go find out what those two are up to. You want to come along?"

"I do. I think we'd better know where we stand in all of this. Neither of us can go back to work in peace until we have this settled."

Eliza stood up from the chair she was sitting on. "Angela, we'd better get going, too." Then she turned to Stephan and Dianna. "You have my card with my cell number. Let me know what's happening."

Angela hugged her friend and Eliza bent over to hug her too. "Rachel, you know I'm here for you.

Do you have any legal questions for me before I go?"

"Not right now, but I have a feeling that I'm going to have plenty as the days go on."

"Take care of yourself."

Stephan and Dianna hugged their sister. Dianna said. "Yes, take care of yourself and try not to worry about Mom and Dad. We'll get 'em packing for Ethiopia."

Stephan turned to Jerrod and shook his hand.

"Thanks man, for what you've tried to do to help."

"I wish I could be of more help. And I plan on hanging around more now that mid-terms are done."

Rachel gave Jerrod a big smile. The guy was really growing on her. There was that warm feeling again.

Jerrod kept his eyes on Rachel as the group left the room and Violet came back in with the blood pressure cuff. He started to step away toward the door but Violet waved him back.

"Don't go anywhere. I'm just taking Rachel's vitals. Unless you make her blood pressure go up just by looking at such a handsome dude."

Rachel and Jerrod laughed. The two stayed quiet until after Violet left. Then Rachel turned the TV off.

"So fill me in on what's been happening at school and all. What's been keeping you so busy?"

Jerrod moved closer to her. "Can I sit on the bed here closer to you?"

Without waiting for a reply, he sat sideways with his arm supporting him and looked into Rachel's face.

He whispered. "Well, I'm not supposed to tell or talk about it. But I'm just busting. Promise not to tell?"
Rachel whispered back. "I promise. So what's the big news? Did you get a 4.0 for the semester? Did you already get your grades? What...."
"No, I haven't got my grades yet. O.K... The secret is that I'm going to be testifying in the Bence trial."
Rachel looked at him suspiciously and elevated her voice. "You are going to what?"
"Shhhh." Jerrod looked around at the door, and then he continued his whispering. "Rachel, you're going to know this sooner or later. When I first talked to you at the college I was working undercover for the police department."
Rachel just stared back at Jerrod. "So why did you approach me? Did you think that I'd done something wrong?"
"Well, I thought you were the prettiest girl on campus and I really did want to date you. However, there were rumors started about you running off with Brent's van. In addition, Brent was implying that you hijacked his vehicle and all sorts of things. Since I was working undercover to unravel the car theft ring operating in this county, I had to find out if you were involved somehow." Rachel half chuckled and it came out as, "Huah." as she tried to keep up the whispering. "You don't believe me."
""I believe you... I guess. You're... I'm just flabbergasted. Why are you telling me this?"
"Because I know that it's going to come out that I was the undercover agent and witness at the chop shop and on campus. I don't want you to think that's the only reason I wanted to take you out."
"Ah, Wow. So you're a police officer?"
"Not yet. I'm in the police academy program at college and I guess you'd just call me an informant."
"So what were you doing at the chop shop?"
"'I got a job sweeping down the floors and cleaning up so that I could gain the evidence needed to put those guys away."

"Oh my God. A real private eye. I never would have guessed it."

Jerrod laughed. "Oh yeah. I guess I don't exactly look the part. But then, that gives me an advantage."

Rachel put out her hand and put it on his shoulder. "I'm impressed with your abilities and I want to hear...."

"That's all I can tell you about it right now. You've got to remember that you promised secrecy."

"I promise, Jerrod. So tell me about you. Is it true that your parents are missionaries like mine?"

"That's true. However, they aren't as idealistic as yours. They are down to earth. I talked to them last night. They are in town to speak at special services at the church."

"Did you tell them about your undercover job?"

Jerrod laughed. "Ho. Oh, no. They aren't the type to lecture me, and they know about my training for law enforcement. However, they picture me behind a desk at a police station or on a safe investigative team...down the road when I'm in my thirties. They would've been worried if they knew I was doing something like that now. So I just talked with them about my psych classes, etc.

And I'm going to go listen to them speak at the 8:00 p.m. service."

Rachel shook her head. "So they haven't pressured you to be a minister or missionary?"

"No. They raised me as a free spirit. I got verbally disciplined just like other kids and a few times, I got grounded. Of course, I had to go to church, church school and Bible classes, but they never preached to me in our home. We said grace at meals and our bedtime prayers. That was the extent of it."

"So do you have siblings?"

"No, just me. Mom miscarried a lot, though. I was their one blessing, I guess."

"You are a blessing. I'm sure they're extremely proud of you."

Jerrod was speaking at a normal level now.

"I'm sure that your parents are proud of you, too, Rachel. They've just got some hang ups to get over."
"I hope they do it soon."
A bass voice sounded from the door. "Do what soon?"
Jerrod jumped and stood up turning toward the door.
Dorothy and David came in and stood at the foot of Rachel's bed.
"Hello, Mr. and Mrs. Brooks."
Dorothy smiled. "It seems time that you call us,
Father and Mother Brooks. I believe that you and Rachel have been discussing something very personal."
Jerrod's face turned a deep red as Rachel looked at him and chuckled. He cleared his throat. "Well, if you are insistent on taking Rachel off to Ethiopia, I guess that Mr. and Mrs. Brooks would be more appropriate."
"No, we just came from a meeting with the minister of the local Brethren Church. We also had the pleasure of meeting your parents, Jerrod. It seems that they are going to be speaking at the special services tonight."
"Yes. I'll be leaving to go to the services soon."
"Well, have you had dinner yet, Jerrod? We just dropped by to see Rachel before we head out to the restaurant, and to the services."
"As a matter of fact, I have eaten. I need to go back to campus to shower and change."
Jerrod shook David's hand and gave Dorothy a quick hug. Then he walked over and lightly hugged Rachel. "I'll be back tomorrow." He gave her a wink and then left.
Rachel sat starring at the door. David walked over and gave Rachel a hug. "How're you feeling, dear?"
Dorothy hugged her and they stood waiting for Rachel to reply. Finally, she shook her head and said, "I'm fine. I'm just a little confused. When the two of you left today, you were both irate and ready to take me to court with a crooked lawyer, no less. Now you're in here acting as if nothing happened. I'm not complaining, but what's going on?"

Dorothy picked up Rachel's robe. "It's so stuffy in here. Let's go for a walk down the hall. You're in this bed every time we see you. You need to get your exercise. Come on."
Rachel let her mom help her up and out of bed. "Mother, it's late. If you're going to services at 8:00, you've only got an hour and a half to get dinner and freshen up."
"It's o.k. We'll make it in time." Dorothy guided her out of the room.
Halfway down the hall, they ran into Stephan and Dianne. The two glanced at each other and then at the entourage moving down the hall. They joined the walk.
Stephan spoke first. "Mom, Dad. We've been looking everywhere for you. It seems that we missed you at every hot spot in town."
"Hot spot?" David gruffed.
"Yes. The motel and then Brethren Church."
Dianne asked. "Well, did you speak with the minister or Jerrod's parents?"
Dorothy laughed. "Well I can tell by the confused look on your faces that you didn't talk to anyone there."
Dianne said. "No, just the church secretary. She said that you two had been there, but nothing more."
Dorothy was bubbly. "Well, we're going to go to the special services tonight. Jerrod's parents are going to be speaking there. Jerrod is going, of course. The two of you need to go so that you can meet his parents. He's going to be a part of this family, you know."
Rachel stumbled and she stopped walking. Her mouth was open. "Why am I surprised?" She looked at Stephan and Dianne's amused expressions.
Dorothy looked puzzled. "Surprised about what, dear?"
"Nothing, Mother, nothing."
They had reached the elevators. David looked at his watch. "We really should be going to dinner, Dorothy. Since Stephan and Dianne are here, they can walk Rachel back to her room."

David pushed the elevator button and then the two giddy parents hugged Rachel.
The elevator door opened. David pointed his finger first at Stephan and then at Dianne. "We'll see you at the services." They stepped on it and were gone leaving Stephan, Dianne and Rachel standing and gawking at the closed elevator door.

Chapter Twenty

"You're an addlepated bantam rooster, Ray. I swear," spouted Herbert. "It's bad enough that you took Delilah's car to your own shop, but you had to go and add rape and assault. Rape and assault, Ray. And with your own cousin's woman."

"Ah sware on my mama's Bible 'at 'hit was unbeknownst ta' me she was Brent's woman. He never brought her around us. 'At filly was jest in the right place at the wrong time. Ah mean..."

"You idiot. Didn't you know better than to spill the beans about what you did to that girl before you even talked to me? I told you over the phone to keep your mouth shut until I got there."

"Ah din't spill the beans. Ah ain't 'fessed up to nothin'. But them cops tricked me. Ah had ta' have some reason fer whar ah was 'at night the girl's car got stole. Thay aweady got my fangerprints off'n the van. So ah jest told 'em 'at ah was fixin' on Brent's van 'n never touched another vehicle 'til the next mornin'. Ah told 'em 'at ah parked 'at van back on the college lot 'n walked on down ta the garage, and 'at part's true. Then thay said thar were a witness 'at seed Brent's van up near whar 'at gal was found."

"Did you ask who the witness was?"

"Naw. Ah jest told 'em the witness mistook another van fer Brent's, 'cause Ah was working on Brent's van 'til late. But thay wanted a witness ta 'at fact. Ah tol' 'em 'at Delilah could vow fer me. But thay said 'at under the circumstances, 'at weren't good enough."

Herbert drew in his breath and then belched loudly. "Well, don't be telling nobody nothing else unless I tell you to do it. And if they asked you to give them a DNA. sample, refuse it without a court order."

"What's a DNA sample?"

"Don't you ever watch cop shows?"

"Don't hav' no use fer T.V. or movies."
"Ignorant. Well, it's a newfangled way to get some of your skin cells or put a swab in your mouth to get some spit. They might even take a piece of your hair and then they do some scientific test on it. They do the same thing on a DNA sample they took from the girl after she was raped. Then they check the results of the two samples up. If they match, then they've got their suspect and can use that in court to convict."
"Kin they git a sample 'afore askin'?"
"Well, they could use hair or skin cells from something that belonged to you. However, those samples could come from anybody. They've got to have proof that they're your samples. That would take a court order and with my cousin as the judge, we've got it made. You just got to keep your mouth shut."
"My word of honor, Herbert. I'll not say 'tother word."
"Good." Herbert got up, hurried out the door, and growled at the guard. "Take care of my client."

Back in his Mercedes, Herbert Snow drove absent-mindedly down the thoroughfare toward his mansion at the edge of Echo Valley. He slowed to 10 miles per hour as he passed the Mountain View Brethren Church.
"That bunch of do goodin' pious fools ought to be run out of this county." He spouted out loud. The big car jolted ahead as he pressed his foot harder on the gas pedal. That bunch had been more trouble to him and his Glory Mount Holiness Church than Satan himself. They held great exception to the true test of God's faith, the trial by poison snakes...rattlers. He had been bitten and lived to tell about it. That proved to the true Christians in this county that he was among the chosen of God's kingdom. It sure didn't hurt his credibility as an influential member in the running of the county.
Gloating in that thought, Herbert spotted Sarah Yoder's car. That clan had been a thorn in his side since he was born. He started mumbling to himself. "Yeah, that Dan Yoder. That meddlesome sheriff gave me no end of trouble with his

righteousness. His death came as no consternation to me. He was the only law enforcer in the whole county. Then the population grew and with that the law enforcement structure. The state came in and backed the new rich people who started resorts and tourist businesses. They appointed Dan Yoder's son, Greg, to the head of a new detective unit and he was now taking his Daddy's place with a different title. What a thorn in the side that one has turned out to be."

Herbert shifted in his seat and looked back through his rear view mirror as he neared the stop sign.

Yup," growled Herbert. "I've still got a lot of housecleaning to do in this government. It's my county and it's just a matter of time...."

The screech of brakes interrupted the thought pattern and speech of the grumbling lawyer and he looked forward. Time moved in slow motion as Herbert realized that there was going to be metal to metal very soon.

Meanwhile, in the Mountain View Brethren church, Jerrod glanced back over his shoulder to check out the beautiful soprano voice singing, "Rock of Ages" in the second pew. At the same time, a loud sound resonated through the church, but the organist picked up-tempo and the congregation continued to sing with the choir. Eliza glanced up, looked around, and then smiled back at Jerrod.

Jerrod's gaze turned to look into the eyes of Dorothy Brooks who was sitting next to him in the front pew. *The poor woman can't sing for beans.* He thought. In that fleeting moment, he noticed that Stephen and Dianna were not sitting with David and Dorothy.

His attention was drawn to the podium where Greg Yoder's bass voice led the choir and the congregation. His parents sat ready to take their turn in the service. He wished that Rachel was sitting beside him. But then again, she would be embarrassed at the way her mother smothered the life out of his family in her own subtle way. Dorothy Brooks was quiet and demure for the most part, but she could change in an instant when it was apparent that something wasn't going the way she judged it should.

His attention was diverted to the stage as Yoder said, "I know we've all been inspired by the sermon of Rev. Showalter and the beautiful voices of he and his wife. Now they asked me to sing this song that meant so much to them when they were traveling in the choir with the Billy Graham crusades. I am honored to sing George Beverly Shay's "How Great Thou Art" and I hope that I don't mess this up." The congregation laughed.

Yoder turned to the organist. Jerrod turned and looked at Eliza again. It was apparent to him that she was totally in love with Greg Yoder as he started to sing. Jerrod was right. Eliza was enthralled by the smooth clear, bass voice. Her heart beat faster and she felt warm all over as she remembered the record that was played repeatedly in her mother's sick room all those years ago. She was amazed at how much Greg sounded like George Beverly Shay himself. Tears welled up in her eyes and seeing this, Angela took Eliza's right hand. Another small hand grabbed her left hand and Eliza looked down at Greg's mother, Sarah. She smiled at the little woman that she had been introduced to just tonight... She looked up again into the approving stare of Greg's eyes.

'I wonder what Greg would think if he knew that I love God in nature and that Angela and I have always spent our Sundays worshipping in the sun on the Lake Michigan beaches.'

All too soon, the song was over. The congregation applauded loudly. Greg left the podium and came to sit by his mother. Sarah let go of Eliza's hand and turned to her son. She took her son's hands in hers and they sat that way for the rest of the service. Something about that scene was disturbing to Eliza and she was confused by her feelings. I'm being silly. There's nothing wrong with show of devotion between parent and an adult child. She thought. Eliza looked at Angela. She was watching the

Brooks. Angela leaned over and whispered in Eliza's ear. "Do you realize how many times, Dorothy Brooks has whispered in her husband's ear? I wonder what they're cooking up."

"What makes you think they're cooking anything up?" Eliza whispered back into Angela's ear.

"I don't trust them. That's all I'm saying."

Eliza tried to focus on the podium as the service was ending. She glanced over again at Greg and his mother. She started to feel like an outsider and her spirits dipped. 'I'm not sure that I'm good enough, or maybe I just don't fit into his lifestyle. This devotion to his mother...we are so different...I'm sure that I can never measure up...even after she's gone.'

She looked back at the podium. She could hear the faint sounds of sirens down the street and the echo of the wolves from the mountain. She imagined that either the emergency was far away, or the walls of the church were extremely well insulated. She looked back at Greg. She noticed that he was looking toward the stained glass window ever so often.

After the prayer and the service ended, she followed closely behind Angela and moved through the receiving line at the door as quickly as possible. As they moved through the outside doors, Eliza and Angela walked into the congregation.

Groups of people were standing in the glare of the streetlights, and gawking at the commotion down the street. Twirling red, blue, and flashing bright lights surrounded what looked to be a car and truck pile up.

Eliza turned and looked toward the church door as Greg and Sarah exited. The Yoders walked to where she and Angela were standing. Greg assessed the chaos and turned to Eliza. "Eliza, that mess looks like I need to investigate. Would you see to it that Mom gets home?"

"Sure."

He turned to his mother. "Mom, I'm sorry. I'll be home shortly. "

"Go ahead, Greg." Sarah turned to Eliza. "I'm used to it." She laughed and continued. "I hope you don't mind."
"Of course not. I'd love to see your place, so maybe I can get a quick glimpse of the outside before I come for a full visit tomorrow."
As Eliza helped Sarah into the front seat, Sarah said, "You're welcome to come inside tonight. You can't see much from the outside in the dark."
"I'd love to, but Angela needs her rest. She just got out of the hospital."
"I'm fine, Aunt Eliza." Angela spoke up. "I think I'll give Rachel a ring. When I talked with her before services, she said Julie and Sadie were there and suggested I call her later."
"Don't you think it's going to be too late to call her now?"
"No, Rachel said I could call her as late as eleven."
"Wait until we deliver Sarah, Angela. A little later won't hurt."
"O.K. But I can't wait to hear about Julie and Sadie. They haven't had a lot of time to leave the campus lately. Julie's been finishing her midterms. She's going home soon for holiday break; which reminds me of all the catching up I'm facing."
"You'll make it work. Step at a time, you know."
Eliza looked in her rear view mirror. The crowd had dispersed from the church steps and was starting to merge into the traffic behind her. She could see emergency lights leaving the scene, but blue and red from atop the cruisers still flashed in the dusk as she pulled down the cross streets toward Sarah's house.
The closer they got toward the mountain, the louder the wolves sounded, but Sarah talked right over the noise. By the time Eliza pulled up in front of Sarah's house, she felt like she knew every neighbor in the eight town blocks preceding and surrounding the big Victorian farmhouse.

"Oh my, Sarah. That's a lot of house." She opened the door and started to step out. The echoes from the mountain seemed even louder. A shiver ran up her spine.
"I know, Eliza. But wait until you see the inside. I know that it'll be just right for you and Angela, and you could rent some of it out to other college students." Sarah rambled on as they sat in the drive looking up at the two large dormers.
"Yes, well..." Eliza looked up at the brightly lit house. It seemed so overwhelming and a lot of upkeep. "We'll talk tomorrow, Sarah."
"Now Eliza, you reserve judgment until you see more of it."
"O.K. Sarah." Eliza got out of the car to come around and help Sarah out, but the little woman was already making her way up the drive. They met at the front of the car.
Sarah kept babbling on and Eliza had a hard time convincing Sarah that she had to leave. She glanced in the front seat of the car and noticed that Angela had changed seats and was talking on the phone.
She looked up as the lights of Sarah's car pulled in next to her driver side on the wide driveway.
Greg got out, leaving the motor running.
"Hey, I guess the timing's right. Could you do me another favor, Eliza?"
"Sure. As long as I can get that girl in the car to bed before she falls asleep."
"I need to put Mom's car in the garage first. If you could drive me on to my place, you would save me the walk. It's about a mile down on the lake."
"O.K. Sarah can I walk you up to the door? I hate to interrupt our conversation, but you heard your son."
"I did indeed. But I can get myself to the door."
She stood on her toes, stretched up toward Eliza, and kissed her cheek. "I'll see you tomorrow, dear."
Back in the car, Eliza watched as Sarah opened the door and went in. Greg appeared, and jumped into the back seat behind Angela.
"Angela, hang it up now."

"Bye Rachel. We'll see you tomorrow." Then Angela turned to Eliza. "Rachel says that Stephan and Dianna just left. They're going be there to pick her up the first thing in the morning. The doctor signed her release papers tonight for 8:30 am and she's free to go then."
"So where's she going from there?"
"They're hoping that we'll help them figure that out."
"We can try."
As Eliza backed to the end of the drive, Greg said, "We're going east and then north from here, Eliza."
Eliza maneuvered the car east. Then she addressed Angela. "I thought maybe the Brooks had mellowed out and were giving Rachel free rein."
"Ashley doesn't trust them. She said that Stephan and Dianne are a bit worried about their parent's erratic behavior and change of mind from one time to the next. And with them having that Snow family as lawyers, she said she doesn't trust what'll happen next."
Greg said. "Well, if you're worried about the Snow family, they're going to have their hands full for the next few days. Herbert just got his neck broke in that accident down by the church. That's really why I needed you to drive me, Eliza. I need to pick up my car at the lake house and get back to the office...turn to the left up here at the light."
"So that's what all that commotion was about.
What happened?"
"Herbert ran a stop sign right into the side of a large transit truck. They had to cut him out of the car. He was alive as they got him onto the board and hauled him out. However, he'll most likely be paralyzed. Anyway, his sons can't seem to do anything unless their daddy's there to oversee things. I imagine that Henry'll be preoccupied in the morning and for a few mornings to come...depending on what's happening with Daddy
Snow...O.K; turn to the left again up here."
The road had narrowed and was winding now through dogwood and mountain rock wall. A wide creek bubbled

along the right roadside. Lights flashed against the wet rock where streams of water formed into waterfalls into the side ditches along the road.
"How pretty. I bet it's beautiful in the daytime." Eliza said.
"This roadway is breathtaking. You'll have the chance to come back to see it often. Now, see where the road forks off, and the left side winds away? Stay to the creek side on the right and follow the gravel drive."
Just as suddenly, they were there. A large log cabin loomed up in an expansive landscape.
"The lake is out in the back of the cabin. The creek is on the right and nature's garden is on the left. I have to leave right away, but next time you come out here, I'd like to show you around. This is my heaven on earth."
"I believe that." She stopped the car and put up her hand.
"Listen, the echoes have stopped."
Greg listened. "Yes, I believe they have. I'm so accustomed to hearing them, that I don't notice anymore."
He got out of the car and bent over to look inside. "Keep me in touch, Eliza. If you need me in the morning, let me know."
Greg jumped into his car, backed out and was gone.
Angela's phone rang. "Hello."
"Calm down, Rachel. What?" ... "O.K. We'll be there in just a few minutes." " What?" Eliza asked.
"Let's get to the hospital. It seems that the Brooks have gone off the deep end. They came in to visit Rachel late, and she got into an argument with them. They packed her things and tried to wrestle her out the door. The nursing staff got security involved and called the police. They kicked them out, but now Rachel wants to leave on her own.

Chapter Twenty One

Security escorted Eliza and Angela to the third floor of the hospital. The head nurse was waiting with Stephan at the station outside the door.

The nurse was saying, "I just talked to Rachel's doctor. After he talked with her on the phone, he agrees that it might be best to release her tonight. She's waiting in the wheelchair inside the room here. Her papers are signed and she's ready to go."

Rachel wheeled herself out the door before Angela could step inside. Dianne followed Rachel, loaded down with a suitcase and flowers.

Angela bent down and hugged her friend. "I'm sorry you've had so much trauma. But you can stay with us."

"Thank you, so much. Angela, how're you holding up?"

"Keeping busy and trying not to dwell on the negative. Nevertheless, you'd be a great help to me if you and I could be together at night for a while. I just dread the dreams."

"Oh, I know. I've been sitting here thinking about the fact that my parents are staying in that same motel. I need to find a place where they can't reach me."

Eliza was quick with an answer. "Then we can all pack up and go up to Dad's cabin. You and Dianne as well, Stephan. You know that when they find out that Rachel left the hospital, they're going to start hounding you."

Stephan shook his head 'no'. "I agree that Rachel needs to get away. But that's a long way from the doctors if she has problems." Dianne was nodding in agreement.

At that moment, Yoder walked up with Jerrod at his side. "Hey, I was here on the hospital grounds and heard the report about what's going on up here on the third floor. Jerrod called me and said that the Brooks came to him and his parents for help to get Rachel released to them. Rachel are you alright?"

"I'm fine. We're just discussing what to do with me to keep me away from my parents...you know...since my folks, Eliza and Angela are all staying at the same motel."
"I think I have the solution for you. You can all stay at my cabin and I can stay at my mom's."
They all exchanged glances. Then in the silence, Yoder added. "Eliza and Angela were just out there. It's secluded, but close enough to the hospital. There's four bedrooms, two baths and a pull out sofa in the office. And... if that's not enough room, there's a big couch and a recliner in the living room. Please say that you'll stay."
"Wow, that doesn't sound like a cabin to me...and that's a great idea." Diane said. "But we don't want to put you out, Lieutenant Yoder."
"Aught...Not Lieutenant Yoder to anybody here. I'm just Greg. It wouldn't be putting me out at all. In fact, I've been staying with my mother a lot these days. She refuses to come live with me until I get her house sold. She's been trying to get me to sell my place and just come live with her all the time. But I've been resisting." He looked hopefully at Rachel. "Please say that you'll stay at my cabin until you can figure this mess out."
Stephan looked at Rachel. "What do you say? Rachel?"
"It sounds perfect. Let's do it. Is that o.k. with you and Angela, Eliza?"
"If no one else has an objection, but we'll have to get our things from the motel and that might be tricky with you along, Rachel."
Greg said. "No problem. I can drive Rachel out and since Eliza knows where the cabin is, she can lead you, Stephan and Dianne out there."
"O.K. I guess that's the plan then."
"I'll go get my car and pull it up to the door." With that, Greg headed for the elevator.
Eliza looked at Jerrod who had been standing quietly by Rachel's wheelchair. She took her breath in and then said,

"Jerrod, I'm sorry, but we've left you holding the bag, so to speak. You can't let your parents know where Rachel is because they might let it slip to Rachel's parents...."
Jerrod held his hand up and shook his head 'no'. "It's o.k. I've just said 'goodbye' to my parents and I'm going back out to the college campus. I just wanted to check on Rachel before I left. I'll see all of you in the morning early."
Rachel looked up at Jerrod. "Thank you so much for your support, Jerrod. Please tell your parents that I'm sorry about the way my parents acted."
"It's o.k. They understand. When I left my parents motel room, they were still talking with Dorothy and David. Dad and Mom had them convinced that they need counseling and Dad set up a meeting for them with the local pastor for in the morning. He also called the Brethren Mission's main office in Pittsburgh, and the chaplain on call talked with your dad. If your parents don't keep their appointment, the main ministry will cancel their participation in the trip to Ethiopia."
Rachel put out her hand to Jerrod. He took it and knelt down beside her chair. Everyone else looked at each other and with a nod from Angela, they all moved down the hall to give privacy to the two young people.
The nurse looked at Rachel, "I'll have to push you down to the car, Rachel when you're ready.
Just let me know."
"I'm ready. I guess we have it all figured out as to which chariot I'll ride in and to what castle I'll be going....abiding in... Oh, whatever." Rachel embellished.
Everyone was giggling, trying to keep the volume down. Stephan quipped. "She's back. Our witty, little sister's herself again."
Jerrod walked beside Rachel's wheelchair behind the others. "I never knew you were witty,
Rachel."
"Oh, there's a lot you don't know about me."
"Promise that I will."

"That's a promise," she said as she looked up at him with a wink.

Everyone lined up into the elevator. Dianne looked down at her little sister through the large plant that she was carrying. "Must be you're just so happy to get out of here that you've reverted to your childhood, Rachel."

"Oh, I am. I'm still worried about Mom and Dad, but for the first time, I feel relieved that they're going to get help in coming to terms with the empty nest syndrome."

Dianne and Stephan chuckled. Dianne said. "I think you've just hit on the diagnosis, Rachel. Mom and Dad have always been flighty, but never so irrational. I think that's the root of their problem,
I really do."

Entering out onto the first floor from the elevator, Angela had to use the restroom. Stephan and Dianne decided it was time to go back to their motel rooms and pack.

Eliza met Greg as he was coming back through the door and they stood away from the nurse aide, Rachel and Jerrod.

"Angela's in the bathroom." Then she asked. "What's happening with Herbert Snow? Is he going to be alright?"

"He's alive, but he may end up in a wheelchair or worse. That whole Snow bunch was in the emergency area, demanding rights and giving the emergency teams holy hell."

"Holy hell?" Eliza grinned at Greg. "You're a choir director and deacon in the Brethren Church and you swear?"

"That's not swearing. Swearing is when you condemn. I'm not condemning anybody. I'm just stating the facts."

Eliza cocked her head sideways, still grinning.

"Since when is hell, holy."

Greg laughed. "O.K. You've got me. Get out the soap bar. I promise to get forgiveness for that one."

"Don't promise me anything. I'm not passing judgment. I'm just surprised. I guess I was expecting perfection from someone of your standing in the church and with your mom."

"Well, fortunately for me, my church does not preach perfection for any human. In all perfect things, there is imperfection. Does that make sense?"

Eliza nodded her head yes. Greg continued.

"We can strive to be perfect in God's eyes. Doesn't mean it will ever happen. God accepts the fact that no human can ever truly reach that goal."

Eliza looked sober. "I guess that's how it was in our family. Maybe Carrie was trying to be perfect in Dad's eyes, but I don't think that she realized that Dad never expected her to be perfect."

"How about you, Eliza? Were you trying to be perfect for your dad?"

"No, I never tried to please anyone else. I've always tried to do the right thing for as many people as possible and follow my gut instincts. However, I know that I failed Dad. I just assumed that he was content to stay on the mountain and wallow in Mama's memory. The day I moved down here to the valley, he took off on a trail and didn't even say goodbye. He wasn't home. He didn't know what time I left. He just knew that one of my high school teachers was picking me up to go to work and to college. Four years later, Carrie followed. When I went up to pick her and her things up, Daddy was out on the trails and we left before he came home." Eliza paused. "You know, I should look up that teacher while I'm here, but that's been so many years ago, I don't remember her name...." She suddenly stopped. "What was the name of the college teacher that they've been talking about...the one that was in the hit and run?"

"Ila Bence."

Eliza gasped. "How old was she?"

"She was seventy-five, I believe."

"Oh my... I've been hearing that name and now I remember. It just dawned on me where I've heard that name from the past. That would make her about the right age. I haven't paid attention to the TV accounts or the newspapers. But what would be the odds of two young teachers in the area by that name who were not married. Of course, the Ms. Ila Bence I knew was young at the time."

Eliza sighed. "I left home while Daddy was still grieving over Mama. I was seventeen. My guilt is that I should have known what he was going through and now it's too late."

"Too late for what?" Angela interrupted as she joined Eliza and Greg.

"Too late for ice cream...that's what." Eliza laughed. "Hey, let's get this show on the road." "Aunt Eliza, could I ride out to Greg's with Rachel?"

"Sure, I still have your things in the car."

Eliza turned and realized that the nurse aide was still with Rachel behind the wheelchair. "I'm so sorry that we're holding you up."

Violet giggled. "No problem. Rachel, Jerrod and I have been chatting away here. We've just been trash talking."

Rachel swatted at the nurse aide. "We have not been trash talking, Violet"

Violet pushed the wheelchair forward. "You couldn't prove it by me."

Outside in the parking lot, Eliza confirmed that Angela and Rachel were safely buckled in the back of Greg's car and she and Jerrod continued across the parking lot to get their cars. Eliza asked Jerrod. "Did you know Ila Bence?"

"Yes, she was an excellent professor."

"What did she look like?"

"She was an older woman. She had graying hair that was still mostly black, but her back was very straight....sweet smile, still had her own teeth...She spoke with a bit of a southern accent. She never married and never had children."

Eliza nodded her head. "Do you know how long she had been a teacher?"

"Yeah, she taught high school for thirty years before she became a professor at the college."

"That would be her then. I think her family lived up on the road to Starlight Plateau and I heard she was killed on that road."

"Yeah..."

Suddenly a vehicle came barreling directly at them. Jerrod grabbed Eliza and pushed her quickly toward her car. They both stood shaking as they watched the car speed out of the lot and down the road.

Stunned, Eliza and Jerrod stood and looked at each other for a moment. Finally, Jerrod asked, "Do you think we should report that?"

"Did you get a good description?" Eliza asked.

"I didn't get a clear view of the license plate."

"It was a black car. Couldn't make out the model, but the license plate number was BAD B the number 0 Y and the number 1. BAD BOY 1.

I'll not forget that."

"A vanity plate shouldn't be too hard to trace. I'll call it in to Greg. He can have them run it." Eliza retrieved her cell phone and motioned for Jerrod to get into the car with her. "It will be safer to sit in here." She said as the two of them settled into the seats.

She leaned over the steering wheel, feeling the pain in her back from being jostled into the car, as she waited for Greg to answer the phone.

She talked to voice mail. "Greg, Jerrod and I almost got run over in the hospital parking lot by a black car with a vanity license plate, BAD BOY1. BAD, B, the number 0, letter y, and the number 1.

The car raced out of the lot and turned right down Pitcher Street."

Eliza sighed and put her phone in the console.

"Jerrod, where's your car parked and I'll drive you. If Greg needs to talk to us, he'll get back to us later. I'm beat and I need to get to the cabin, tuck the girls in and get to bed."

Jerrod grabbed the door handle. "I'm parked over on the end there. I can walk."

"No. I'll drive you over there. I don't know who else is lurking in this lot. So hang in here."

Eliza eased her car up in front of Jerrod's at the end of the lot and watched as he got in. When he turned the lights on, she left.

Jerrod pulled out of the lot and headed toward the college. What a night. He thought. 'What a crazy week.'

He looked into the rear view mirror as he pulled up to a red light. That car in back seemed close and with the bright lights on, it was hard to see anything else. He looked forward just as the light turned green. He pulled forward and headed straight for the mountain range. The college campus was just a mile out of town and he was going to be happy to hit that hard dormitory mattress tonight.

The lights moved in closer blinding him. He flipped his rear view mirror up to avoid the glare. Then he sped up and the car pulled in closer to his bumper. Come on jerk. Back off. This is a four lane with no cars in the passing lane. In fact, there were hardly any cars at all on the highway.

He came to the mountain road that passed by the college. He moved into the left turn land and stopped at the signal light. The car with the bright lights pulled up behind him.

'Awhh...just my luck.'

The light turned green and Jerrod had to wait for oncoming cars that turned their bright lights on as they were blinded by the lights of the car behind him. Judging from the incident earlier, I'd say that it's not safe for me to be on the college road alone, but the sign says no U Turn here.

The light changed and Jerrod impulsively pulled up as if to cross the highway, then he made a sharp U-turn, and headed back toward town. He looked in the rear view mirror. The car with the bright lights, a black car, bounced across the intersection and took the college road.

Jerrod let out a big sigh. To be sure that he had avoided the car, he turned to the right the next road. It would be safer to take the long way around to the back of the college campus. He looked into his rear view mirror before he got to the top of the hill and spotted a black car flying across the intersection.

Chapter Twenty Two

Rachel woke to the sound of the water lapping on the shoreline. A cool lake breeze moved the thin curtains gently. She jumped up and shut the window. A squirrel chattered as he scurried away among the tree branches. She crawled back under the heavy quilts.

The smell of bacon drifted in and she heard the footsteps of someone running up the stairway. The door burst open and Angela came running across the room in pajamas with her red curls swinging over her face.

"Hey, Sleepy Head. I've been down to the lake already. It's great. Come on. Get out of bed."

Rachel burrowed further under the quilts. "No, it's too cold." She peeked out. "You were down by the lake in your pajamas?"

"No, I was down by the lake in your pajamas. Remember these? I took them in the shower room that day."

"Those aren't my pajamas. By the way, what did you do with my clothing that you stole?"

"Here on the foot of your bed. Now get up. It will not be cold after you get up and start moving around. Come on. We've got lots to do today."

"But I want to have a pajama day today."

"Hey, you've been having a pajama day almost every day for the last two weeks. Today is Saturday and Greg promised us a ride on the pontoon. Come on, Jerrod's downstairs. He just got here."

Rachel threw the coverlets off and sat up.

"Well, I hate to leave this great bedroom, but o.k."

"Isn't this neat? Now get up and let's get dressed for breakfast. Aunt Eliza is almost done. She's been cooking up the deluxe of all meals downstairs."

Angela bounced across the room to the twin bed that she had slept on and dove into her suitcase.

Rachel grabbed her clothing and moved slowly to the hall. "I've got to go to the bathroom and take a shower first."

"Took mine last night." Angela was almost dressed.
"I was too whooped to shower. By the way, you don't move as if you're sore anymore. I feel as stiff as an old woman." Rachel reached the door and stood looking back at her giddy friend.
"No, I feel great...fresh mountain air, and being here on the Lake. Rachel, you missed a wonderful sunrise this morning. Aunt Eliza and I sat on the pier and watched it peek between two mountains. The lake was like glass and reflected every detail of the mountains...you know...as if I was looking at the mountains upside down. Sometimes fish would jump out of the water, a ripple would form, and the image of the mountains would wave. It's so beautiful here."
"I couldn't go to sleep last night, Angela. The wolves were howling and the way you were moaning and groaning...well, I thought maybe you were having nightmares."
Angela stepped over to the window and looked out. "I'm fine. I'm sorry if I kept you awake. I don't remember any nightmares, though." She turned and went back to her suitcase on the bed.
Rachel stepped back into the room and stood looking at her friend rummaging through her socks. "Angela, if you ever need to talk..."
Angela threw up her hand without looking up and made a motion for Rachel to move on. Rachel turned and went out the door.
In the bathroom, Rachel dried off, dressed, and made a face at herself in the mirror. God, I look terrible.
As she made her way down the staircase, she could see Dianne and Eliza preparing breakfast in the kitchen area of the Great Room. Angela was sitting within view on a stool at the dining side of the counter. There was an arm on the counter beside Angela, but she couldn't see who it was because of the overhang over the island counter.
She looked toward the lake and mountain view through the window wall. Wow. She stopped and stared at the mesmerizing scene for a moment. Then she looked down on

the deck through the double French doors. Greg and Stephan were leaning against the rail, engrossed in conversation.

Rachel's attention was drawn back to Angela as she spotted her and called out. "Hey, Sleepy Head. Come on down and join the party. The women looked up and started throwing silly little comments at her.

"The day's half over."

"Yeah, make hay while the sun shines."

Rachel continued down the stairway. When she reached the bottom, she realized that the arm on the counter belonged to Jerrod. He grinned at her, the doll face with silky ivory skin and big blue eyes shadowed by long brown eyelashes.

"Hello Beautiful."

She swung up on the bar stool next to him and leaned against the counter. "So what do you want, Mr. Smooth Talker?"

"Come on, can't you take a compliment?"

Dianne pushed three plates of food across the counter. "She never could. She's just never known what a cutie she is."

Rachel looked down at her plate. "Hey that's a lot of food."

Dianne rolled her eyes up. "She's ungrateful, too."

"I'm sorry, Dianne. It smells and looks delicious. I'm sure that it's better than hospital food."

"I would hope so. Thanks for the compliment."

The men came in from the porch. "Hey." Eliza called from the stove. "I knew you'd show up when the grub was on."

Greg and Stephan took a seat at the dining table. Eliza and Dianne came out carrying two plates each. Dianne served Stephan and Eliza served Greg. Then the two women seated themselves.

It was a great time with lively conversation and laughter. After the food was devoured, Greg said, "I need to talk to all of you. Stephan and I have been talking this over out on the deck. There are going to be some undercover officers in and out of here today...maybe for a few days. I want you to make them seem like part of the group. Everyone needs to stay in the back part of the property. Don't go out to the front of the house at all."

Everyone was quiet. Then he continued. "Jerrod and Eliza had an incident in the hospital parking lot last night involving a black car. Later when Jerrod was on the way back to the college, a black car was following him. I picked him up at the college this morning early, so his car will stay in the college parking lot." He cleared his throat and looked at Eliza. "We need to keep everyone together."

Stephan got up from the table carrying his plate and silverware. "Dianne and I are going to be going back today. He put his dirty dishes in the sink and turned to Rachel. "Are you sure you don't want to go back and stay with one of us?"

Rachel shook her head. "No, I'll be safe here. Angela needs me and I want to be ready to dive back into my studies."

Eliza had been staring out toward the lake. She stood up and grabbed her table service. "I think we would be safer at Dad's cabin."

Greg picked his dishes up and followed her to the kitchen. "Well, if we do that, I want to have undercover men out there. Is there room to house at least one man in the cabin?"

"Yes, there are two beds upstairs for the girls and room for another cot for me. Jerrod can sleep in the master bedroom downstairs and the undercover men can use the cot that's in the Great Room area."

"You do know that whoever it was knows your car as well as Jerrod's. A deputy of mine lives next door to me here with his dad. His dad has a hummer. He'd love to drive you up there in that. You can leave your car out of sight."

Eliza nodded. "I'm willing to do anything that'll keep the young people safe."

Greg looked around the room. "Is this acceptable for everyone?"

Jerrod spoke up. "I don't want to put anyone out. I'd feel better if I could be close to the women. If I stayed behind, I'd be worried about them all the time." He hesitated, had a

strained look on his face, and then continued, addressing Greg. "Oh the other hand, do you think that I'm the target? If I'm the one they're after...and it would seem that's the case, perhaps the women would be safer without me around."
Greg thought about it for a moment. Then he spoke. "I'm going to leave it up to you, Jerrod. If you'd feel safer here, then you're more than welcome. You can use my computer and phone to get in touch with the college to keep up on things. But, I'd still want to keep an undercover person here and you'd have to stay in the cabin and out of sight."
"It's not that I'd feel better off anywhere, but I think the women might be safer without me there, if I'm the target."
Eliza said, "You're more than welcome at the cabin, Jerrod and I think we'd be more secure with two strong people around. I think that none of us are popular with the people who are behind all this."
The room was silent. Then Jerrod looked at Rachel. "What do you think? Would you be uncomfortable with me staying at the cabin?"
Rachel laughed. "Why should I be uncomfortable? Of course, not. Please come with us."
Eliza added. "If you're worried about classes, you can all use my laptop. It has wireless service anywhere. I've already got Angela set up with the college to take her midterms on line and get back in sync with her studies."
Greg said, "I'll take a cot up to your cabin for you, Eliza."
"Thanks, Greg." She looked at the floor in deep thought. Then she said, "My cabin. I keep thinking of it as Dad's cabin, but I guess it belongs to Angela and me now." She looked over at her niece and noticed that her eyes were wet... She walked to her side and hugged her. "I guess we'd better get going."
Dianne was already loading the dishwasher and cleaning the kitchen. Eliza went to help her.
Dianne waved her off. "I'm already packed, Eliza. I can take care of the kitchen. You go and get your things around."

She turned to Stephan. "Hey Bro, will you get my bags out of my room?"

"Yeah." He winked at Eliza. "That's why she travels with me."

The girls scrambled up the stairway to gather their things. Stephan carried all the packed bags down from the upstairs loft and Eliza brought hers from the master bedroom downstairs.

Rachel stood in the front foyer with Stephan and Dianne. Dianne gathered her up in her arms. "It's so hard to leave you little sister. I'm tempted to be like Mom and Dad and take you with us. But it would have to be your decision." Rachel started to cry. Dianne folded some tissues in her hand. The crying subsided. The three clung to each other for a while. "I don't want you to go. I wouldn't mind going with you. But I know I need to stay here to be with Angela. You've got to know that it was Mom and Dad's over protection and control that I couldn't and can't live with...and I feel so depressed that Mom and Dad are going to be leaving. I won't even be able to tell them goodbye. Things are so bad between us."

"Do you want us to check on them before we leave?" Stephan asked.

"Yes, I know they're supposed to be going to see the counselor and I don't know where they'll go from there. But if you could just try to keep tabs on them and let me know how things are going, I'd be so grateful."

"We can do that. You hang in there, Little Sis. We want to hear from you every day."

Rachel watched sadly as her siblings backed out and headed toward town. Jerrod came up behind her and put his hand on her shoulder. "Are you o.k.?"

She patted his hand. "I'm fine. Thanks." Then she turned and grabbed her rolling suitcase handle.

"Is everyone ready?"

Eliza came in from the garage door. "All the bags are in the hummer but yours, Rachel. We're all set."

Jerrod and Rachel followed Eliza into the garage. The hummer was parked there next to Eliza's car. Jerrod put Rachel's bag into the rear and climbed in the back seat beside her.

They looked ahead at a white haired gentleman who was in the driver's seat. He turned and looked around. "Is this everyone?" He said in a high pitched, but distinctly male voice.

Eliza spoke from her passenger's seat. "We're all accounted for. Everyone fasten their seat belts.

That means you, too, Angela."

"Don't worry, mine is fastened securely. No one knows better than I that a seat belt can save your life."

"O.K. then. We're on our way. If you haven't ridden in a hummer, you're in for a treat and there are dark windows all around. You can see out, but no one can see in." The man said proudly. "By the way," he chuckled, I'm Sam Gibson, I'll be your driver today, and Eliza here is the navigator

"Hello, Sam." Angela chuckled. "I guess you have a new job, Aunt Eliza." "Where's Greg?" Angela asked.

Sam said... "Greg explained everything to me. He's gone ahead to check out the cabin. He has some undercover cars covering all the roads up to the mountain top road. We won't know who they are, but they'll be on our bumper, in front and to the side of us, most likely."

With Eliza's instruction, they pulled out onto the mountain road and turned to the right away from Echo Valley. A blue car pulled in front of them and a white one was in back. As they passed by the college entrance, Jerrod slid down in the seat.

"Why're you doing that?" Rachel asked him.

"I still feel like I'm the target." He said. "If someone's watching the college and recognizes me, they'll follow us."

Eliza looked through the rear view mirror. "Silly, no one can see you in here. Even if they could, I'm sure the undercover people will be on the lookout for anybody following us. Believe me, when we get further up the mountain to the old ranger road, any vehicle is going to stick out like a sore thumb."

Rachel had a tug of recognition as they passed the fork where she had gone down by mistake that fateful day. A tan car sat at the stop sign. As they passed, she noticed that the white car behind them turned and left the entourage. Then the tan car pulled in behind them.

Her spirit draped over her like a cloud. She felt like she was being watched and turned to look into Jerrod's eyes. He smiled at her, and then he reached over and took her hand. "We're going to be passing by the Bence place going this way." He said.

"You've been up here before?" Rachel asked.

"Yes, I've driven a lot in the mountains. There are several small roads that wind in and around to the top and back down again. The road back there passes through the park and leads back to the main highway. The ranger road is up further."

Eliza said, "We could have taken that road back there for a smoother ride to the cabin, but it's a long way around. It leads to the new highway that was built after I left for Chicago."

"This is the shortest route and the best way to stay unnoticed. We could have gone back by the hospital and caught the highway up to a paved road that winds around and down to the community on the other side of the mountain as well. It's faster for people who live up there to get down to the hospital and downtown Echo Valley area."

Everyone became silent as a black car with blacked out windows came speeding by. They all leaned forward and all eyes followed it as it crested a hill. The license plate was unmistakable.

Jerrod pulled out his cell phone and did a fast dial. "Shoot. No service." He leaned toward Eliza. "That's the car that followed me last night, but I can't get a signal to let Greg know. Can you try with your cell?"

Eliza had her cell out and dialing as well.

Sam reached forward and started pushing buttons on a call unit of his dash. "Don't fret Jerrod. I've got it."
At just that time, Sam swerved toward a mountain bank. They all caught their breaths, startled and jostled by the near missed collision when another large black vehicle pulled in close to the hummer and sped around a curve.

Chapter Twenty Three

Sam spoke first. "Is everyone O.K.?"
The unison of "yes" confirmed that all was well.
"I can't stop here, obviously. There's not enough space."
The older man was hanging on tight to his wheel.
Eliza reached over and started pushing buttons on Sam's call system. "The car ahead of us is in chase. Look up ahead on the road."
Everyone looked up the mountain road. A blue car with bubble lights flashing on top was tail gating a black Mercedes.
A voice answered from the call unit. "Sam, what's up?"
"Hey, Greg. Your front cover car is in hot pursuit of the black car that just tried to run us off the road."
"Is the back car still behind you?"
"It is."
"Jerrod, is it the same car that chased you last night?"
The same license plate, Greg. Did you run that from last night?"
"But there were two black cars. The one from last night passed us and then this last one tried to run us off the road. I didn't recognize the make or model of either of them."
Sam spoke. "I see that one of your under covers just pulled the last jerk over on the side. It looks like the guy's giving up rather than go over the side of the mountain."
Greg's voice sounded relieved. "Good. Let the officer's handle that one and just get on up here."
There was static, and then Greg asked. "Is the tan car still behind you?"
Sam checked the rear view and everyone turned and looked back. In unison, everyone said, "Yes."
Jerrod asked. "What about the first car?"
Greg said. "I just signaled another car out to chase that one down. Don't worry, we'll get him."

The tan car kept going straight as the hummer pulled off onto the old ranger road. A covered jeep pulled in behind them.

As Sam pulled the Hummer in front of the cabin, Dog came bounding out across the yard with Trek right behind him. Both animals went to the business of sniffing the car tires and barking. Zeb came from around the backside of the cabin and called the dogs off.

Greg was nowhere to be seen and there were no other cars there except for Joe's jeep.

Eliza got out and introduced herself. "Thanks so much for taking care of things, Did Greg...Lieutenant Yoder fill you in on anything?"

"He's a Lieutenant? Army 'er what? Didn't hav' no uniform on." Zeb didn't wait for an answer. "A feller...Greg, yeah... Ah recollect he said he was, Greg Yoder. Said he was a friend. Said he jest wanted to make shore ever thang was up ta snuff fer ever body. He put one of them folding beds in the loft. "He looked around the group. " Ah guess ya'll be needin' it."

By the time the slow talking Zeb had finished his first sentence, everyone was out of the
Hummer. Sam got out and was helping Jerrod load the bags out onto the porch.

"I can't thank you enough for watching after the place and taking care of Dog."

"No worry, 'Liza. But my how you've changed since you was a youngun'." He turned and looked at Angela and Rachel as they got out of the car and joined the group. Jerrod stood behind them.

"'Ere these all yore younguns?"

"Well, not biologically. This is Angela, my niece and these are her friends, Jerrod and Rachel." " Ah, so Carrie must be yore mama." He said to
Angela. "And how's she?"

"Carrie passed away when Angela was born. I raised this one." She said as she hugged her niece to her.

Eliza realized at that point that Zeb not noticed the package with Carrie's urn sitting on the bed. At least, he didn't know what the package contained if he had seen it.

"Oh, Ah'm in remorse ta hear 'at."

He turned his attention to their driver, who was now leaning against his Hummer. "Who's 'at good lookin' feller or'er here?" He motioned to Sam.

Then he walked over and started inspecting the big square, but shining vehicle.

Sam laughed and said. "Well, I'm not exactly good lookin', but I'll take the compliment. I'm just the driver and I'll be heading back now."

Eliza turned to Sam. "Thank you so much, Sam. How much do I owe you?"

"Not a thing, Eliza. I owe Greg more than I can ever repay him. I think that most of Echo Valley can say the same. Good luck to everyone, and let Greg know I can drive for you again. I get a kick out of showing off my Hummer."

After Sam left, Zeb pointed to the vehicle at the side of the cabin. "Ah took the jeep 'tother day 'n give 'hit a test drive. Thar's plenty ah gas in 'hit. Ah took 'hit down ta the community station 'n the folks thar filled 'hit up fer free. Said thay was obliged ta yore daddy 'n ta tell ya'll how grieved thay 'ere about his passin'"

"Thank you, Zeb. Tell them that I appreciate it. But I'll repay them for the gas."

"Ah'll do 'at. But these mountain folk ere mighty proud. Thay won't take good to offerin' to pay fer what thay give in kindness."

Zeb's attention was drawn to the jeep that had followed them up. The driver had backed up into the tree line across the road. He pointed to the man still sitting in the driver's seat and talking on his mike.

"Who's 'at?" Zeb inquired.

Not knowing how to explain it, Eliza said, "He's going to be mapping out the place and helping us to make some changes to the cabin. We'll all be staying here for a few days, maybe a week. So you and your dog can take a break."

"Well, hit's pleasurable watchin' after my old friend's thangs. Me and the dogs, we've stayed at my place for the most part 'n jest hiked up here during the day ta check thangs out. Dog patrolled the property most all the time. Ah let him hav' his freedom 'n sometimes he jest disappeared, night or day 'n ah knowed he'd come up here lookin' fer Joe."

"You've done a wonderful job taking care of him, Zeb. How much do I owe you?"

"Now don't ye go offerin' up anythang for 'at. Thar's nothin' ah wouldn't ever do fer Joe or his'n. Ah hav' ah lot ta be beholden ta Joe fer. 'At remembers me. When 'er you funeralizin' yore daddy?"

"We're bringing Daddy's ashes up here and sprinkling them with Carrie's near where Mama's are. We'll let you know when we'll be doing that memorial service. You can invite all his friends to come."

"Wall, yeah. Ah reckon' Ah'd do 'at, but most mountain folks up here on Shady was a mite upset with Joe when he sent yore mama out lack 'at. Thay stayed his friend, but cremation's agenst the religion...'at is for religious folks up here, hit's a sin to put a body away like 'at."

Angela moved next to Eliza and took her hand. Eliza looked down at Angela. She noticed that Dog had stayed close by Angela's side for the whole time. Angela had been petting him and whispering to him.

Zeb turned and whistled. Trek came bounding out of the woods behind a rabbit. Dog's attention was distracted until the rabbit doubled back and disappeared into the woods again. Dog never left Angela's side.

Trek came trotting up beside Zeb. Zeb looked at Dog. "Now Dog's awares of somethin' 'bout 'at girl. He knows hit's Joe's kin."

Angela reached down and petted Dog's head, and she and Eliza exchanged looks and both were thinking the same thing. Dog recognized Angela's scent from when she was lying on the cabin porch all beat up that night.

Rachel moved closer to Angela. Eliza smiled at her. Then she looked toward the driveway and realized that Jerrod had gotten in the undercover car and the two guys were in deep conversation.

Zeb shuffled his feet, looked from Eliza to the Angela, and then out to the car. He whistled to his dog and said. "Well, Ah thank hit's time Trek 'n me got on back down ta my place. Ah jedge 'hit's gonna snow tanight. You let me know when I kin be of help agen. Thar's plenty ah firewood in the firebox in on the harth. But if thar's anythang else, I'll be jest on the 'tother side ah 'at radio in thar."

Eliza, Angela and Rachel stood and watched as Trek and Zeb disappeared through the woods at the side of the cabin. Dog stayed faithfully by Angela's side.

Jerrod got out of the car and headed toward the cabin. The undercover agent got out and followed him. Jerrod introduced the man as Detective Dan Bolger.

Eliza said, "Let's all go inside. I'll see if I can find something hot for us to drink. It's getting cold out here today."

The door closed behind them and they found places to sit around the great room. Eliza found that the wood stove was already stoked and a good heat was ready to put the cast iron kettle with water on the top. Then she opened up the cupboards and found the six tin cups that Daddy had always kept, some instant coffee, creamer and some tea bags.

Bolger said, "I'm waiting right now for a call from Yoder. He's giving me the latest on the people they're questioning from the car that tried to sideswipe the hummer. They still hadn't tracked the first car down yet, the last I heard."

Eliza sat down on a chair with a glass of water.

"So they've still got them in custody."

"Yes, all I know so far is that the driver and a passenger of that car are denying being a part of the Snow family, but Greg thinks they are."

"Ah, well that wouldn't surprise me." The pot whistled and Eliza served up the hot drinks, according to preference. She realized as she walked around the room that Angela was missing.

"Excuse me." She said as went to the front door. Opening it up, she looked down at Dog snuggled up to Angela as she sat propped up against the side of the cabin.

Eliza stepped out, closing the door behind her.

She sat down on the floor beside her. She brushed Angela's hair back away from her forehead. "Is this where your grandpa found you?"

Angela brushed tears from her eyes and combed her fingers through Dog's hair. "Yep. Dog knows. I've been pretending to be strong. It was easy to gloss my feelings over when I was in a different setting. Now that I'm right here, the reality of what happened is back. I can cry now. I can let it go."

"Are you sure that the memories are just too close here? Maybe I shouldn't have brought you back up here so soon."

"No, right here is where I feel close to grandpa." She patted Dog's side. "Dog and I have a positive memory of Grandpa right here in this spot."

Eliza and Angela sat with Dog for a few minutes. Neither said anything.

A whistle sounded and laughter exploded from inside the cabin.

"I guess we ought to go in. The police are questioning two people who were in the second car. We're waiting for Greg to call and give us the information."

Eliza helped Angela up. Dog barked, and then followed them inside. Jerrod was standing in front of the desk beside the fireplace.

Rachel was still giggling in the corner on a stool. "Jerrod just about jumped out of his skin. The ham radio whistled and he was sitting in front of it."

Bolger moved over to the desk from his seat on the cot. "That may be Yoder trying to reach us so that he can talk to us all at the same time. He said that he might try to signal us on the radio."

The whistle blasted again. Bolger picked up the receiver and called back. "This is Joe's cabin. Out."

"Bolger, is everybody there? Out."

"Yeah. What's up? Out."

"We got the studs who tried to sideswipe the Hummer. They're tough guys from out of Chicago. We've got 'em jailed for possession of a large amount of weed and about ten pounds of cocaine. They deny knowing anything about the Snows, or trying to scare you and Jerrod, but get this, they had an address book and a map of the county. You won't believe this one, but every x on the map was on the location of a Snow property. Out."

"So is there any word on the first black car? Out."

"Can I talk to Eliza? Out."

Eliza stepped over and took the receiver. She pressed the button. "I'm here. Out."

"We got the passenger to talk. He had a notebook in his shirt pocket. It had your name, your description, and the description of your car, right down to the plate number. He also had Jerrod's info on that page underneath a notation "Snow". Out."

Eliza looked at Jerrod and then at Angela who was sitting, like the rest of them, with mouth and eyes wide open.

"So do you think the Snows put that contract out? Out?"

"Well, they definitely had something to do with the whole mess. However, I need you to come back down here and check these guys out. I have a hunch that you knew them in Chicago. Out."

"I'll get the jeep ready. Out."

"You still have to have a guard. Stay there and I'll come and pick you up. I'm on the way. Out."

The radio was silent. Eliza turned and looked at the stunned group. She looked at Angela.

What could she say? "Angela, would you like some hot tea?"

Angela shook her head as if to shake off the reality of it all. "I'll get myself some, Aunt Eliza." She went to Eliza and hugged her. "But I want to go with you."

"I'll be safe, Angela. They've got the threat taken care of. Greg is just being overly cautious. Besides, Dog's not going to be happy if you get out of his sight. You're probably going to have to take him for a potty walk."

Angela looked down at Dog who was looking up at her with soulful eyes. "I see what you mean. O.K."

Eliza looked up to see Greg's car pull into the drive. She hugged Angela. "I won't be long." She said. Grabbing her jacket, she opened the door, waved at the others and left.

Angela looked over at Rachel who was sitting close to Jerrod on the cot. She stepped to the kitchen area and busied herself with making herself a cup of tea. Dog started growling deep in his throat and hovered at the back door. Angela looked up through the kitchen window. She turned half around, without taking her eyes from the window. She motioned with one hand for the others to come to look.

Bolger drew his pistol, moved close behind Dog, and peeked around the window frame. Everyone else crowded behind Angela and looked out. About three hundred feet away, on the rocky overlook ledge stood the most magnificent animal. In broad daylight, the Alpha Male stretched his neck out and lifted his nose skyward as snowflakes started falling down around him.

A chilling memory filled Angela from head to toe as the wolf's howl echoed down the valley.

As soon as the howl started, Dog went spastic and wound himself around Angela's legs.

Everyone was focused on the wolf as he finished his howl, turned and looked at the cabin, then faded into the woods to the side of the cliff.

Bolger put his gun back in the holster and shook his head. "I've lived in the valley and the mountains all my life. I've never seen or heard of anything like that. Not in broad daylight."

"What do you think it means?" Rachel asked. Angela knelt down and cuddled Dog. She started to cry. "Dog knows. I know."

Chapter Twenty Four

Eliza sat down in the observation room next to Greg and waited as two men were led into the interrogation room. She stared at the two men and said, "That's Ralph and Jason Masterson. Those sorry creeps must have served their time."
"So you know them from Chicago." "I do. I helped put them away several years ago. They didn't get enough time, obviously, or they wouldn't be out and in trouble again."
"What were they in for?"
"Possession and trafficking. Didn't you run their bio and fingerprints through the system?"
"I did. The results are not back yet. We don't have the latest in technology with all the computer programs." Greg looked deep into Eliza's eyes. One horrible thought came to his mind. "Did they threaten you?"
"What? Oh, yeah, they made the usual big, trash talk toward the whole legal team. Nothing I hadn't heard before. But I'd like to call my old law firm and find out what they know about all this."
"Then you ought to call Rachel and get with her. Looks like you're going to be helping to put them away again. While you're doing that, I'm going to get my team together to go over what we know about the Snow involvement in this."
"Is there any change in Herbert's condition?"
"Doesn't look too good for him. But from our perspective, the longer he's out of commission, the better."
"I agree. Can I use your office?"
"Sure. I'll show you the way."
Greg led her to the main office and to his office door. He let her in. "I'll be in a meeting with my team. When you're done, let Stella know." He turned and walked back down the hall.
Eliza sat down in the big chair and pushed the speed dial on her cell phone for her old office.

After several connections, she said, "Hello. This is Eliza."

After a pause, she spoke again. "Yes, I know, I didn't expect to be calling you so soon either. How is everyone?"

Eliza got up and walked back and forth looking out the front window as she listened to the voice on the other end.

"Well yes, actually I would like for you to check something out for me. Ralph and Jason Masterson. What's the..."

Eliza sat down as she listened. "Out on early releases?" She grabbed a pen on the desk and took some notes. Then she stepped back toward the window. "O.K. Leave a message at this number, 812-555-1395."

Redialing, she called Rachel's office. Rachel answered her phone with enthusiasm. "Eliza, I'm surprised to hear from you so soon. Are you ready to go to work?"

"No, but it looks like I've been brought in on a case." Eliza briefed her and ended the call.

When Eliza stepped out of Greg's office. Stella said, "Greg wants you to join the meeting. I'll show you the way."

'O.K. I'm expecting a call back from Chicago. Please let me know right away.'

"I will and I can send the call into the meeting room if you'd like."

"That would be super."

Eliza was aware of her tight fitting jeans as she stood before the meeting door. Not exactly dressed for my new profession. She thought.

Greg was giving the main report. He stopped and introduced Eliza as the District Attorney Assistant working on the case. Eliza nodded at the three detectives and took an empty seat at the nearest end of the table. She looked around at the officers who were dressed in varied forms of attire and decided that she fit right into this group.

"Eliza, we're discussing the Mastersons." He picked up a report copy and passed it to her. "The rap sheet was too thick to make copies."

"That's a copy of the report we just received on them. What did you hear from Chicago?"
"I'm sure it's all in the report here. Someone from that office is going to call back with anything new. If we're still in this meeting, Stella will send the call to us."
"I'll update you on what we know about what's going on right now. There's evidence that the Mastersons have been in cahoots with the Snow clan for a long time. They've been trafficking illegal drugs into the mountains for quite a few years. Their distributors here in the mountains have been identified as working under the direction of
Herbert Snow and his kin."
Eliza whistled one trill as she surveyed the report. "Oh what a tangled web they weave."
"Not only that, we also have evidence that members of the Snow family are responsible for the car theft rings, illegal gambling, prostitution, and moonshine operations and have been in operation since the clan immigrated here from
New York City in the early 1900's."
Eliza shook her head. 'Unbelievable. When I was growing up on the mountain, I never realized there were any crimes committed here."
Greg said, "I guess at that time, my dad had to deal mostly with moonshine. But in the last twenty or so years since you lived here, other crimes have developed."
"Guess Rachel's going to have her hands full for a few years yet. This mess is going to take a long time to get untangled and it's going to be hard to fight with a relative of the Snow's as the judge."
"Yeah, I guess that bunch has ties that run through the whole state. It's going to take some work to get this straightened out. But Rachel has you to help her get it done now."
"Thanks, but..." Eliza waved him off, and then turned toward the ringing phone in the middle of the table.
Greg motioned to one of the detectives who reached over and grabbed the phone.
"Yeah...Sure."

He handed the phone to Eliza. "This is Eliza Hardigan." She listened.

"Hello, Chad. Thanks for looking into this for me. Can you hold for a moment? I'm going to turn on the speaker."

She looked at Greg, who leaned over and pushed a button. She put the receiver in the cradle. "O.K. Chad, I want to introduce you to Detective Lieutenant Greg Yoder of the Young County police force at Echo Valley, Pennsylvania. He can introduce you to the deputy detectives."

"Hello, Lieutenant Yoder."

"It's Greg, please. Can I call you Chad?"

"You can."

"O.K. I have my three deputies here. John Davies, Mark Jones, and Lanell Graves. What do you have for us?"

"The Illinois governor gave the Mastersons an early release due to the overcrowding in our jails, along with a number of other creeps that are no doubt going to boomerang on us. I've faxed you another report on them. According to our latest information, the Master sons picked up a car at the airport that is registered to Eli Cromwell, a suspected drug lord here in Chicago. The car plates then underwent another change, when the title ended up as belonging to Benjamin Snow of Champaign, Illinois. The Mastersons are still on parole and I'd appreciate it if you held them on charges of parole violations. They're not supposed to leave the city, let alone the state."

"Snow, eh. Any chance Benjamin Snow could have roots in Pennsylvania or New York?"

"I couldn't say, but it's a possibility. When can we expect the Masterson's back here?"

"Well, I'd like to send them back to you right away, but I've got a few issues to settle with them first. We're going to be charging them with a couple of misdemeanors, and major felony charges."

"Hauling drugs were they?"

"They were indeed."

"Eliza, when you get done prosecuting our old friends, we'd like to add a few more years for parole violation. If we work hard enough as a team, we'll put these crooks away until they're ninety, if they live that long."
"That's just fine with me. Chad. I'll let Rachel Donovan, my new boss and the county prosecutor here, know that. I'll introduce her to you in our next call. Maybe we could set up a conference."
"Great and tell her that I'm never going to stop trying to get you back here. I don't know what they're paying you, but it's got to be good."
"Chad, you know I've never been materialistic.
It's not about money."
Greg looked over at her and smiled. That's my kind of woman. He thought.
Chad laughed. "Yeah, well, I'll never understand that, I guess. Anyway, keep in touch, Eliza."
"Same to you. I'll drop in when I come back to settle my apartment and affairs in the windy city."
"Looking forward to it, and Greg, please keep me up to date, as well. It's great to talk with you."
"You, too, Chad."
Greg leaned over and hit a button and the call was gone. He turned to the group. "Well, I guess there's no doubt in our mind what we need to do.
The call was taped, so we can have Stella type that report up and get it into the Masterson file. I want you, Davies to work with forensics on the reports, on the fingerprints and other evidence from the car that the Masterson's were driving. Jones, I need you to cover the reports and secure the drugs found in the car. Graves, you and I'll work together on interrogation of those two fools." The deputies dispersed to their assigned duties.
He turned to Eliza. "Well, Eliza, I guess you've started back to work sooner than you anticipated. Let's drive over and report to Rachel. Then I'll get you back to the mountain."

"Yes, I need to get back to Angela. I know that she's in good hands with her friends, but she's so vulnerable right now."
"Then let me take care of the report to Rachel."
"That would be good. I really don't want to deal with this until after the memorial for Daddy." " I don't blame you.
Greg took the main highway back up the mountain and then cut off through the community highway. He looked over at the reserved and quiet woman sitting in the passenger's seat. Eliza felt his stare and looked back smiling, a question in her eyes. "What?"
He summoned up his courage and said, "Eliza, you didn't say two words all the way down the mountain and you haven't said a word since we left my office. Is there something I can help you with?"
"Oh, Greg. I don't know. I'm thinking that I made a mistake in deciding to stay and keep Angela here."
"Why is that?"
"Angela's not handling things very well. She's trying to act brave, but she lost it today when we were at the cabin. I may have to rethink this whole thing." She sighed, and then continued. "I haven't yet brought up a really big fear to Angela. That is the possibility that she could be pregnant with her attacker's child."
Greg suddenly felt extremely depressed. He kept his eyes on the road, but his heart was in the driver's seat.
"I guess Chad will have your job open for you for a while."
"Yeah, even if it's not my old position, he'd have something for me." She gave a big sigh. "One minute, I'm confident that I've done the right thing and the next I think that I've made a big mistake. I just don't know what to do."
Neither of them spoke for a minute. Then Greg said, "Eliza, I think you ought to give it a few days on the mountain and grieve for your dad. Then you can face reality. The problems are just too overwhelming right now."
After a quiet moment, Eliza said. "I'm wondering about something, Greg. We both grew up in this area. How come we never met before?"

"What year did you graduate?"
"1980."
"I left high school in '77 and joined the marines and was stationed all over the world in one place or the other. I was still in the service in '91 when trouble erupted in the Middle East and I was there for two years before coming back here."
"Ah, well, that explains it. I went to school at our community school up through the eighth grade.
Then I bussed down to high school. You would've been out of school and out of town by then."
"So you didn't come to the valley for movies or to the doctor or anything?"
"No, even when Mama got cancer and had to come down to the clinic ever so often. My parents kept us on the mountain. My sister and I were late in life children. Mama was about eighteen years younger than Daddy. "
"I'm sorry I didn't get to know you sooner. But I guess things happen the way they do for a reason."
"And many of them are because of the choices that we make. You know why I chose to go to Chicago, why'd you make your choice to come back to the valley?"
Greg maneuvered the car onto the community road. "Well, my Dad was diagnosed with a bad heart and I knew he'd be having to retire soon. I wanted to keep the legacy going. When I got my discharge, the county was growing and the law enforcement team was hiring officers to help Dad. I signed on as a deputy and then when he had his fatal heart attack, I wanted to continue this fight against the Snow bunch. Besides, Mom needed me more than ever."
"You don't have any siblings?"
"No, I'm an only kid."
"No marriage or girlfriends?"
"No, never tied the knot. I had a serious girlfriend or two, but they couldn't take me being in law enforcement. And in this county, the women were either kin of the Snow Clan or afraid of that bunch of no goods."

"With any luck, the Snows have reached the end of their dynasty. With all that's been happening, I think that the honest, law abiding people finally have the upper hand."
"Whatever happens, I hope that you and Angela will stay here. I know that you have a lot of issues to deal with, but Mom and I are fond of both of you. Besides, putting the Snows and their kind away is going to take a long time."
Eliza didn't answer. She stared ahead at tree lines along the road as the darkness settled in. Once she thought she saw a large dog slip into the woods ahead of the car. As they passed, she was sure that large eyes glowed from the brush. As they turned into the drive, it was dark. Greg turned the car lights out before turning in to keep from waking people in the house. Flickers from the oil lamps flashed in the windows. As they got out and walked toward the front porch, something brushed against Eliza's leg. She shrieked and two figures jumped up from the porch swing.

Chapter Twenty Five

Eliza jumped closer to Greg and he put his arm around her.
"Who's there?" Greg said.
"It's me, Rachel."
"I'm here, too," said Jerrod.
"We were just out here talking." Rachel's words came fast and her voice was shaky.
Eliza stood with Greg's arm around her. She chuckled. "It's o.k., Rachel, Where's Angela?"
"She's in bed. She took the bed next to the window in the loft."
"Was she o.k.?"
"Eliza, I'm a little worried. I caught her taking her prescription pain pills three different times today. Do you think she could be getting addicted?'
"I hope not. I'll check her pills when we go in. It would be easy for her to get hooked. She's pretty vulnerable." Eliza moved away from Greg and started toward the cabin.
Rachel leaned toward Eliza. "Please don't let on that I told you. I don't want her to be mad at me, but I thought you needed to know."
Eliza turned back to Rachel. "Thanks for telling me. I won't break your confidence."
"Thanks, Eliza."
Jerrod stepped forward. "I think maybe the wolf incident might have had something to do with
Angela taking the pills today."
"Wolf incident?"
"She didn't want us to tell you." Rachel told the story of the wolf howling in the daytime on the cliff and everyone's reactions.
"That's spooky." Eliza remembered the big dog like creature she had seen on the roadside, and the eyes as they passed. She started to tell the story, but she didn't want to add to the fear. "By the way, where's Bolger?"

"He's staked himself out in his car in the wood clearing across the road."

Jerrod said, "He said that another guy will be relieving him at midnight, so we'll have someone else here in the morning ...and he said he felt more comfortable watching the cabin from the outside than sleeping on a cot in the house."

Greg spoke. "As long as you're covered. I believe that the danger is over. But I don't want to take any chances."

Eliza asked, "So what did Angela do after she got over the initial shock of seeing the wolf this morning?"

Rachel answered. "She took a pill and tried to make us promise not to tell you about what happened on the point. Then she took Dog for a walk with Bolger following them. As soon as she got back, she headed up the steps. She didn't say goodnight or anything. It was as if someone had deflated her... like pricking a balloon with a needle. Dog followed her upstairs and he's sleeping beside her bed."

"She's been in bed since just after I left?"

"Yep. Well, just about. We cooked hot dogs and corn on the cob. We tried to get her to get up and eat. About three this afternoon, she got up, fed Dog and took another pill. Then she went back to bed and back to sleep."

Jerrod spoke. "We lit all the kerosene lamps in the cabin, even the one in the loft. But with all our noise and the light, Angela just kept right on snoring."

Eliza turned to Greg. She took his hand. "I'm going in to check on her. Thanks for driving me back. I'll call you in the morning."

Greg reached over and put his arms around Eliza. "Hey, thanks for making the trip down." He squeezed her. "I'm there for you anytime, day or night. Just give me a call." He hugged her again and she hugged him back.

"Thank you, Greg. I really appreciate you."

He watched her until she disappeared into the light of the great room. Then he turned to Jerrod and Rachel. "You two stay inside now. Even if we don't have any problems from the two legged variety, that wolf's still out there."

Jerrod shook Greg's hand. "O.K. Thanks, Greg. You have my cell number. So call me if anything comes up or if you're worried. I plan on doing my part to keep these ladies safe."

"Don't get too brave, Jerrod. You have our force to rely on. You're going to make an excellent police officer, but remember you're just a cadet yet."

"I know...wet behind the ears. Don't worry, I won't do anything stupid."

Greg watched as the two walked to the cabin arm in arm. Jerrod dropped his arm and opened the door for her. The relationship was apparent to Greg when the door closed. He watched through the window as Jerrod pulled Rachel to him and kissed her. Rachel's arms went over Jerrod's shoulders. Greg felt like a window peeper and turned his back on the scene. He crossed the road and got into the car partially hidden in the bushes.

"Bolger, I hear the wolf spirit echoed his warning from the point today."

"I never thought I'd see what my great grandparents vowed was the truth."

"Me either. Maybe, it is not a wolf spirit. Maybe, we're just spooked."

Greg looked up at the light through the loft window. He wondered if Eliza had seen the wolf on the road and his eyes peering at them from the brushes as they passed. He hoped not. However, if there was something out there, it was a living, breathing animal.

His attention was drawn to the window facing the staircase. He could see Jerrod go into the bedroom and Rachel disappear into the loft.

Bolger was watching, too. "What do you think about those two?"

"Just hope Jerrod stays alert and focused tonight. If there's any trouble, he'll be in the thick of it. We both know that. So he'll need to have a clear head."

Bolger cleared his throat. "Are you going to head back home now?"

"I need to check up on Mom. Make sure you call at the first sign of trouble."

Bolger watched as Greg got in his car and headed down the community road. He looked up at the window at the shadow moving in the lamp light. He chuckled as the lamp light from upstairs moved back down the stairway. He could see Rachel slip through the bedroom door. He thought about what he had just seen. Is this the kind of trouble I'm supposed to report on? He laughed. He decided against it. He watched the light as it settled near a window in the bedroom.

Inside Eliza curled up close beside Angela. She lay quietly thinking about the pills that she counted in Angela's bottles. In her mind, she ran over her actions again. She had read the labels in the flickering lamp light. She replayed the opening of the sedative bottle and the counting of the small white oval pills into a small tray. She had looked at the label again. The label said that twenty-four pills were prescribed and no more than two pills a day were to be taken, as needed. There were only 16 pills left. If Angela had taken them as prescribed, there would be 20 pills left. Of course, Angela probably read the "as needed" and ignored the rest of the label. Anyway, that would mean that Angela had taken two more sedatives than she needed since Eliza had picked them up at the hospital pharmacy. The pain pill count may have been as directed, but she had no idea how many pills she had taken at the hospital.

Eliza found the artery in Angela's neck. She counted the pulse rate and estimated the time. The pulse rate was normal, but Angela's breathing was so deep and slow that Eliza had to get close to detect it. Eliza figured this was not healthy, but she was more worried about Angela's mental and emotional state than the two extra pills.

Eliza thought about the medications she had just now hidden in a secret cubbyhole that she remembered from childhood.

She hoped she didn't have to have a row with Angela, but she was not going to give them back to her until she called the doctor in the morning.

As Eliza drifted off, she thought she heard movement in the room. Then the lamp light dimmed and left the room. She willed herself to wake up and check things out. She followed the light from the great room and felt her way down the stairway. As she got half way down, Eliza saw Rachel sitting at the desk, bent over the wireless computer. Keeping her voice low, she said, "Rachel, what're you doing up so late?"

"I hope you don't mind that I took the loft lamp. Jerrod needed a lamp in the bedroom. I knew I wouldn't be able to sleep and I wanted to keep this one to work with here."

Eliza sighed and sat down on the cot. "I can't get relaxed myself."

"I logged into the college website, but I'm not having any luck with the password information you gave me."

"Well, I'm not too swift right now. Let me get some sleep. If you don't figure it out by morning,
I'll help you. But don't stay up too late."

Rachel turned and looked at Eliza. "Could I talk with you about something personal?"

"Sure, how can I help?"

"Jerrod and I are now a couple."

Eliza smiled. "I thought so."

"But Jerrod wanted me to stay in the bedroom with him tonight. I'm just not ready for that."

"Good decision. Is Jerrod pressing you?"

"No, I think he understands, disappointed, but resigned. But that's not what I really want to talk about." Rachel shifted on the chair. "I heard from Dianne and Stephan. My parents want us all to meet with them in their counselor's office. The counsel won't allow them to go to Ethiopia until they can get a better understanding of our personal family business."

Rachel annunciated "personal family business" with a whine. "When?"

"I don't know yet. Stephan's going to call me tomorrow to arrange to come get me when it's all set up."

"O.K. We'll have Greg drive you back down the mountain if we're still sequestered up here."

Rachel leaned in her seat toward Eliza. "What about you and Greg? Are you a couple yet?"

Eliza grinned and slapped her hand toward her.

"Haven't given it that kind of thought."

Rachel chuckled. "Of course, you haven't. But there's nothing wrong with it if you have."

"Didn't say that. However, my mind and life are just too busy for a relationship. Besides, I'll be working in the prosecuting attorney's office. That may cause some people to talk. In fact, that's one reason why I never had a relationship during my years in Chicago. The only people I had any close contact with worked in our office. There has always been a policy -against dating a co-worker or boss."

"Well, hopefully, people here will be supportive. I think they'll be saying positive things. You two deserve a life together. Angela was telling me that she was hoping that Greg and you could have a chance at happiness."

"Oh, so you and Angela have been discussing my love life."

"Well, we did... at Greg's cabin after we went to bed last night."

"And just what arguments can you submit that will support your case?"

Rachel laughed. "Oh, come on. You're a lawyer to the max, aren't you?

Eliza and Rachel were startled by the howl of a wolf from the direction of the point. The sound of Dog's growl made the two of them look toward the loft.

Rachel shivered and shook her head. "What's he trying to tell us tonight?"

Eliza laughed. "Probably it's a bad omen that Greg and I should be a couple."

"A lawyer that believes in the supernatural?"

"No, it's just my way of saying, it's time for bed and I don't want to give opponents of our county legislation any fodder. Try to get your mind sorted out, Rachel, and come on up to bed."
Jerrod peeked his head out the bedroom door as
Eliza headed up the stairs. He said, "Good grief,
That wolf was close by." " Probably out at the point again."
    Eliza said.
Jerrod looked toward Rachel. "I'm not decent or
I'd come on out."
"It's o.k. I'm going to bed now."
Rachel shut the computer lid and picked up the lamp. As she passed the bedroom door, she leaned over and gave him a kiss. Jerrod grabbed her arm and pulled her close to the door.
"No, Jerrod. That's not our agreement."
"I know, but a guy can try."
"Yeah, well, try to go to sleep." Angela hurled back at him as she continued up the staircase.
Outside, Bolger had been watching all the movement through the windows of the cabin. He had been surprised when Rachel left the bedroom. Then more surprised when she disappeared up the stairs to the loft. That said a lot for those two young people. He was impressed with Jerrod's restraint. He was going to make a fine police officer.
He thought about the wolf's howl. He wondered if the wolf population was going to be a problem for the farmers.
Wolves had been unheard of in the Alleghenies until the last few years. There hadn't been any reports of wolves feeding on farm animals. Some problems had been reported with the Coyote, but that problem was resolved by the hunters.
Wolves had stayed clear of humans and the recent sightings were unusual.
Bolger saw the lamp go off in the loft and the cabin was dark. His eyes adjusted to the dark around the cabin. Then he saw the movement cross the yard, very close to the porch.

He quickly turned on the headlights, illuminating the front of the cabin. At the same time, Jerrod and Dog shot out the door and chased after the man who was running down the road. Bolger started the jeep and pulled in behind Jerrod and Dog. The pursuit continued down the road and they all stopped at once. In front of the escapee, the largest wolf that Bolger had ever seen, stood with hair bristled up and in a charge position.

Dog stepped forward and continued past the man. Bolger couldn't believe his eyes at what happened next. Dog walked up toward the wolf. As Dog got near, the hair on both animals laid down.

They communicated in low grunts, and then Dog turned and stood by the wolf. They both bristled their hair up and assumed attack position toward the man.

Bolger got out of the car with his gun cocked, and moved slowly toward Jerrod, standing barefoot with just his under shorts on. The man started slowly retreating. Bolger was sure that the animals would attack at this point, but they stood their ground. When the man backed up beside Jerrod and in front of Bolger, the look on Jerrod's face told Bolger that this was someone familiar. Bolger grabbed the man from behind and clapped handcuffs on him.

Jerrod spoke. "What in blazes are you doing out here, Brent Morse?"

Brent had not taken his eyes off the animals. He remained silent. Jerrod and Bolger looked back toward where the canine team stood. Dog nudged the wolf and grunted. The wolf turned and ran off into the woods

Chapter Twenty Six

As Bolger turned Brent around and headed him to the jeep, shadows appeared from the side of the road. Dog ran toward them. He licked Angela's hand as she stepped out into the car light.
Brent stopped and Bolger held him tight.
Angela walked up to Brent and stared into his eyes. "What are you doing here? I thought you were in jail where you belong?" She snarled at him. Dog was growling low.
"I'm out on bail...Angela, they've been keeping me from seeing you."
Angela slapped him hard in the face and turned away. Brent tried to pull toward her, but Bolger held on. Dog lunged at Brent and gave a warning bark.
"Why did you do that?" Brent yelled.
"You allowed your cousin to beat me up and rape me." She yelled back. "You almost destroyed my life. I'm not giving you the pleasure of hurting me again... You're scum."
"You've got it wrong, Angela." Brent yelled.
Bolger nudged Brent into the back seat of the jeep.
Angela turned back and ran into Eliza's arms. She choked back her sobs. "I'm not going to break down again." She was breathing and talking in short shaky gasps.
Rachel walked behind them as they headed back to the cabin. "I'm so proud of you, Angela."
Jerrod stood behind the jeep and watched the three women and the dog in the moonlight, until a cloud cover brought rain pelting down.
Jerrod stepped over to the driver's side of the jeep and spoke to Bolger. "I've got to get inside the cabin before I catch pneumonia. I'll call you later." Bolger put down his radio mike. He looked Jerrod up and down and laughed. "Yeah, I guess you didn't take time to dress for the weather. Get in and I'll back up to the cabin door."

Jerrod dripped all over as he slid into the passenger seat. "Sor-ry... to make your car... seats wet." He stammered as he shook.

"It's o.k. They're leather. But I'm getting a shower."

Brent spoke up through the cage panel from the back seat. "Hey, Jerrod. Get them to let me loose, you back stabber. You know I'm innocent."

Bolger stopped the jeep as close to the cabin door as he could.

Jerrod said, a little less shaky, "Do you want me to sit here with you 'till your relief comes?"

Bolger said, "No, Lanell's coming early. He'll stay and I'll take this one down for questioning. I'll get back with you in the morning. You'd better get inside and get dry clothes on."

Jerrod looked at the cabin windows. The lamp was lit in the bedroom and the only other light was filtering down from the staircase.

"O.K. Thanks for all you've done tonight." Jerrod opened the door as Brent yelled out at him.

"Tell Angela to go to hell, you little prick."

Jerrod shook his head as he ran for the cabin door. "What an idiot." he said out loud as he opened the door.

"Who's an idiot?" Rachel said as she was making her way down the steps with a kerosene lamp. "I found another lamp upstairs." She said.

Jerrod jumped and held his arms out. "Want a hug?" He grinned.

She jumped back. "No. You drenched duck." She said. "Go get some dry clothes on." She added as she pushed him toward the bedroom.

Rachel laughed. She felt her warm face as she headed for the kitchen area. "Looks like you've been working out."

"What was that?" Jerrod called from the bedroom.

"Nothing." She said.

Rachel went to the wood stove, stoked up the dying embers, and put in some more kindling. By the time Jerrod came into the room, dry and dressed, Rachel had hot water for tea.

She smiled at him. "Hey, you look like you might survive that fiasco."
Jerrod stopped close to her and gathered her up in his arms. "I've got a lot to sort out about all that.
It was the weirdest thing I've ever seen."
The couple broke apart as another voice was heard. "Fill us in on the rest of the story, Jerrod. We won't be able to sleep until we hear every detail." Angela said.
"O.K. But let's get settled down here."
Eliza and Angela took the last steps from the stairway and everyone found seats around the great room with cups of hot tea. Dog ran to the door, sniffing.
Angela followed him. "Do you have to go out, Dog?" She opened the door. Dog started then backed up and looked up at Angela. He whined, "Well, I guess I'm going to have to go out with you." She said.
Jerrod came and looked out the door toward the trees on the other side of the road. "Bolger's out there, Angela. He's got Brent secured in the back seat. You'll be safe to go out with Dog. I'll go with you as well."
Jerrod stepped out behind Angela onto the porch, and they left the door open. Jerrod said, "Another deputy, Lanell, is going to be coming out to relieve Bolger and Bolger will take Brent on into town."
Dog ran to the edge of the woods, and then shot out across the road. A flash of lightening lit up the trees.
Rachel stepped out carrying a lamp. She said.
"That's further than Dog's gone away from you,
Angela, since the beginning."
Dog could be seen running and sniffing around Bolger's car. Jerrod said, "I hope nothing's wrong over there."
Angela said, "There isn't or he'd be going spastic. He's just checking things out. It makes me feel creepy. That means that Brent can see me."
Jerrod shook his head, "Maybe not. The trees limbs hang low there, so maybe he can't see well from the back seat. If he can, he's probably just seeing shadows."

Angela looked back at Jerrod. "So what made you and Dog go barreling out of the cabin like that…what alerted you?"

"There was a noise and when I looked out, I saw a shadow creeping toward the door. Dog must have heard it too. He came bounding down the stairway and just about knocked me over when I opened the door. Bolger saw us, I guess and we were all in pursuit."

"The noise sure brought the rest of us out of the house. " Angela said. "I wish that Deputy Lanell would get here so that Bolger could get that creep out of here."

Suddenly a rabbit streaked across the road with Dog right behind him. Everyone gasped and then started to laugh. They watched as the animal disappeared behind the house.

Eliza stepped outside. "What happened after Dog went barreling down the steps tonight?" She asked. "The noise was so loud that it woke Angela."

Jerrod related the story of the wolf and Dog.

Rachel watched him intently as he spoke. Eliza and Angela kept looking at each other as Jerrod talked about the unusual understanding between Dog and the wolf.

Eliza took a sip of her tea from the cup she still had in her hand. "Angela, do you want to tell the group what I found upstairs."

Angela pulled a book out of her pajama pocket.

"It's my mom's diary."

Rachel stepped closer to Angela with the lamp.

She asked, "Where'd you find it?"

"Aunt Eliza found it someplace up there. She won't tell me where."

Eliza said, "There are passages in the diary that I think Angela should share with you."

Angela moved to the lamplight, opened the book, and started to read.

July 10, 1979
"I found some wolf pups today. The Park

Service says that wolves don't exist in the Alleghenies. The locals say that the wolf howls are ghost, haunts of ancestors long dead. Nevertheless, these are real wolves. They were out in the woods near the caves. I started to go near, but Mama Wolf came back. I watched them for a while. Mama Wolf spotted me and stared at me for a long time. She looked thinner than she should. I heard Daddy say that food for the wild animals was scarce this year. I stayed quiet. She seemed restless and I could hear a low growl. I was afraid she'd come after me, so I backed away slowly and ran for home. I think she's in tune with my spirit. I'll visit her again tomorrow. I'll take her some food. I think she'd like that. "

Angela stopped and turned the page and read on.

July 11, 1979
"Mama Wolf was standing alert at her cave door when I went today. I stood and stared at her. She stared back. It was as if our souls connected. I took a dead rabbit that was in Daddy's trap and laid it as close to the cave as possible. Mama Wolf waited until I left, then she sniffed it. I was afraid she'd reject my offering, because some farmers poison meat to kill wild animals that frighten them.
I watched her from the wood line and she finally started to chew on the rabbit. Then she looked up at me. Raising her neck to the sky, she howled, as if to dismiss me and say thank you.
As I was about to leave, a dog...I'm sure it was a dog, came and stood at the top of the ridge. It looked like the young male German Sheppard, Bailey, Eliza brought home from Joan Davis' house that last year before Mama died. Daddy wouldn't let her keep it, because Mama sneezed every time the dog came near her. Eliza tried to find a home for him. One day when we came home from school, Bailey was gone."

Angela closed the book. She looked down at Dog as he returned to her side. "I think there's a connection between the German Sheppard in Grandma's diary and Dog." Dog rubbed his head on Angela's legs.

Eliza said. "Dog was a stray. Daddy told me about how he picked this little German Sheppard mix pup up on the side of the road. He could have been dropped off there, but his mix could be half wolf."

Jerrod said, "It would explain why the wolf hasn't been vicious or threatening to people or farm animals."

Dog started panting fast and looking down the road. He became restless and hopped around barking.

"Listen," said Jerrod. "A car is coming."

Headlights signaled the arrival. The headlights stopped in front of the house just short of where Bolger was parked. Everyone watched as the black car backed into the trees.

Eliza almost dropped her cup of tea. "Is that the car…?"

Jerrod stopped her. "No, it looks like it in the dark. But that's just Lanell's undercover car."

"Whew." Eliza turned toward the door as lightening lit up the sky. The two cars were visible in the light for that second.

"We'd all better get inside and try to get some sleep." She said as they all watched Bolger's car head away down the road.

Angela laughed. "I think I've had enough sleep."

Rachel hugged her after they passed through the door. "Do you feel better after unloading on Brent?"

Thunder clapped loudly and a lightning strike lit up the whole cabin. Dog wrapped himself around Angela's legs.

"Wow. That was close." She said. She turned toward Rachel. "Yes, I somehow feel in control, now that I've vented on that creep."

Rachel smiled. "Isn't it amazing how much we've had to grow up in the last weeks?"

Angela hugged her. "You have that right."

Jerrod sat beside Rachel on the cot. He looked across the room at Eliza who was sitting near the fireplace in a wood and hemp-rope bottom chair.
"Did your dad make that chair?" He asked.
"Yes, daddy was very handy with his hands that way. He made all the furniture in the house. He loved to carve and made all the toys for Carrie and me. We always knew that he was Santa, but we never told him that. When Carrie was very little, she would argue with me that Daddy had a hidden sleigh and reindeer in the woods. She was sure that the furniture and toys that he had carved and stashed in his workshop to the side of the cabin were for all the little boys and girls all over the world. She insisted that we should be helping to make some of those toys...like Santa's elves. Mama started teaching us how to make quilt dolls like the ones that were under our tree every year."
"You mean, like the ones that are upstairs on the shelves?" Rachel asked.
"Exactly. Those were made by Mother. The ones we made disappeared, and we thought that our Santa Dad had probably delivered them to other boys and girls."
Jerrod pointed at the mantle where there was a line of small and large animal figurines. "Did your dad whittle the figurines?"
Eliza got up and stepped to one-step to the mantle. She picked up a large wood craving of a wolf and ran her fingers over the smooth surfaces. "This looks exactly like our wolf as he's howling on the point."
She took the figurine and handed it to Jerrod.
"What a fine made piece. It's so much better than the work that I've seen in the handicraft shops in town, and that's saying a lot."
He handed the object to Rachel. She examined it quickly and handed it to Angela.
Angela smoothed her fingers over the wood. "Brent gave me a carved doll that I thought was beautiful. He made it on a lathe in workshop class.

It was not made nearly as well as this piece."
Rachel looked at Eliza. "What's going to happen to Brent?"
"I can't say for sure without looking at the laws for this state more carefully. But I know that he violated his bail by coming up here against the restraining order."
Jerrod asked. "Are you going to be involved in prosecuting him?"
"Probably not in court, but I may be asked to help with the paperwork leading to the trial. I won't be working on anything until after the memorial service."
Angela handed the figurine back to Eliza.
"When is that going to be?"
"Your granddad's ashes will be brought up on Saturday. You and I will get together and plan the service for Sunday. I'll be reporting to the prosecutor's office on Monday."
As Eliza placed the figurine back on the mantle, Dog ran to the back door and started whining. Everyone gathered at the window and peered out as lightening lit up the whole mountain top in repeated strikes.
The eerie silhouette on the mountain ledge flashed, and the howl reverberated down the mountain from the magnificent animal on the point.

Chapter Twenty Seven

Mournful sounds of "How Great Thou Art" flowed from Eliza's computer that sat on a nearby picnic table behind the cabin. The music echoed down Shady Mountain. The beautiful choral melody could be heard by a small group of mourners standing on a trail near where they could see the "Outsiders."

Zeb turned to his neighbors. "I shorely understand ya'll can't brang yerselves ta assimilate with Joe's kin 'n all, but I'd be obliged if'n ya'll wouldn't hold hit aginst me fer goin' ta say my regrets."

He turned and finished the end of the trail and stood beside Rachel, Jerrod, Greg and his mother as they faced Eliza and Angela. Eliza and Angela smiled at Zeb and Eliza nodded her head at him.

He smiled and nodded back at her.

Behind Rachel stood Julie, Dean Johnson, Sadie, and Joanna. They all looked toward the man who had just joined them.

Standing side by side with their backs to the point, Eliza and Angela waited for the last note to end. Dog stood between Eliza and Angela.

Eliza looked down at the bronze urn in her hands. She read, "Joseph Hardigan, Jan. 1, 1913 to November 13, 2000."

Angela held a silver urn with pink flowers engraved around the cup, the stems leading around the center plaque. She said. "Carrie Lee Hardigan Pike, December 9, 1965 to December 10, 1983." Angela looked up and spotted Stephan and

Dianne as they walked up. They had their fingers on their lips to shush her from alerting Rachel. From behind them walked David and Dorothy.

Eliza smiled at the growing group and then settled her eyes on Zeb. "I want to start by extending our gratitude to all of you for coming out to this ceremony. A special thanks to you, Zeb, for being Daddy's friend, for being there with him when he passed on and for taking care of Dog and the cabin." Zeb smiled and nodded at her. She looked to the side down the trail. "I know that this goes against the beliefs that some of the community hold deep in their souls and I appreciate their respect of our beliefs. You're all true Christians and God will bless you for your humility and understanding."

Eliza drew a trembling breath and then started. "Joseph Wilson Hardigan was born the son of Joseph Wilson Hardigan, Sr. and Miriam Geneva Graves Hardigan on January 1, 1913 at home in Coaltown, West Virginia. He worked his way through High School and then worked for the forest service while he attended Virginia University and graduated in 1933 with a degree in Forestry. He taught for twenty years at Virginia University where he met Jessie Mae, they eloped, and the two were married on June 1, 1953. His life's dream was to live in nature. He accepted a position with the Echo County Forest service in August of 1953, and moved here to this land where he and Jessie lived in a tent for the first summer while Zeb and some of the other forest service people built this beautiful cabin. On October 21, 1960, I was born, then on December 9, 1965, Carrie Lee was born. Eighteen years and one day later, December 10, 1983, Carrie passed away.

Today, we are honoring the wishes of my father, and according to his will, we are scattering his ashes from the point where the ashes of his wife and our mother were scattered after her death on December 9, 1976. We are also here to honor Carrie and our mother, Jessie."

Eliza drew a deep breath in. "I want to take a few moments to remember our mother. Jessie Mae Jaynes Hardigan was born July 21, 1930 to Veronica and George Jaynes in Virginia. She passed away December 9, 1976. She was 46 years old. As a vibrant mother and wife, she was active in quilting and soap making and belonged to the Eastern Star.

She was a Sunday School teacher at the Shady Mountain Methodist Church. Joe and Jessie lived their dream until one spring she found that she had cancer. For five years, Jessie fought her battle with Joe working from morning through many nights as a Forest Ranger and Caregiver.

Tears welled up in Eliza's eyes and her voice shook as she continued. "I was 17 years old when Mama passed away and Carrie was 12 years old. I remember the day that Daddy, Carrie and me stood on the point and had a little private service for her. After the service, Carrie said, "Bring my ashes here, and spread them with Mama's when I die." At the time, I thought that Carrie was just being dramatic. Since I was older than she was, I never thought that she would be the one who joined Mama first. As for Daddy, he seemed indestructible. He was vibrant. There was never a trail that he couldn't cover in a day's time. When I saw him again after I had been gone for 19 years, I could see the aging, but he still had that same vibrancy. He walked a little slower, pure white had taken over his once auburn hair and beard, but he was still walking trails." She stopped to wipe away the tears. "He tried to get me to stay and walk a trail with him the day he died." The dam burst and Eliza and Angela stood sobbing. Greg walked forward and stood between the two women. He put his arms around them both and pulled them close to him.

Their tears subsided as they wiped their faces with one hand, holding their precious containers close with the other. Eliza spoke again. "If anyone here would like to say something, please feel free to step forward. You're welcome to share a memory if you'd like."

It was quiet. Then Eliza looked toward Zeb. "Zeb, I would love it if you could share a story or two with us. I remember you when you were a ranger with Daddy. He thought a lot of you and you probably knew him better than I did."

Zeb looked toward the trail where the community group had walked closer to the ceremony. One of the men nodded his head, "Yah." and Zeb stepped forward. The community group walked closer.

Zeb looked at Eliza. "Ah 'member yore paw from 'afore you was born, Liza. Him 'n Jessie labered hard ta git this here place built. Thay never thowt thay'd ever have younguns. But the Lord allowed the two of 'em needed a blessin' 'n he sent the purtiest lil' dark haired babe 'at you'd ever want ta see. Yore Daddy'd show you off by stickin' his fangers in the curls on 'at lil' head ah yore's 'n tell you ta dance. You'd spin 'round 'n 'round 'n ever body'd laugh. 'Hit was warmin' ta see how much he loved you 'n yore lil' sister when she come along."

Eliza stood smiling and wiping tears as Zeb talked. He wiped his face with his kerchief, and then he continued. "Joe Hardigan wasn't much of a church goer, but he was the straightest man on this here mountain. Ah always knowed ah could trust him with my life. Weren't nothing' he wouldn't do fer anybody. Weren't no human truer than Joe Hardigan."

Eliza and Angela were surprised to see the man who had nodded his o.k. to Joe step forward. He said, "Joe saved my little ones life. He was walking a trail and come past our house. My lil" Grayson had crawled into the hawg pen on the side of the trail. A sow was in thar' with all her new piglets. Joe jumped into the pen 'tween that sow 'n Grayson n' got that sow ta run after him with them piglets. Now sows kin run fast fer thar size. So Joe was really hoofin' it. Ah was able ta crawl inta 'at pen 'n grab Grayson. Then when Ah hollered, "Got 'em Joe. Now git outta 'at pen.', Joe run ta the rail fence 'n climbed out." Ah could never thank 'at man enuf n I'll never forgit 'em. So when ah got 'at newer truck, ah drove 'at old one up here 'n give it ta 'im. He made a fuss over takin' hit, but ah tol' 'im 'at ah'd be put out if he didn't take my offerin' of thanks fer savin' my youngun'."

The man stepped back to his group. Eliza noticed that the two women had been staring at the urns and frowning. She figured that they were probably more curious than anything. One of the younger women walked closer to stare at the kaleidoscope display on the computer screen. She counted six men in the group. All of them except one were wearing overalls. One man stood out in his suit pants and white dress shirt. He stepped forward.

"I'm Dan Raeburn. I'm not a native of the mountain. I've only been here for about 15 years. But I fast grew to respect your dad. One day before Joe got his truck or his Jeep; Joe came down to the community store and bought his month's groceries and supplies. He had me cash his pension check and then when he got home, he went through his purchases and did his bookwork. He realized that I had made a ten-cent mistake in his favor. He walked the hour walk all the way back to the store to pay me that ten cents. I told him that he didn't have to do all that, but he insisted."

Eliza smiled as she listened to the people. She waited for a moment. Then she said, "Thank you for sharing all your stories. You don't know what wonderful gifts those are. Does anyone else have a story?"

One of the older women stepped up. "Ah come up here 'n helpt take kere of yore mama when you and yore sister was at school."

Eliza laughed and said, "Yes, I remember you. You're the lady that Mama named me after. Eliza Ann Cahill. Isn't that right?"

The old lady nodded her head. She started to walk toward Eliza and then looked down at the urn she was holding and stopped.

Eliza noticed her reaction, but kept smiling. "Thank you for taking such good care of Mama." She said.

The old lady smiled and nodded. "Hit were my pleasure. Them two was the finest God ever made."

"Thank you, Mrs. Cahill. Thank all of you." She took a deep breath and turned back to the group. "Now I'd like to remember Carrie."

"Carrie was born on December 9, 1965. She went to Kinsey Community Elementary School and graduated from Echo Valley High School in 1982. She was bright and creative. She excelled in college classes in art at Echo Valley Community College. Carrie passed away at Butterworth Hospital in Chicago Illinois, one day after she gave birth to a beautiful baby girl. Her daughter, Angela, and I brought her here to join her spirit with her father and mother.
Rachel stepped forward and stood beside Angela. She opened up Carrie's diary and held it for Angela to read. Angela looked up at the group and her voice quivered. "I never got to know my mother. She died giving me life. I will always be grateful for her sacrifice and that she left the legacy of my grandfather. Her dying wish was that Aunt Eliza raise me and keep me safe. You see, she knew that Aunt Eliza would sacrifice her right to her own children in order to honor that wish."
Angela's tears flowed and Rachel handed her a tissue. Angela regained her composure and continued. She looked down at the diary. "Mother left this diary and I would like to read this entry to you. She wrote this poem when she was 16. It is entitled, "Echo from Shady Mountain."

"Howls of the alpha wolf dog
Send a mournful trumpet sound
Out of the thick blue fog
Across the valley and every mound.
The music of the mountain Sends shivers in the wind.
Rushing water over Crystal Fountain
Through Allegany Glens.
He knows, the wise wolf dog knows
As his warning echoes mournfully
Through the valley and the coves,
While his wolf mate waits soulfully,
Listening, protecting her pups
From predators and wicked foe
The humans who would climb up

From Echo Valley down below.
At night the wolf dog's pleading
Haunts me in my dreams
His time and cause is fleeting
Help him stay free, I scream.
No matter where my spirit flees
The Echo from Shady Mountain
Will forever follow me."

Angela stopped speaking and stared down at the urn with tears flowing, as Rachel closed the diary.
Eliza spoke again. "Our father had a hard time trying to balance fatherhood, caretaker, and childcare. He left most of the rearing of Carrie to me. After Mama died, Joe continued his job as a Forest Ranger and retired at the age of 75, staying on here at the cabin. He still volunteered for many projects for the forest service.
Eliza looked down at Dog who was now lying beside Angela's feet. "One day, he was walking on one of the trails and came upon a German Sheppard mix pup. He named him Dog and from that moment forward, he and Dog were constant companions"
At the mention of his name, Dog's ears perked up and he stood and watched Eliza as she continued.
"When Carrie and I were young, while mother was sick, a friend of mine gave me a little German Sheppard pup that I named Bailey. It's a long story, but one day the pup disappeared. We took Dog to a vet the other day and the vet says that Dog could be descended, as we surmised, from one of the wolf pups. Daddy would be so happy to know that his Dog is protecting his granddaughter."
Eliza wiped her tears, looked at Greg, and nodded her head. He walked over to the picnic table where his guitar laid. He picked it up and strummed the strings, then he started the opening chords and sang a baritone version of "Go rest high on the mountain...." a song by his favorite country singer, Vince Gill.

Rachel felt Jerrod's arm around her. She looked out across the yard to where her family stood. She spotted Stephan and Dianne and smiled. She had to fight to contain her joy at seeing them. Then she looked to the side. She almost dropped the diary.

The last people she expected to see were her parents. Jerrod guided her to a spot in the front row.

Greg strummed the last chords of the song and laid the guitar down.

Angela turned as she realized that Eliza had turned around facing the point. Eliza reached over and took Angela's free hand. They started walking to the point. Dog was walking between them.

Eliza and Angela reached the edge of the point. They knelt together and sat the urns in front of them. The group stood and watched as the two figures knelt with their long black coats spread out behind them. Then they opened the urns together and leaning out they scattered the ashes over the edge of the point.

Dog stood and stretched his neck up toward the sky and his howl echoed across the valley. Eliza and Angela left the urns, stood, and hugged each other.

Dog stopped his howl and walked over beside Angela and the three figures started their walk back to the group. The black dresses and capes floated in the wind taking away any signs of debris from the leaves.

Eliza looked out toward the trail and realized that the community people, except for Zeb had left.

Zeb spoke to those close to him. "At's the first time I ever knowed of Dog howling lak 'at. Look at 'im. He looks lak a wolf. Jest lak 'at wolf 'at runs these here hills."

Jerrod felt a chill run down his back as he remembered the wolf and Dog facing off Brent Morse. "How long has the wolf been seen around the mountain?"

Zeb said, "Well now, thar's allais been packs ah wolves 'round these here mountains, even though the gov'ment denies it. But jest lak 'at poem 'at Carrie wrote, hit's

believed 'at a Sheppard dog mixed with a wolf runs here-a-abouts 'n ah believe 'at Dog thar is a off sprang. Yes, sir, Carrie knowt
'bout hit when she was jest a youngun' "
Jerrod looked at Greg who had been listening to Zeb.
Well, that explains what happened between those two animals that night. He thought.
Rachel stepped forward to hug Angela and Eliza as they returned to the group. As Rachel dropped back, she looked into her mother's eyes.
"Hello, Sweetheart." Rachel let her mother hug her.
"Rachel, you're so tense. This has got to be a stressful day. That service was so ungodly."
Rachel gasps. Stephan and Dianne were immediately on each side of their mother. They guided her back and away, but not before Eliza and some of the others heard the remark. She was aware of Joanna, Sadie, Julie and Dean Johnson standing nearby within earshot.
Rachel looked at Angela and Eliza. "I'm so embarrassed. I apologize for my mother."
Eliza hugged her. "It's not for you to be embarrassed, Rachel. You can't control what another person does."
Joanna took the steps toward Rachel and Angela and hugged each of them. "If you need to talk, I'm available anytime."
Angela hugged Joanna tightly. "Thank you so much for being so supportive of us during all of this."
"That's o.k. I'm very proud of how much you've grown and how strong you two girls are. Your grandfather would be so proud." She said and turned her attention to Eliza, who had turned and had been talking with Dean Johnson.
The two women and Dean Johnson stood talking as Julie stepped forward and hugged the two girls. She spoke to Rachel. "It's so good to have you back, roommate. Maybe things will settle down now."
"Thanks Julie, for all you've done."
"You're welcome. Are you coming back to the dormitory tonight?"

"No, I've got to get this session settled with my folks counselor tomorrow. But I won't miss any classes."

Dean Johnson stepped forward and hugged the girls. "I'm so proud of you young women. Let me know if I can be helpful to you in the next few weeks as we wrap up the semester."

Angela spoke. "Thank you for all your understanding and help in keeping us up to date on our college classes."

"You're so welcome. We all have to get back down the mountain. We'll see you when you get back on campus."

Angela and Rachel hugged all of them one more time. Eliza thanked them again and shook hands with each of them.

As Rachel and Angela watched the college friends leave, Rachel noticed that Stephan and Dianne were walking around the corner of the cabin with her parents. She looked at Angela. "Excuse me, I'll be back."

Jerrod put his arm around Rachel and they hurried to catch up with Rachel's family. Stephan and Dianne had their parents in the car before Rachel and Jerrod could reach them. Dianne hugged Rachel. "We're so sorry, Rachel. They were so convincing when we met with them today. They were upset that you hadn't come to meet them and insisted that they could handle coming to the service."

"It's not your fault. I know how it is. I realize that it's going to take a long time before I'll be completely comfortable with our parents again."

Stephan spoke to Jerrod. "Jerrod, we're feeling so grateful to your family for convincing mother and father to see counselors. But it's going to take a lot longer than we thought."

They all turned and looked as they heard the car doors open. Dorothy and David were climbing out of the back seat from either side of the car.

Dianne and Stephan rushed to the side of the car. Rachel said, "Wait, let them get out. I'll talk to them."

Rachel walked toward her parents who were at this time standing in front of the car. David got to Rachel first. "Your mother and I have to get back and get packed for our trip.

However, we need you to come meet with our counselors. Will you go with us now?"
"I'll be down tomorrow, Father."
Stephan said, "Father, it's Sunday. Your next appointment with Reverend Gray is tomorrow.
Rachel can come join us for that meeting."
Dorothy sighed. "Stephan, you and Dianne are going to lose your jobs if you keep taking off like this."
"We have everything taken care of Mother.
Don't worry about it."
Dianne said, "Come on Mother, Father."
Rachel looked at her mother as Dorothy fixed her eyes on the woods beside the cabin. She looked to see what Dorothy was looking at, but saw nothing there. Dorothy put her hand on her husband's arm. "David, let's go. There's evil here."
David looked down at his wife and patted her hand. He led her to the back seat of the car, opened the door, and helped her in.
Stephan and Dianne hugged Rachel. Dianne said, "I think we're going to need more than counseling for mother."
Rachel nodded her head. "I agree. Maybe for the both of them."
Rachel bowed her head and sighed. Then she looked up. "As for travel, haven't they missed the departure date on their airline tickets?"
"Yes, but they still think the tickets are good. We'll call you tomorrow morning and set up a time when we can meet with the counselor."
"That'll be good. We're all leaving the cabin tonight to go stay at Greg's place on the lake. Eliza starts work tomorrow."
Rachel gave her siblings a last hug and waved goodbye as they closed the car doors.
The car backed out and disappeared down the community road. Rachel and Jerrod were silent and stood watching until the car was out of sight.

Angela and Dog joined them, followed by Eliza and Greg. Rachel looked around toward the back of the cabin. She asked, "Where's Zeb?"
"He's gone back to his cabin."
"What about Dog?"
"We're going to attempt to take him to the lake with us. I don't think we'll have a problem with that as long as he's close to Angela."
Angela knelt down and Dog licked her face. "Dog, you're not going to mind leaving the mountain for a while, are you?"
Dog hopped around and made circles as he ran toward the woods. Angela said, "No, Dog. I cannot go with you. Come back. You can go with us.
We'll come back another day."
Dog ran into the woods. "Dog! ...Dog!" Angela yelled frantically. She whistled and ran toward the woods.
Eliza yelled. "He'll come back before we leave, Angela. Let him be."
Angela walked back slowly, turning to look toward the woods where Dog disappeared. *No, he won't. He won't leave Grandpa.* She thought as she got into the passenger's seat of Eliza's car.

Chapter Twenty Eight

Jerrod and Rachel stood on the long veranda and watched the Christmas lights dance on the snow covered lake. The orchestra version of "Silver Bells" surrounded them. Jerrod took Rachel in his arms and starting dancing with her.
Rachel said, "We'd better get to the college chapel. Angela wants me to help her with the last minute preparations for the cantata, and we only have an hour before the first song starts."
Jerrod pulled Rachel closer. "Just a few minutes more."
"Just a few minutes more." Rachel repeated as an answer. Then she kissed him lightly on the cheek.
"Rachel, I love you."
"I love you, too, Jerrod."
"Then let's get engaged."
"I've got a long way to go to get to that degree."
"I know. That's all the more reason to start planning."
He stopped dancing and looked down at her. He reached into his pocket and brought out a small object. He took Rachel's left hand and slipped a small ring on her finger.
"It's a promise ring." He said. "It's a promise to become engaged. A promise that I will love you for now and always."
Rachel swallowed hard and stretched her hand out in front of her. She let the blinking colors of the Christmas lights on the veranda dance in the tiny stone.
"It's beautiful, Jerrod. Thank you." She turned and hugged him tightly.
The two lovers looked down on the landing below to see Greg and Eliza dancing to the Christmas music.
"Wish I could hear what's going on down there." Rachel said.
"I'm sure we'll hear soon enough."
Greg hugged Eliza tightly. "Did you notice the young lovers on the balcony?"

"I did. What do you think is going to happen with those two?"

Eliza didn't answer. Greg hugged her tighter as she shivered. Eliza stated. "Greg, we'd better be picking up your mother for the college cantata"

"In a few minutes. I have something to take care of."

He took an object out of his pocket and slipped it on her finger. Eliza looked down at her hand in surprise.

"What's this?" She stared at the large opal surrounded by diamonds.

"It's just a promise. It belonged to my grandmother. She gave it to me to give to my first love. You're my first, one and only and last love."

Eliza gasps." It's extraordinary, Greg. I've never seen anything so gorgeous. But I can't believe at your age I'm your first love."

"At my age?" He laughed. "I'm hardly an old man...not just yet. And, well, believe it or not, I've dated plenty, but you're my first true love. We can call it a promise ring if you don't want to marry me."

"A promise of everlasting love...that's sweet.

Thank you, Greg. However, you know your mother isn't going to be happy unless we get married. Do you think she'll think this is an engagement ring?"

"If that keeps her happy to think that, we'll let her."

"And she'll be telling everyone in the church that we're getting married."

"So... they think that anyway. Anyway, it could be true someday."

Eliza put her arms around Greg's neck and kissed him.

"Thank you Greg." She sighed. "Speaking of your mother. She's waiting for us to pick her up."

"Where're we supposed to meet Angela?"

"She should be at the chapel right now. The Christmas events have kept her busy and I'm really happy about that. I wonder how long it will take her to notice this ring and what

she will make of it. I guess we'd better gather the troops and get to the church."
"I know. I'd love to just stay right here on the veranda with you." Greg hugged Eliza close to him. "Eliza, if you don't want to get married, could we live together here? The kids will all be going back to the campus after holiday break, and you need a place to live. Why not just live here with me?"
Eliza pulled back from Greg. "Oh, now that ought to really set your mom off, and get the people talking. Don't you think I'd have problems earning public trust with that kind of set up?"
"Public trust? Is that what you're worried about?"
"Well, yeah. This county is mainly conservative, religious, and most of them fanatical about marriage and godly appearances. How're they going to trust you as their chief public protector and me in the prosecuting office if we're committing what they consider to be carnal and indecent?"
"So you don't feel about me the way I feel about you? You'd be surprised at how many people could come to accept our relationship. Besides, we don't have to broadcast to the world that we're living together."
"Greg, it's got nothing to do with how we feel about each other. Your mother would know. And you can't tell me that church congregation is not going to know. There are enough self-righteous little mothers and spinsters in that church to spread that news clear to Chicago. Not only that, if the Snow family got wind of it, they'd use it to push you right out of office, especially with a new election coming up next year."
"What's the difference if I'm sleeping over at your place or if we're living together here? They're still going to gossip."
"Greg, you keep saying, 'if you don't want to be married.' Is that your choice? You haven't come right out and asked me to marry you. Seems to me you just want your cake and eat it too, as the old expression goes."
Greg pulled Eliza back to him and hugged her. "Oh, Eliza. I was afraid to come right out and ask you. I was afraid you'd

say no. Would you consider the ring our engagement ring. Will you marry me?"

Eliza looked up into his anxious face, his eyes damp with impending tears. "Greg Yoder. What a coward you really are. You've got a lot to learn about me. You've got to be straight forward if our relationship is going to work."

"You didn't answer my question. Will you marry me?"

Eliza kissed him slightly on his lips. She whispered. "Yes, but to everyone else, this is a promise ring. We can make it official after all the trials are done."

"That may take years and in the meantime, you'll still be living with me, right?"

"Greg, I have the money. I can afford an apartment, you know. We can take trips up to the cabin away from prying eyes."

"Yeah, but..."

"Greg, I said yes, I will marry you, and you're still negotiating for more. What more...."

Greg interrupted with a big whoop, picked Eliza up, and swung her around the porch.

Jerrod and Rachel started laughing as they looked down from the balcony. The celebrating whoops and laughter echoed across the lake.

Greg and Eliza stopped dancing and waved up to the young couple. Eliza shouted. "We'd better get to the chapel."

Jerrod and Rachel waved back. Greg walked to the door and shut the stereo button off on the wall. A cold breeze drifted across the balconies, the sudden quiet of the lake was broken by the echo of the wolves from the top of the mountain. A sudden quiet followed as the couples stood and looked toward Shady Mountain. Then one distinct howl echoed loud and clear.

Angela stepped outside the college chapel and snuggled in her heavy, winter coat. She looked up to the sky and drew in the crisp, mountain air. The stars mesmerized her and she searched for the North Star, the star of Christmas songs. A shiver went down her spine and she looked toward the

mountain point behind the cabin. She listened to the lonesome howls of the wolves. Then all was quiet. She smiled as she saw the small distant shadow of a wolf dog in the full moon. The minute she heard the trumpeting notes, she knew the sound.
"Dog." She whispered.

Chapter Twenty Nine

Angela stood quietly in the darkness, listened to the sound of Dog, and felt the cold wind as it whipped through the Balsam firs and up to the bell tower. The involuntary rings of the gongs on the sides of the bell brought Angela to reality and soon she could no longer hear Dog. She strained to see his shadow as the clouds moved over the moon. The movement in her stomach brought back the uneasiness that she felt about the continuing morning sicknesses. She had so far been able to hide the occurrences from Rachel and Eliza. She was sure that it was just nerves. After all, stress could cause a lot of health problems and delays in monthly periods. Her attention was drawn to headlights pulling into the parking lot in front of the chapel. That was most likely her family. 'Her family...what a great sound. Rachel was like her sister, now. Aunt Eliza and Greg were going to be like her Mom and Dad, soon. 'I just know they're going to be married. Rachel and Jerrod will be married and I'll have a brother-in-law. It's going to all work out.'
Rachel and Jerrod met Angela in the foyer of the church. "O.K. you two. Let us get to work. We've got lots to do." She said, and then noticed the glitter from Rachel's left ring finger.
Her mouth flew open. "Ah!" She grabbed Rachel's hand. "What's this?"
Rachel giggled and winked at Jerrod. "It's a promise ring. Don't go bananas, yet."
"Well, a promise ring is...well, a promise. That's good enough. Congratulations, sister."
Angela hugged Rachel and then Jerrod. "Congrats, Brother-in-law."
Jerrod was grinning ear to ear as Eliza and Greg appeared, escorting Sarah from the sanctuary hall. He grabbed Eliza's hand as she walked by. "How about this one?"
Angela jumped up and down gleefully. She looked at the bigger ring, a large opal with diamonds and grabbed her

aunt. "Congratulations. Oh, wow." She turned to Greg and started hugging him.
Sarah looked down at the ring. "When did you give Eliza this, Greg? " "Tonight, Mother. "
Greg put his arm around his mother. Sarah looked up at him and gave him a nervous smile. Then she turned to Eliza. She volunteered, "That was Greg's grandmother's ring."
"It's beautiful." Then she quickly added. "It's just a promise ring. We don't even know the dating policies for this county, since we both work for the government. So, we may have to back off and just be friends."
Sarah said, "It seems to me that you should have checked policies before you got involved. That is not 'just a promise' ring. Greg, your grandmother's ring should have more meaning than that."
Eliza took Sarah's hand. "I will treasure this ring and guard it with my life. It means a great deal to me that Greg is letting me wear it. Ownership will stay in your family, Sarah."

      Greg smiled at Eliza over his mother's head.

327

The chaplain opened the main doors to the sanctuary and peeked into the foyer. "Where are my helpers?"
Angela stepped toward him. "Oh, I'm sorry, Reverend, this is my family." She introduced everyone.
The group moved forward to shake the chaplain's hand. They followed him into the mid aisle and saw a group of people waiting at the front. As they neared the front, a young woman stepped forward toward the group
The chaplain turned and introduced her. "This is Anna Marie Taylor. She's our Junior Choir Director and a student of theology and music here at the college."
Anna's eyes were glued on Eliza. She shook her hand and asked. "You're the new Assistant District
Attorney, aren't you?"
Eliza looked at Greg. Then she asked. "Yes, I am. Are you a native of this county, Anna?"

"My name's Anna Marie. Yes, I am, but I disown the Taylor that's in the jail."
"It's o.k. I'm not going to judge you."
"Well, I mean, I don't hold to the thefts and all the other crooked things that he's done, but I figure that the girl he's accused of raping probably asked for it. That's the only kind he gets involved with."
Everyone in the group froze. Eliza's face showed shock. She stood and stared at the girl and then turned just in time to see Angela running out into the vestibule.
Rachel was right behind her. She caught up with Angela in the ladies bathroom down the back vestibule hall.
Angela ran into a stall and locked the door. Rachel stood helplessly outside as she listened to Angela throwing up. Eliza opened the door and came in. "Angela, it's o.k. honey. No one knows that you're that girl.
Your name was not released to the media."
Angela stopped barfing for a moment. Then she started again. Eliza gathered paper towels and made a wet pack of them. She moved to the stall and passed the toweling under the door. "Here,
Angela. Take the wet towels."
Then Eliza stood quietly with Rachel until Angela grew quiet. Angela opened the stall door and came out, shaky and pale.
"I don't think that pizza settled too well in my stomach." She said.
Eliza felt Angela's forehead. "Come sit on the bench, Angela."
Angela sat down next to her aunt and looked up at Rachel. "Aunt Eliza, would you go out and let everyone know that everything's o.k. Blame it on the pizza. Rachel can stay with me for a moment.
The choir needs to start practicing." Eliza hesitated, her face showing confusion.
She got up, looked at Rachel, hunched her shoulders…whatever…, and walked slowly out the door.

"Angela, why'd you send Eliza and not me?" Rachel said as she sat down on the bench beside her.

Angela started to cry. "How can I tell Aunt Eliza that I may be pregnant?"

Rachel sighed. "I was afraid you were going to say that." She put her arms around Angela as she sobbed into her hands.

Angela sobbed for a little, and then dried her eyes and nose on the tissues Rachel gathered for her. Rachel spoke. "What makes you think you're pregnant?"

"Periods late, morning sickness. Sickness after being stressed. I get really hot and sweaty, then I start shaking, my stomach starts rolling and then
I'm barfing."

"Do you want me to take you to a doctor?"

"I've been thinking that I could get one of those drug store tests, but I'm afraid that if I buy one, someone will see me and start asking questions. You know that a lot of people from the college and others have guessed that I was raped, since it was reported at first that I was in an accident. Then the word was that I had been beaten up. If someone hasn't told them, you can bet, they guessed it.
Especially after that report on the news."

"So you think Anne Marie was purposely acting like she didn't know, but she does."

"Yes, especially after I ran out at that obvious time. She's got to know."

"Well, I'm thinking that you shouldn't care what anyone thinks. The rape was not your fault."

"Logically, I know that. But I still feel responsible, no matter how I try to make it…"

At that moment, Eliza poked her head in the door. "Angela, how are you doing?"

Angela waved her in. "I'm fine, Aunt Eliza, but I may be coming down with the flue, so I'm asking that someone take me back to the cabin. I don't want to spread a virus."

"O.K. I'll take you home. Rachel, you go on in and help with the Cantata."

Rachel looked at Angela. "We'll talk later." She said and left the room.

Eliza helped Angela find her things in the coatroom and they were soon on the way. Eliza maneuvered the car toward the cabin.

Eliza asked. "Angela, how did you feel before you ran for the bathroom? Did it come on all of a sudden, or had you been feeling ill?"

"Well, I'd been a little queasy, so I thought it was the pizza. I still think it might be, but I didn't want to take the chance."

"Why didn't you want to talk to me in the bathroom, instead of Angela?"

"Aunt Eliza, your lawyer sense is showing."

"That's right. I'm not liking it that you're not talking to me."

"I'm not doing that intentionally. I'm handling things well. My counselor said she's impressed with my progress."

"You're talking about Joanna."

"Yeah."

"Just yeah? Can you open up to me? How are your sessions working for you?"

"Just fine. Aunt Eliza, stop worrying."

"Well, I'm not going to just drop you off at your next session. I'm going in and talk to Joanna myself."

Angela sighed. "Aunt Eliza, Joanna can't tell you what we've been talking about."

"Then you need to talk to me."

Eliza let out a frustrated sigh as she pulled into the driveway. "I want to check your temp before I leave you here."

"I'm old enough to check it myself, Aunt Eliza. I'll drink some orange juice, take a pill, and go to bed."

Eliza pulled out of the driveway toward the college campus. "You've never brushed me off before, Angela, and you know that you've never been able to keep secrets with me.

Besides, the truth is going to come out sooner than you're going to be ready for."

Then a feeling of glum came over her. She verbalized her thoughts as she pulled up to a stop light. "Oh…wow. All those drugs they had her on, the tests they ran…." She sighed. "If she's pregnant…"

Eliza was so entranced with her thoughts; she did not realize how she got to the campus. As she pulled onto the grounds, she scolded herself out loud. "Come on, Eliza. You've never been a worrier or paranoid."

She could hear the choir outside the chapel as she pulled her car into a parking space near the back. The parking lot was filled. She stepped out of her car, hardly noticing anyone or anything as she walked into the vestibule. She left her coat in the coatroom, slipped through the door and took her seat beside Greg in the front row.

When the chaplain announced the last song, Eliza realized that she had not heard most of the service.

Rachel knocked on Angela's door and peeked in. "Angela, are you awake?"

"Yeah. How was the cantata?"

"Great. How are you feeling?"

"After a nice shower and clean clothes, my stomach settled down. I was hoping you'd come in to talk. I've made some decisions."

"And what decisions are those?"

"I'm going to disguise myself and go to the farthest Wicks Drugs from here and get a pregnancy test. If it's positive, I'm going to find a clinic and get an abortion. Then I'm going to live my life and forget about this whole thing."

"Bad plan."

"What do you mean, bad plan. Do you have a better one?"

Rachel sat down on the edge of Angela's bed. "There are a lot of holes in your plan, Angela. First, how are you going to get to that far away without Aunt Eliza knowing about it? Who's going to drive you there, since your car hasn't been released from the impound with all the other vehicles confiscated from Taylor's chop shop?"

"I'll get it released."

"Good luck. Then there's the abortion clinic idea. There aren't any abortion clinics in this county. Are you going to drive all the way back to Chicago?"

"I'll find a clinic closer, maybe Ohio."

"Alright, now let's see. You're planning on driving to an abortion clinic someplace, getting a procedure that's going to rip an embryo out of you, then you're going to get yourself back in your car, bleeding and in excruciating pain and drive yourself all the way back here without Aunt Eliza knowing it. And how much time do you think this is going to take?"

"O.K. If you can't help me, I'll call Julie. She knows a lot of people in a lot of places. She'll help me."

"I want to help you, Angela. However, abortions are hard on a woman's body. You don't want to put yourself through that unless you have a life-threatening situation. Abortions are life threatening."

"How would you know?"

"I don't know first-hand, Angela. I've heard about it in health class and from other people. Haven't you ever watched the talk shows on TV? There's got to be a better way if you're pregnant, and the big word is IF."

"I thought you were the protected one. You sound more street smart than me."

"I don't know about that. Promise me you won't do anything crazy and impulsive. Julie and I'll help you figure this whole thing out. Give us time."

"The longer I wait, the bigger the kid gets...that is if I'm pregnant."

"O.K. Then just wait until I call Julie in the morning. We'll invite her to the cabin and we'll work it out."

"O.K. it's a deal."

"What were you feeling when you tore off to the john tonight?"

"Awful. I've been fighting it off and then all of a sudden, I was hot all over, shaky and I just felt hypertensive."
"Doesn't sound good. You know, I think Eliza knows. She's a smart woman and she was with your mom when she was going through her pregnancy when you were born. She knows the signs."
"Just don't tell her, Rachel. Keep your mouth shut."
Rachel got up and raised the palms of her hands. She shook her head. "I'm not going to tell her. That's your job. She's hurt that you aren't talking to her and being truthful. I can see it in her face."
"Don't tell her!"
"I'm not going to, Angela. However, she's extremely observant. She most likely already knows. I'm going to get ready for bed now. I'll help you figure it out tomorrow." Rachel picked up her pajamas from her bunk and headed to the door. Angela rose up on her elbows. "Rachel, I'm sorry. I didn't mean to be nasty."
"It's o.k. Angela, I'll see you in the morning."

As the sun peeked through the blinds, Angela woke drenched in sweat. She looked at the numbers on the lighted digital clock by her bed. The aroma of coffee drifted into her senses. She jumped up and ran for the bathroom in the hallway.
The dry heaves left her sweaty and shaking on the floor in front of stool. A knock came at the door and she looked up expecting to see Angela. Eliza stepped in and sat down on the floor beside her. She reached over and gathered her startled niece in her arms.
"It's not the flue, is it? You can tell me."
Angela moved away from her. "Aunt Eliza, you're going to catch this bug. Now, just let me take care of myself and get well."
Eliza stayed seated. "Well, if it's a bug, you're going to the doctor today. No arguments."
"I'll have Rachel drive me. You need to get to work."

"I can work on my research here on my laptop. You come first. Now I'm going downstairs, look up a doctor's number, and make an appointment for you after the office opens. You get back to bed and I'll bring you something to settle your stomach."

Angela agreed. "If it will settle your need for parenting, go ahead."

Eliza got up shaking her head. She met Rachel coming up the stairway with a cup of coffee. Eliza said. "I'm taking Angela to a doctor. Maybe one of the doctors from the hospital will be able to see her today."

Rachel frowned. "Oh, well, why don't I just take her out to the college clinic? It's probably just the flue and she wouldn't have to wait long. The only students left on campus are ones that couldn't go home for the holidays. I can get Jerrod to drive us."

"I can drive her, but I'd prefer to get her to a doctor in town."

"One of the doctors in town does go out to the college for a few hours per day. Let me look into it for you."

"O.K. She might be more acceptable to that idea."

The house phone rang and Eliza went down the stairs to answer it. "Eliza, new evidence has come in that we need to go over together."

"Could I do it from here, Rachel? I have a sick girl that I need to get to a doctor."

"I'm so sorry. However, I'd really prefer that you come in to the office. The information isn't on the computer. Can you make the doctor appointment for this afternoon, and come in this morning?"

"Hold on for just a moment."

Eliza looked back up the stairway. Walking with the portable, she looked up the stairway to the girls' closed bedroom door. The light was trickling through around the cracks. As she was coming up the stairs, she could hear the low voices. As she got to the top, she hesitated and stood to listen. The voices stopped.

She walked to the closed door, knocked once, and opened it. She stuck her head through. The girls were sitting on the bed. "Angela, would you allow Rachel to drive you to the doctor today?
Promise me that you'll go."
"Rachel convinced me. I'll go if you'll stop worrying about me."
"O.K. Then try to get some more sleep and let Angela take care of everything. April needs me to come in to the office."
"Alright. That's fine. I'll be fine." Angela lay back down and curled up under her comforter.
Rachel got up, picked up her coffee cup, and left the room with Eliza, turning out the light. As they went down the steps, Eliza said. "Go in with her to the examining room. Let me know what the doctor says. She won't talk to me and I can't help her if she won't tell me what's wrong."
When they got to the bottom of the stairs, Eliza stopped and turned toward Rachel. "Rachel, I know that you're loyal to Angela, and I'm glad about that. Nevertheless, you won't be doing her any favors if you help her keep secrets from me. You and I both know that there's a possibility that she could be pregnant. If that's true, she's going to need me to help her."
Rachel stood looking out the large window toward the lake and watching as daylight started to reveal the snow covered ice. "Eliza, Angela is worried about that possibility. Right now, she's trying to be in denial about it. She worries about going to a doctor here in Echo Valley. She doesn't want Ray's family to find out and to be a part of the decision as to whether to keep any child from this rape. I can't say that I blame her."
"Then you need to let her know that I support her. I can help her with a lot of options and we can work it out so that she never has to face Ray or his family again, unless she wants to." She sighed. "She thinks she's letting me down. I just wish she could believe that this was done to her and that none of what's happened is her fault."

"I know. But she was saying just a while ago that if she hadn't gone downtown that day, she wouldn't be in this mess now."
Eliza shook her head and walked in a little circle. "Maybe I should just take her back to her doctor in Chicago. Would you tell her that I'm offering that option to her when she wakes up? After today, we're going to be on Christmas break.
Going back into Chicago to go on the Christmas shopping tours would be a great excuse for leaving town."
"Hey, that sounds like fun. Could I go along?"
"Sure if you can break away from Jerrod long enough."
"He'd just have to deal with it. If Greg can live through a week or so without you, then Jerrod can be without me."
Eliza smiled weakly. "Keep talking to her, Rachel. I'm going to go take a shower and get myself to the office."
Rachel took the phone book from a drawer and hid away in Greg's office.

Angela woke up when she heard the door to the garage close. She got up and sat on the side of the bed. Rachel walked in with a glass of milk.
"Hey, how's the tummy?"
"I'm better, thanks. I heard you and Aunt Eliza talking downstairs. You didn't tell her anything, did you?"
Rachel sat down on Angela's bed. "Eliza did the talking, Angela. She's worried about the same thing that you are."
"Why, what did she say?"
"She said that she's been concerned that you might be pregnant and that you need to know that she's behind you and will help you in your decisions.
"What did you say?"
"I told her that you wouldn't want to see a doctor here in town and that maybe you could see the doctor at the college."
"So you did admit that I'm worried about a pregnancy?"
"Yes, I pretty much had to."

"Crap! " Angela plopped back on the bed. "Did you call Julie?"
"Yeah, she's still at her folks until after New Years. I didn't tell her the reason. She said she'd call you later today."
Angela sat back up. "Good. Maybe she knows of some doctor who would be discreet."
"Eliza wants us to go on a Christmas tour in Chicago. Would you agree to see your doctor there, if Eliza can get you an appointment with her?"
Angela sighed, got up, and started gathering her clothes from the drawers and closet. "You know, Aunt Eliza may say that she will support me in whatever I decide, but I know her. She made the sacrifice to raise me. My mother made the sacrifice to have me instead of having an abortion. I know that Aunt Eliza is going to point that out to me if I decide not to have a baby."
Rachel bent down to pick up a sock that Angela dropped. "Angela, aren't we being a bit premature?
We don't even know that you're pregnant."
"Well, we're going to find out today. Will you walk into town with me today? There has got to be a drug store somewhere that can sell me a pregnancy test."
"I called Jerrod a while ago. He's in town, but he's coming back by here. I'm getting his car. When he comes, we can drive him out and drop him off at the college. I also located a drug store in Clarkston off the highway. I called them and they carry pregnancy test. It's a large town, so they're not going to be asking questions or recognize us."

Rachel and Angela sat on Angela's bed waiting for the minutes to tick away. When the alarm went off, both girls jumped up and ran to the bathroom. Angela picked the stick up and both girls glared at the indicator. Then Angela kept holding the stick as they walked arm in arm back to the bedroom. They both burst into tears, holding on to each other on Angela's bed, rocking back and forth.

Finally, Angela stopped, put the stick in the torn package, and sat it down on the stand. "Could you drive me someplace else, Rachel?"
"Sure."
"I need to go see Brent at the jail."
"What on earth for?"
"Don't worry. I'm not telling him anything. I just need to convince him that he needs to help himself. None of what happened to him was his fault any more than it was mine."
"Be careful, Angela."
"I will. He can't hurt me where he's at. And I don't have to see his creepy uncle."
"I'm surprised, Angela. All of a sudden, you're sympathetic toward Brent, of all people."
"Well, I'd like to think that the whole family is not like Ray and the rest of that bunch."
"So are you thinking that you're going to keep the baby?"
She rubbed her stomach. "I don't know yet.
Knowing for sure kind of changes reality a little.
I'll tell you after I talk to Brent. I just want to see if his attitude has changed. I just don't want to have to be affiliated with that family in any way."
"Angela, did you ever meet your father?"
"No, Aunt Eliza always kept me from his family. Not one of them was worth my knowing. I don't want my child to grow up knowing that the father and his whole family are criminals or trash the way I did."
"Are you going to tell Eliza?"
"Yeah. Tonight. I guess we could still go to Chicago. Maybe I could still see the doctor. You know this package says that there are cases of false positive results. Maybe mine is a false positive."
"Do you really believe that?"
"Well, there's always hope." She hugged herself and the tears came. "I always dreamed that when I had a child, I would have a loving husband, and we would be overjoyed when we found out we were pregnant."

Rachel hugged Angela. Her mind was busy. She grabbed on to her old faith. How can I help her, dear God? What can I do to help my friend?
Angela stopped sobbing. She stepped away from Rachel and picked up the package with the test kit. Placing it back in the market bag, she said. "I'll dispose of this away from the house. Come
On, let's go to the jail."

Angela sat and stared at the dishelmed Brent through the visitor window. She clenched the phone next to her ear. She listened as Brent rattled on and on. She had hoped he'd changed. His rhetoric was full of blame. He still couldn't admit to his faults.
Finally, she stood and placed the receiver in the cradle. It was useless.
As she turned to leave, she could see Brent with his hands up in a "What?" gesture. But she didn't care. He wasn't ready to listen. His world was totally absorbed with how he was being railroaded.
Rachel stood up in the waiting room and walked to meet her friend. "Well, how did it go?"
Angela snickered. "I couldn't get a word in edgeways. He was hopped up as soon as he picked up his phone receiver. I know all about how he's going to beat this rap, and that cop, Yoder and Prosecutor Donavan are jerks and what his beloved Snow lawyers told him. He still has no clue why I was there, and what I had to say about it all and he didn't care."
Angela wiped her tears as Rachel put her arms around her shoulder. "Well, let's get out of here.
We need to go do something more productive."
'Yeah, like packing. I'm excited to be going to Chicago. This is going to be a great trip, not that I'm all that excited to go to face the doctors. But it will be good to get it over with."

As Angela was talking, Rachel was guiding her toward the door. Out of the corner of her eye, she caught glimpse of a group of men in suits, one of which looked like he might be related to Brent's team of lawyers. She pushed open the door to let Angela through and turned to look back. The men were gone.

Chapter Thirty

Angela stood with Rachel and Eliza in the observation deck of the Sears Tower and looked down over the bustling windy city. The view with all the Christmas lights was spectacular. She wished Brent could be here with her instead of in that miserable jail cell. Her feelings for him were up and down. So he wasn't admitting where he was wrong. He had nothing to do but sit there and get depressed. He was bound to be a bit self-absorbed.

She thought back over the last two months and the roller coaster feelings that she'd had about the guy she had loved and hated all at the same time. Her talk with Brent last week had cleared the air between them. They had talked about his difficult position he was in. He was feeling grateful to his extended family for helping him finance college, but felt that he had been used in a lot of ways. His parents had died in a car accident in another county when he was seventeen. He had moved to stay with his grandmother after he graduated. The price for his relatives help was high. She had stayed away from telling him about her drug store pregnancy test until she saw a doctor. Now she knew.

Here on the tower, she thought about what her doctor had said this morning "…almost three months pregnant." She would wait until she saw him face to face to tell him about it. Aunt Eliza wanted her to keep it a secret, because the baby could be used to go against her as a witness in the trials. She rationalized that, "the baby can't be Ray's," but she knew she couldn't tell anyone else that just yet. She had gone in alone for the examination and the doctor agreed to let her tell Aunt Eliza. Then this morning, the doctor called the hotel room to tell her the results of the tests. The doctor confirmed to her that the date of conception was at least three weeks before the rape. The fetus was almost three months along. My conscious won't let me get an abortion. Of course, now that I know that it's not Ray's…

Angela came back to reality as Eliza hugged her. "Do you remember coming here when you were little?"
"I remember being here on the tower on our Christmas shopping trips every year of my life,
Aunt Eliza."
"That's right. We didn't miss it this year, did we?"
Rachel said. "Whoa. That wind makes the tower feel like it's bending."
Angela grabbed Rachel's hand. "It's not bending, but the wind does make it feel unsteady.
Are you ready to leave now?"
"Sure, but I'd like to walk down. I guess you need to take the elevator."
"No, it's like I told you on the way up. Taking the elevator is silly. I'm pregnant, not disabled. The doctor said that I can run a marathon if I want to. "Eliza hugged her tighter. " Don't blame us for being protective of you, Angela. If something's going to happen, it'll happen in the first two months."
Angela felt a pang of guilt. All the same, she wasn't going to tell her yet. If Ray's lawyer knows this baby's not out of rape, it will weaken the case. It'll make me seem promiscuous. I can't tell anyone.
Eliza dropped her arms. "Let's go back to the hotel. I'm glad that we got our personal stuff from the apartment before we checked into the hotel, but we need to get the car packed up properly, and since we're going back with more than we came with, it's going to be a job finding the room. We may have to leave some things behind for the hotel to donate to the homeless shelter."
Angela giggled. "Well, I'm not leaving any of my things, I'll just have to put my maternity things on top of my regular clothes and wear everything home."
Rachel joined in the laughter. "That would be a sight."
"Just a preview of the next six months."
Eliza intervened. "You mean the next seven months, don't you?"

Angela coughed. "Yeah, my math's bad. Well, I mean, at least six months, I'll probably look like a butterball."
Eliza took another look out over the city. *This is de ja vu. I stood with Angela's mother here that last Christmas before Angela was born.*
She looked at Angela. *She looks and acts exactly like her mother, flamboyant, giddy, and ready to turn whatever happens into a dramatic and glorious event.*
"Come on, Aunt Eliza. It's getting cold up here."
Back in the Chicago Regency, Eliza and Rachel left the room to take the first of the packages to the car. Eliza told Angela, "You finish your packing while Rachel and I put these pieces in the car and go for some carry out lunch."
As the door closed, Angela took a small journaling book and pen out of her suitcase and began to write.

"Dear Brent,
I hope that you'll be able to read this someday. It's with hope that I write this on behalf of our unborn baby. Yes, it's ours. I'm sure of that now. I'm sorry that I couldn't tell you about my pregnancy when I visited you in jail. Anyway, I wasn't sure and I thought it would be Ray's kid. I can't tell you now until after the rape trial. I can't present my babies' mother as a slut. You see, that's what the defense team for Ray will say. If I tell you the truth, you'll be too excited to keep it a secret.
Maybe someday, you'll be able to see your relatives for who they are, and you'll beat all the charges against you. Then if it is too difficult to live in Echo Valley, you, the baby and I can move here to Chicago where no one will judge us.
I'm scared, Brent. I don't know how this is going to end. Mama died in childbirth. Of course, she was beat up a lot and she didn't see a doctor until the end when Aunt Eliza took her to the hospital. Aunt Eliza told me one time that Mama had injuries that caused her to die.
When I was in the doctor's office, I told him about the drugs they had me on for what Ray did to me. Aunt Eliza made

me promise to do that in exchange for not going in with me to the examining room. Anyway, the doctor looked at the prescription list and said that he couldn't see anything that could initially harm the baby. I hope he's right. I know one thing for sure, I'm not taking anything from here on out unless it's absolutely necessary. It's a wonder that there wasn't a miscarriage from the rape. It's a miracle and I'm going to be the best mother in the world.
As I told you in jail, Brent, I don't hold you responsible anymore for the beating and the rape. It wasn't your fault. You can't help that you were born into that family. They led you down the wrong path. Now you have to start taking control of your own destiny. You promised that you would. You promised that you would testify against Ray, the Masterson's, and the Snow family. I know you'll keep your promises and help my Aunt Eliza to clean up the county. Who knows, maybe Aunt Eliza will do such a good job, we'll be able to stay in Echo Valley and raise a big family of great kids."

Angela jumped when she heard the key card in the door. She quickly put the book and pen into her purse and got up grabbing her toiletries and packing them into the front of her small case. Eliza and Rachel came in the door juggling food bags and drinks.

"Oh wow, it's colder outside. I think Chicago's going to get more snow. I'm not going to regret leaving the lake effect winters, that's for sure."
Aunt Eliza talked quickly as she set out the food.
"I checked on the mover's while I was out, Angela. They packed our apartment things in a large van and they're already on the way to Echo Valley.
Our lease will be up the first of January, so I'm glad I was able to get that all taken care of while we were here. They'll take everything to the storage barns that I was able to locate

in Clarkston. It's a ways from Echo Valley, but when I get a house, we'll move everything out."
"We really did get a lot done, didn't we?"
"Yes, aren't you glad that I never let you have a pet? That would have been another problem."
"I still missed having animals growing up. Not that I blame you, but my babies are going to have pets. Brent told me at the jail that he has a dog. His cousins are taking care of it."
Eliza stopped chewing her food and swallowed, almost choking. Wiping her mouth on a napkin she said, "I heard that you went to see Brent. Is that all he talked about? You didn't tell him anything about possibility of pregnancy, did you?"
Angela pushed her empty food box into a plastic bag. She swallowed hard. Darn, she thought. Slip of the tongue. She kept her composure as she said. "No, I didn't mention a thing about that. I just went there to clear the air about everything. Joanna told me that I needed to forgive if I wanted to have peace of mind. She said that a grudge was a heavy burden to bear. So I just wanted Brent to know that I had forgiven him, so that I could go on with my life."
"So are you going to forgive Ray in the same way?"
"For my peace of mind, I will. However, it's going to take a lot longer. I'm still not over the hurt and the nightmares."
Eliza put her empty containers in a plastic bag and stood up. "Angela, have you thought about adoption? This baby is going to be a constant reminder of the pain that was inflicted on you."
Angela looked at Rachel, who was putting her coat on. "Aunt Eliza...no, I won't allow my baby to be placed in a home or adopted. This baby is going to know who his real parents are. And everything is going to be o.k."
Eliza put her coat on. "I hope you're ready for the responsibility. Your life won't be yours anymore."
"Is that how you felt when you took me into your life. You put your own chance at happiness on a back burner."

Eliza looked shocked. She walked over and took Angela's hands. "I didn't mean it to sound like that, Angela. I'm sorry. I made the choice. I didn't have to take you as my own. I took one look at you in the hospital and knew that you were my happiness. You have a different situation. A man raped you. That's not…"

Angela pulled away from her. "Aunt Eliza, let's go. We can talk more at home. We need to get going."

As Angela picked up her purse, grabbed the handle of a pull suitcase and headed for the door, Eliza and Rachel exchanged looks. Rachel knew by her look that Eliza needed answers to what was going on in Angela's head. Rachel hunched her shoulders to indicate that she was clueless.

Nothing was said about Angela's condition as Eliza maneuvered through the traffic on Wacker Drive, winding through the city and out to the toll road interchange. Angela and Rachel had insisted on riding together in the back seat, leaving Eliza to listen to their chatter about their purchases at places like Akira's and the Water Tower Place.

Rachel's phone rang. "Hello, Jerrod…Yes, we're on our way home…Don't worry…O.K."

Rachel leaned forward. "Eliza, Jerrod wants to talk to you." She leaned over to hand the cell phone to Eliza. Eliza waved her hand and shook her head. "No, tell him that I'm driving. I'll call him back today, when we stop."

Rachel leaned back in the seat with her phone. "Jerrod, Eliza said she'd call you back when we stop."

Rachel leaned back over the seat to talk. "Eliza, Jerrod wouldn't give me details, but he said that the Masterson's and Brent are out on bail and on tethers. He said to be careful driving home."

Angela laughed. "Brent's out. That's as it should be."

Eliza glanced in the rear view mirror at her niece. "Well, this time, I hope he's going to behave himself. He won't have any choice as long as he's on a tether. Did Jerrod say where he's staying?"

"No, he just said to call him."

"I don't understand how they managed to get past the court to give the Masterson's another chance on tethers."

The girls didn't talk again as Eliza pulled through the first tollgate. Eliza turned the radio on to a Chicago news station. She looked in the rear view mirror to see that both girls were already sleeping.

There was no news of interest, except for the usual terrorist activity, robberies, and other negative world chaos. Eliza kept her eyes on the traffic and turned her thoughts to plans for phone calls when she stopped.

At Gary, Indiana, Eliza pulled into a gas station and the girls headed into the restrooms, leaving Eliza to pump the gas and use the ATM at the pump. She finished and pulled the car up in front of the restaurant attached to the station.

Her car mobile phone rang and Eliza saw by the digital display that it was Angela's doctor. She was puzzled until she realized that she had left all her phone contacts with the desk.

She pushed the speaker answer button and said, "This is Angela's guardian and Aunt. How can I help you?"

"Oh, hello, Eliza. This is Miriam, the nurse at Dr. Simonton's office. Is Angela available?"

"No, we're on our way back to southern Pennsylvania and Angela is using the bathroom at a truck stop at this time."

"That's o.k. We just need a doctor's address to transfer her records. She filled out her information on the form, but we need to have a medical address."

"Oh, well, I'll have her new doctor fill out a request form when we make that connection next week."

"Sure. Another thing, Angela forgot her prescription for pre-natal vitamins. She needs to start those right away. She's already about three months and she needs to start a nutrition and exercise program as soon as possible."

Eliza's jaw dropped. 'So my suspicions were correct. That baby can't be from the rape. She's afraid it'll hurt the case. I guess she's picked up a few bits of legal understanding from me after all.'

To Miriam, she said, "If you can fax that to me when we get back, I'll get it into the drug store or if you can suggest an over the counter formula, I can pick it up for her before we get home."

"You could use an over the counter formula, but if you can tell me what pharmacy you use, I can fax the order there. And, please let us know where we can transfer her medical records."

Eliza gave her the pharmacy information for the Clarkston pharmacy. She figured that the druggist there would be more discreet and it would give Angela more privacy. As for a new doctor, she told her that would be worked out later. As she hung the phone up, the girls were coming out of the station. She got out, locked the door, and said. "Let's get a bite to eat here and drive as straight through as possible to get back tonight. If you can't take it and can't sleep in the back seat, we can stop at a motel. The nurse called me on the car phone while you were inside. She said that you forgot a few things, like your prescription. I had her fax it to Wicks Drugs in Clarkston."

Angela fidgeted with her coat zipper. "Oh?"

"Yes. That's no problem. Tomorrow, we'll pick up the vitamins and set up an appointment for a doctor in Clarkston. They can send a transfer form for all your medical records from Dr. Simonton."

Eliza looked up to see a man staring at them. He was standing within earshot of them by a late model black Mercedes Benz. She was certain that she had seen a man somewhere with that familiar look, but it was not someone she knew. His black eyes were penetrating and he did not look away from her, when she stared back at him.

She quickly turned and followed the girls through the restaurant door.

As they sat down in a booth next to a window, Eliza looked back toward their car. The man and his Mercedes were gone.

Chapter Thirty One

Eliza drove with unease. Several times, she had to stop at a rest center so that Angela could use the rest room. At each stop, she searched the parking spaces and the buildings for the man she had seen at the Gary, Indiana truck stop. A thought with reason brought her a sense of peace. I'm probably being paranoid. Black cars make me nervous. That man was probably wondering why I was staring at him. She listened to the chatter of the two girls in the back seat, as she looked up to see the first Akron exit. "Aunt Eliza, can we stop soon. I need to use the rest room again."
"O.K. I'll grab the next exit." She put her signal light on to move into the far right lane. In the small mirror on her left, she could see a black car hanging on her right fender. She stayed in her lane waiting for it to pass. The car moved up so that it was even with the front passenger door. The car lingered there. She sped up and tried to move in, but the black car sped up behind the car in front of it. There was a solid line of traffic. Eliza slowed down, but the black car slowed down to the same pace.
"Aunt Eliza, you missed the exit."
"I know. The guy in the black car is being a road hog. I'll find a way over."
Eliza looked in her rear view mirror and spotted a police car. She slowed down more so that the driver of the black car would look through the rear view mirror to see the police cruiser. It worked and she was able to slide in behind the black car. She turned her blinker off and memorized the Illinois plate number. The next exit came and she quickly turned on the signal and turned down the ramp. She looked in her rear view mirror to see the police cruiser pull in behind the black car.
Rachel and Angela had been watching the scenario. They turned in their seats and watched the police car as it stayed behind the black Mercedes. They clapped. Angela asked.

"Aunt Eliza, who do you think that was and what do you think he was doing?"
"I don't know, but I think I'll take I 77 and head south now. We can pick up I 70 at Cambridge toward Pennsylvania. That will throw anyone following us off the track."
"So you think someone is following us?"
"Maybe I'm being paranoid, but I wouldn't be surprised if the Snows have private detectives out looking for us. I just don't want to take any chances."
"That must be what Jerrod wanted to talk to you about."
"That could be, and I forgot to call him at Gary.
I'll make some calls while we're stopped here." Eliza pulled up to a Pilot Truck Stop gas pump. The girls got out and headed for the bathroom. All the while Eliza was pumping gas; she was anxiously watching other cars pulling in, and the traffic on the road in front of the complex.
She pulled her credit card out of the pump slot, replaced the gas lid, and pulled the car up in front of the building. She was on the car phone as she watched the girls inside browsing through the aisles of snacks and drinks.
Eliza knew that her now former superior, Chad Ellerton wasn't in Chicago for Christmas vacation, but she hoped that one of the assistant attorneys would be in the office. The paralegal that answered the phone took her message, but could not give her any information. She knew that April would not be in the office today. She pushed the fast dial for Greg's cell phone. She couldn't get a signal through. The office number rang through to voice mail. "Greg, call me. "
She pushed his mother's home phone number. There was no answer there, but she didn't leave a message. She was getting frantic.
She dialed Jerrod's number and finally got a real voice.
"Jerrod, sorry I couldn't talk before."
"Eliza, Greg's been trying to reach you. There's evidence that the Snow family has hired private detectives to investigate charges against their clients. He's concerned,

because the detectives are out of Chicago. Have you seen anything suspicious?"
Eliza told him about the black Mercedes.
"Could you have Greg run the plate number? It's Illinois plate XLT 666."
"Got it. What is your travel route?"
"I had planned to follow the toll road a bit farther, but I'm going to grab 75 and go south. I can catch 33 and wind my way over to Clarkston."
"O.K. I'll let Greg know if I talk to him before you do."
"Tell him I've been trying to reach him. Tell him to call me on the mobile car phone. I can use the speaker without having to use my hands."
"Sure. Is Rachel nearby?"
Eliza looked up as the girls came out the door with snacks and drinks. "Hold on a minute." She said.
She motioned for Rachel to climb in the front seat. Angela jumped in the back.
Eliza spoke to Rachel. "I have to use the restroom. Jerrod is waiting to talk to you." She pushed the speaker button on the car phone and got out of the car.
"Hey, Sweet Thing. I'm missing you." Rachel's face felt warm as she blushed and looked in the rear view mirror at Angela. Angela winked at her, grinned, and put her hands to her ears.
"I miss you, too, Jerrod. I'll see you by morning. Eliza plans on driving straight through tonight without a motel stop."
"There's something I want you to do. Call often on the trip. Keep an eye out for any suspicious people. Get a good look at every person or car you see. I don't want to scare you, but you and Angela need to know this. There may be private detectives or goons following you. So if you see anyone who seems to be giving you too much attention, let me know. Eliza is doing a good job of it, but you need to help."
"So she told you about the black Mercedes."

"Yes, and Greg is following up on a lead on the Snow bunch activities. Now, I want to talk longer, but you need to start being alert, and I need to get in touch with Greg about some information that Eliza gave me. Take care of that little blonde head of yours. I love you."

"Love you, too."

Rachel sat the phone down and turned around in her seat to look at Angela who was sitting in stunned silence. Angela became alert and looked up at her. "This is really beginning to sink in Rachel.

"I know." Both girls started looking around the parking lot. Angela looked toward the building as Eliza came out with a drink in her hand. As she got in, Angela said, "Aunt Eliza, are you sure that the route we're taking is going to be safer."

"I'm sure. Now hang on to your seats, girls. If you really need to stop for more than gas, we will. But dinner tonight will have to be drive through and eat in the car."

"That's fine with us." Angela and Rachel said together.

Neither girl slept for the rest of the trip. They wrote down every description of every car, every license plate, and every mile marker. Rachel called Jerrod at every stop. When they reached Cambridge, the mobile phone rang and Eliza pushed the speaker phone.

"Hello Greg."

"Eliza, the Mercedes that you saw was a rental. We tracked it to the O'Hare Airport, Car Rentals.

It was registered to a Jasper Jones from San Francisco. The puzzle is that he rented a car in Chicago, and he was driving it in Ohio. Why he didn't fly into Detroit or Cleveland, we don't know. Anyway, he probably had nothing to do with anything that's going on here. We're keeping an eye out for him, though. If he shows up here, we'll know that he probably picked up drugs in Chicago to transport across the states. Stranger things have happened. I mean, why don't these guys operate from New York City? That's closer. It doesn't make sense."

"We're keeping a close eye on traffic and people, and we're almost there."

"Don't be surprised if you see cruisers following you through the cities. I have a protection alert out, so law enforcement along your route will be looking out for you."

"Thanks, Greg. I feel much better."

"No problem. We have to protect our Assistant Prosecuting Attorney. She's got lots of work to do when she gets back here."

"I know. I'll see you by morning."

"I can't wait."

"Me either."

"Eliza." "Yeah." "Take care." Rachel and Angela giggled. Angela said loudly from the back seat, "You can tell her you love her, Greg. We know." Eliza laughed.

"Oh, Angela. So that's o.k. with you?"

"It's more than o.k. with me."

"O.K. Eliza, I love you."

"I love you, too. Greg. We'll see you, soon."

Eliza glanced in the rear view mirror to see a cruiser pull up behind her. "Well, there's one of our protectors. We'll be fine, Greg." She pushed the off button on the receiver.

On the east side of Cambridge, the cruiser dropped back and exited. Another cruiser picked them up and followed them. At dusk, Eliza pulled in to a carry out restaurant. A car that Eliza recognized as an unmarked car by the lower front lights discreetly set into the bumper pulled into the parking lot. They all got out using the restroom and Eliza picked up carry out.

Exiting the restaurant, Eliza handed the drinks and food to Rachel and Angela. As they walked across the lot, a man bumped into Eliza.

"Sorry, ma'am." The offender said. Eliza turned to look as she saw the driver of the undercover cruiser walk behind her and block the man.

The man put his hands up. "I apologized. I didn't mean any harm."

Eliza stared at the man's face. The officer said, "Ma'am. Would you check your purse to make sure you have everything?"

Eliza realized that the zipper of her purse was open. Her mouth flew open. "I know I zipped this up." She said. She reached in. "My billfold is gone."

The undercover pulled the thief's arms behind him, just as a marked cruiser pulled up. A uniformed policeman got out and the undercover cop pulled the thief over, put him on the back of the cruiser, and searched his coat pockets. He pulled out two billfolds and laid them on the trunk. "Why would you need two billfolds?"

He picked up the green one. "When did you start using a woman's billfold?"

The undercover looked at the identification of both billfolds. Eliza, Rachel, and Angela stood by watching as the officers questioned the man.

"So you're Benjamin Snow?" The undercover asked the man as he looked in the black billfold.

"Yes sir."

Eliza's mouth dropped. The two girls stood in stunned silence. Eliza asked, "Benjamin Snow from Chicago?" She asked the undercover.

"Yes. Do you know him, Ms. Hardigan?"

"I know WHO he is."

Angela and Rachel looked at each other and looked around the parking lot.

Rachel pointed at a car parked next to Eliza's car. "That's the car." She said.

Angela turned to the undercover. "That car has been following us for miles." She said.

The undercover walked over to the cruiser.

"Mr. Snow. What car were you driving?"

"I got dropped off. I wasn't driving."

"You were driving that tan Ford over there?"

"No sir."

The undercover turned to Rachel. "Can you identify the driver of the car you saw?"
She pointed at Benjamin Snow. "He fits the description of the driver."
"Are you sure that's the car you saw?"
Rachel asked. "Eliza, could you unlock your car door. I'll get our lists where we wrote down the plate ID, but I'm sure the plate matches."
Eliza pushed a button on the remote and a clicking sound signaled from her car.

Rachel spoke as she and Angela walked back examining the papers. "Right here it is. A tan Ford, license plate, Illinois, BXT 124." She handed both lists to the officer.
He took it and looked from the list to the license plate on the car.
He handed the list to the uniformed policeman.
"Run this plate." He said.
The undercover handed Eliza's billfold to her. "Ms. Hardigan, I know who you are. I'm not sure how all this fits together, or why you've been tagged for protection to Echo Valley, Pennsylvania, but I'll try to get this sorted out. It might be helpful if you could tell me as much as you can about this Benjamin Snow and anything else that pertains to this."
"I'm the Assistant Prosecuting Attorney at Echo Valley, Pennsylvania. We're working on a series of cases that includes drug smuggling and car theft between Chicago and Echo Valley. A Benjamin Snow is one of the suspects. He sure favors the Snow clan in Echo County."
The uniformed cop got out of the car and handed the undercover cop a slip of paper. The undercover looked at the plate on the car and then at the paper. He turned to the uniformed officer
"Search that car thoroughly, and keep Snow on ice in your cruiser."

He turned to Eliza. "We'll be hauling Benjamin Snow in for theft and questioning since he's wanted on suspicion in Pennsylvania and his car will be impounded. He'll be the least of your worries tonight, but we'll keep the protection order in place until you get home. We'll radio Lieutenant Yoder and let him know the new developments. You're free to go on to Echo Valley tonight, and we'll get in touch with your office tomorrow. Let us know when you're safe."

"Thanks, Officer, we'll most likely be getting an extradition order to get Snow transported to
Echo Valley."

The uniformed officer returned from his car. "I've got Yoder on the mobile. I filled him in.
Says he needs to talk to Attorney Hardigan." The officer handed her the speaker. "Hey, Greg. We'll be there in about three hours."

"Eliza, does drama always have to follow you?"

"Lately I would believe that it does."

"I'll have a midnight snack ready when you get home."

"We won't be hungry, but it'll be good to see you. Is that all you wanted to tell me?"

"Just wanted you to know that we've found more evidence and we picked Brent Morse and Ray Taylor up after they were out free for only seven hours."

"Oh, great. What did they do now?"

"They got caught cooking and dealing meth from Ray's house."

"Do me a favor, Greg. Don't tell Angela about this until morning. I'd like Angela to get a good night's sleep. And tell Jerrod not to tell Rachel."

"Will do. Now get on the road and drive safely."

Eliza thanked the officer and handed him the speaker.
As she got back in the car, she looked back at Rachel and Angela in the back seat. Rachel was finishing her meal and Angela was on her cell phone.

Angela looked up at Eliza. "Brent is back in jail, Aunt Eliza. That creep, Ray was cooking meth and since Brent has to stay with him, he got hauled in right along with that S.O.B."
Rats! Too late. Eliza sighed. "So that was Jerrod?"
"Yes. He called Rachel and wanted to talk to me."
Eliza took a deep breath in and took a drink of her pop. The food no longer smelled appetizing. She put the key in the ignition and backed the car out. She could hear Angela's soft sobs in the back seat. It was going to be a long drive home.

The rest of the trip went without a hitch, although there were sightings of police cars nearby at all times and that, she hoped, would have been enough to deter anyone trying to follow them. A phone call from Jerrod set up a meeting place at a rest stop just before the state line.
Rachel spotted Greg's patrol car first and jumped out as soon as the car stopped. Jerrod got out and went to hug her. They stood talking as Eliza went to the window where Greg was still sitting... He got out and hugged Eliza.
Eliza broke the embrace after a few minutes.
"We girls have to use the little girl's room."
After everyone finished and gathered back at Greg's car, it was agreed that Jerrod would drive Eliza's car and Greg would follow in the police car with the women. Rachel was voted down when she wanted to ride with Jerrod. The women all breathed a sigh of relief when they reached the blue mist that signaled they would soon be home.
Eliza looked back at Rachel and Angela through the prisoner grate from the front seat of the cruiser. They became quiet with their own private thoughts. She looked at Greg.
"Now it's time for us to roll up your sleeves and really get to work on those cases."
Greg reached over and padded her knee.

"Tomorrow will be soon enough. Today you need to rest from that long stressful trip." He smiled and then added, "And you and I have some catching up to do."

The lights of Echo Valley greeted them as they entered the blue clouds. The sounds of the wolves welcomed them as they rounded Python Curve.

"Look." Angela pointed to the rocks and the trail in the trees that led down to the landing below.

In the mist, stood an old man with a white beard and beside him stood "Dog."

Eliza and the others looked where Angela was pointing.

"He's gone." She said looking back through the rear view mirror as the car finished traveling around the curve.

Eliza and Greg looked at each other. "Who's gone?" Greg asked. Eliza's blue green eyes were wide and her face paled in the moonlight.

Angela turned to look forward, sighed, and lay back in her seat. "That's a good omen." She whispered.

Rachel sat staring at her friend. "I saw them too." She whispered. "Yes, that is a very good omen."

Note from Author:

Watch for Justice for Echo Valley, a sequel that will follow sometime in 2014 to 2015.

Your review is welcome at Amazon.com, createspace.com and/or Barnes and Noble.com.

Thank you, readers. You are wonderful.

Clarice Cook, Author

Other books by Clarice Cook, Certified Dementia Caregiver and Author

Non Fiction
　Creating the Dynamic Dementia Care Team, with a new manual, Memory Path Care – The Dynamic Dementia Caregiver

Fiction
Legacy from the Wake Journals
Justice for Echo Valley – Sequel to Echo from Shady Mountain

Made in the USA
Charleston, SC
28 March 2016